What You Don't Remember

What You Don't Remember

Kirsty Cooper and Steve Johnson

Dedication

Kirsty

For Mum, Dad and Chloe.
Together in heart, always x

Steve

For Katy & Liv.
My two best buddies and biggest fans x

1

A Confession

I understand what you're probably thinking — the obvious response is shock and horror. But you're not an obvious person. There's more to you than that, and deep down, you understand. You understand that not everything is clear cut; the world isn't black and white. Sometimes choices have to be made for the greater good.

It may seem a callous, malicious act. Someone ended up dead, after all. But to see it so simply and coldly would be to overlook the passion that lay behind it.

I hope you can see what I was trying to do. I need you to understand why. It was meant to be one casualty to make way for a perfect relationship. Sacrificing one person so that two others could be happy together. Truly happy. Isn't that worth it? I did it for love. But it was not meant to be her that died. I am truly sad about that.

I understand you're upset now but I need you to forgive me or else it will all have been in vain. Don't let it be in vain. Don't let anger drive you for too long. I think it was Virgil who said, "Love conquers all things; so we, too, shall yield to love." I know that love will conquer this too;

you'll understand one day and you, too, will yield to love.

We can still be together. We will find happiness together.

I know we will.

2

Rose

"I guess it all started when I killed my mum."
The words gripped, as if with claws, to the swell of anxiety in Rose's throat — the answer to the latest in a year-long line of questions. Questions from the police, the coroner, her sister. Questions that stomped around in Rose's subconscious day in, day out. And now more probing from yet another professional trying to help her. Hopefully, this could be the start of a breakthrough.

Ironically, it was Nate's lack of questions that had brought the two of them there. He was the only person she wanted to be questioning her. How are you doing? Do you need to talk? How can I help you feel better? But Nate's silence had led her to question their relationship and whether he cared about any of the answers.

Consequently, they were both being subjected to their second round of personal interrogation from this total stranger.

Rose didn't mind the questions so much, but her inability to answer the most important ones was sending her world into darkness: How did it happen? How did such a simple journey end in disaster?

The question, 'when did this all start?', had been easy to answer in her mind, but harder to say the words out loud. The words had hovered above Rose, waiting like electrically charged particles. Her throat was dry, her eyes wet, and her face cold. Nate's hand rested on her knee as she sat next to him, perched on the edge of a two-seater leather sofa that gave no comfort.

She reached to a table beside her for a brushed metal cube filled with tissues. An identical cube mirrored it on a matching square table at Nate's end of the sofa. Hers was now slightly askew where she had welcomed its offerings; Nate's stood straight, untouched. She noticed the meticulous order with which the room had been dressed — the tables, the tissues, two crystal-clear glasses of water. At her end, a small vase containing freesias emitted a nostalgic scent, her mum's favourite. The room was vast and long. At one end was a homely space near the door which housed the sofa on which Nate and Rose were sitting, a single armchair and a large desk. The other end had a more clinical setup with a high-backed chair and another smaller desk. A sink marked the halfway point, above which a medicine cabinet hung from the wall.

Rose had noticed similar attention to detail at the front of the house when they arrived. The well-kept garden was incongruous between the family homes on either side. To the left was the other half of the 1950s-style semi whose lawn displayed one too many garden ornaments; a selection of gnomes and a windmill made for a colourful welcome. To the right, fence panels lined an alleyway between the houses. As they pulled up, Rose had noticed some graffiti on the fence — out of place in the upmarket Derbyshire village. However, the words 'be kind' sprayed in blue paint had restored her faith in the modern degenerate. This house was the only one in the street with such a neatly trimmed lawn, bordered by weedless flower beds and a freshly pressure-washed path. There were no hints of family life or a relaxed attitude toward gardening. A block-paved driveway stretched along the side of the property. It led to an extension which spanned the rear of the house, incorporating what had presumably once been a garage. An entranceway led them through an adjoining hallway to the comfortable office space, different in style from the residential dwelling at the front.

"Stop it," said Nate, his eyes closed. He was facing the doctor but talking to Rose.

"You can't shut me up because you're not comfortable talking about it," said Rose. "It did start when I killed my mum."

"I'm not trying to shut you up," said Nate. As his hand retracted, Rose waited for the inevitable change in his tone. It was how all arguments began. "I wish you would stop saying that. You didn't kill her, it was an accident. A terrible accident that wasn't your fault."

Dr Thomas interjected now. He crossed his legs — the first movement he had made since taking his place opposite them both in a brown leather armchair that Rose assumed was part of a set with the sofa. "Why do you think it was your fault, Rose?"

"I was driving. How could it not be my fault?"

"But you're not sure?" The doctor's head tilted to the side and his pale blue eyes examined her face as he waited for her response.

"It's all a blur," she said. "A big mess of colour right up to the point I was staring into her eyes as she lay there on the roadside."

"Your mother?"

Rose nodded. "It's the only clarity I have — leaving the house in the morning to pick her up, driving a little way, and then her face as she lay on the road. But in between — nothing. I just want to remember what happened. I can't cope anymore with the guilt, the anxiety. It's taking over everything. I quit my job. I've hardly left the house in months, and I'm terrified of being behind the wheel. Nate and I never talk anymore. He shuts me down, thinking he's protecting me, but I need to clear the haze, not bury it."

"Tell me what you remember," said Dr Thomas.

Nate raised his eyebrows. "Is this really necessary? Is it helpful to keep going over it all? She's torturing herself. I thought we were here for, you know, couple stuff."

"Would you say this is affecting your relationship?" The doctor smiled and moved his focus to Nate.

"Understatement," said Nate, examining the grease that lingered beneath his fingernails.

"That's why we're here," said Rose. She gave Nate a sideways glance, and the tears ran warm again as her voice lost strength. She locked her stare on the tissue that was crumpled tightly within her palm.

"OK," said Dr Thomas. "I can see there's tension between you both; conflicting needs. Rose, you want to talk about these feelings of responsibility for your mother's death. And, Nate, you're reluctant to engage in a conversation about it?"

"Sounds about right," said Rose. "I'm struggling. I need to talk about it, but every time I do, he clams up. He wants me to go back to how things were. But I can't. That image is always with me. I try to create distractions but every time I relax, her face is there; when I'm making a cup of tea or doing the ironing, it can hit me when I'm not expecting it. It's crushing me. I need to know why I crashed the car, I can't focus on anything else until I discover what went wrong."

"Not even me," said Nate.

Rose knew they would never get past this without help. It had gone on too long — nearly a year. When her mum died, Nate had been the pillar of support for her and her sister at first. Then, as time went on, he lost patience with

Rose, keen for them to carry on like nothing had happened. But she had no headspace for talk of house renovations and holidays. She didn't want to be discussing inheritance and her childhood home having to be sold. Anxiety now ruled her life — that and all-consuming guilt and frustration. Nate's simplistic determination for her to 'move on', was an annoyance which prevented her from focusing on her new obsession — trying to remember what happened. What had gone so wrong? What had led up to that moment? Why did she crash the car?

Rose had tried grief counselling, self-help books, mindfulness. She had even gone to a hypnotherapy evening with her friend, Helen, but the blur remained blurry and Nate grew less and less tolerant of her self-loathing. Between them, a wall had risen and her capacity to break it down with kindness and generosity had long since disappeared. She had closed herself off, given up trying to talk. She had learned to be alone. Now they spoke only of the mundane and argued with no resolution. Perhaps this doctor was their last chance to work out how to co-exist again.

"OK," said Dr Thomas. "Tell me about the accident, about this image that you do remember."

Rose turned to glance at Nate. He had come willingly, but it was awkward revealing so much of herself to a stranger in front of her husband. It felt intimate when she hadn't shared these demons in such detail with him. That wasn't her fault. She had tried to talk to him so many times, but he always froze up. There was always something else that needed his attention — work, DIY, the football, his mates. Sometimes he would fall asleep while she spoke about the most awful event in her life. The frustration rose inside her like a wave that refused to recede. She focused on the other man in the room.

"Mum's eyes were open. That's how I knew. If they had been closed, then I could have believed she was sleeping. I wouldn't have seen her life trickling away. But she was looking straight at me and her eyes had changed, they were empty. She wasn't in pain, she wasn't afraid, she wasn't anything. My mum wasn't there anymore. I could hear her breaths, rasping and rattling, each one taking longer to come than the last. And then there were no more. The road lit up with blue and it was like someone had unmuted the sound of sirens, engines, voices shouting, my own voice desperately calling for her to come back. But she didn't... she couldn't... she was gone."

Rose's fingers shakily traced the lines under her eyes. She reached for another tissue and considered that emotional outbursts must be prevalent here. The room was warm and decorated in calming blues and greys. There were qualifications hanging in frames across the wall, and she imagined the breadth of sadness this office must have witnessed.

"That's all there is," said Rose. "That image of her on

the road, before the paramedics pulled me away. Everything before that is blank. It's all gone."

"That must be very distressing," said Dr Thomas.

Rose's hands shook harder, and Nate returned his hand to her knee with a tightened grip. She liked that he had noticed and wished he would do it more often.

"Some nights she wakes up crying her eyes out," said Nate, softening his tone.

"I didn't think you noticed." Rose sniffed. "You're always asleep."

"I'm not," said Nate, his gaze locked onto the cushion between them.

"Why don't you say anything, then?" Rose pleaded. "Why don't you hug me?"

Nate said nothing. He picked at the cushion.

"And of course, you clam up again!" Rose turned to Dr Thomas. "It's like this every day. There's no point talking to someone who isn't listening. He wants me to carry on like nothing happened — trying to rush me back to work, inviting people over for dinner."

"You mentioned wanting a hug," said Dr Thomas. "How would you describe your physical relationship?"

Nate cradled his brow between his thumb and index finger. "Look, I'm just not a huggy person, OK? Everything else…" Nate's cheeks became flushed, "… is fine."

Rose couldn't argue with the first part. Nate wasn't a

tactile person, and she had never resented him for that until now. But things had changed. They weren't 'fine'. Nate was even more reluctant than usual to comfort her. There was sex, but no intimacy — just a shot of dopamine in the system when everything else was numb. How could she reveal that to this stranger now, though? Nate didn't need to hear about the tears she had shed over his shoulder. She still loved him, she wasn't out to hurt him.

"It's not fine," she said. "That's why Alannah suggested we come to see you."

"Is there anything in our marriage you don't tell your sister about?" Nate shifted in his seat.

"Who else am I supposed to talk to, Nate? You won't talk to me; Mum's gone." Rose stopped and took a trembling breath. "I can't remember a time when I felt happy. Losing Mum has erased anything good. I need to see the light again. Or I'm done. Maybe we're done."

A silence fell while the doctor made notes. Rose glared at Nate, whose resolve to avoid eye-contact remained strong. She noticed some tiny hints of grey forming in the dark hair on his head and hiding amongst his stubble. She realised her husband's hair had changed, and she wondered how long it had been like that, unnoticed by his wife.

Dr Thomas lay his pen down atop his notebook. "Nate, would you like to respond to anything that Rose has said?"

3

Nate

Nate shifted on the sofa. The warm leather of the seat made the underside of his thighs feel clammy inside his jeans. He locked his fingers together in his lap. He thought for a few beats before answering the question he'd been posed, glancing briefly at his wife.

"I feel like… I feel like Rose has been through a really shitty time. We both have, I mean. But, obviously… mainly Rose." His sentences were riddled with awkward pauses. He knew what he wanted to say. But he needed to choose the words carefully. Rose was better at that than he was. He didn't want the poorly chosen words to appear hurtful or insensitive, as they sometimes did during arguments. Not that they argued lots — no more than any normal couple, he thought. Nevertheless, he was acutely aware of where the wrong words had led in the past. Although on those occasions, his ex-fiancée, Nicola, was usually involved. It was occasionally awkward with both of them having former partners living nearby. Admittedly, that issue was more prevalent in Nate's relationship history than Rose's. Halewood Heath was a small place, making it hard not to bump into the past. Rose's ex, James, was a nice enough guy and he and Rose remained friends. In fact, Nate enjoyed the odd pint with him now and then. However, the same was not true for Nate and Nicola. They had parted on bad terms, and she had lingered in their lives for longer than she should have done. Rose was not always forgiving of him defending his former fiancée's behaviour. His words could be misinterpreted, and it had made him reluctant to be forthcoming on occasions.

"I get that it's an awful thing. Honestly, I feel so sorry for Rose. But I just feel like no one can change the past, can they?" He moved his hands to rub them on his legs. "There's nothing Rose can do about the accident. So, I just think we have to… move on. Together, I mean. Be there for each other and all that. Rose knows I'm there for her. Don't you, Rose?"

Rose chewed on her bottom lip. She inhaled but waited for him to continue.

Nate turned to look at Dr Thomas. "I know it's harder for her, I get that too. Not just because she was the one…" He cleared his throat, "… you know, driving and all that."

He swallowed and felt a damp patch forming under both armpits.

"I'm just trying to be logical about it… practical, you know. That's just how I am, I guess. It's not that I'm not sad about what happened. Of course, I am. It was a horrible thing. But, you can be sad and, well…" he locked his fingers back together, "… still get on with stuff, can't you?"

Rose looked up, away from Nate, staring between the certificates on the wall — or somewhere much further beyond them.

"I'm not a complicated bloke," Nate went on. "I fix cars — find what's wrong with them and fix them. If they can't be fixed, they have to get scrapped. It's… practical, you know? So, the way I see things, you find what's wrong and then fix it."

"How do you think relationships are like cars, Nate?"

"Hang on! Don't twist my words into something they're not."

"I'm sorry, Nate. I was merely asking you to elaborate on your own analogy. You were making a comparison, were you not?"

"Yeah… no… I mean, yeah, but not like you were making it seem. I'm saying we just have to fix… us. We've had this shitty time, but everyone goes through shitty times, don't they? And this was no-one's fault. It's not like we caused it but… it's just—"

"Go on, Nate. You should feel that you can speak freely here."

Nate's words caught sharply in his throat. They formed a lump and scratched to get out. And he knew that speaking them would release the tears forming behind his eyes. He wasn't a crier.

"How does it make you feel to think that you and Rose have drifted apart?" Dr Thomas pushed a little further. Nate felt it was a harsh line from the doctor.

Maybe it was needed. He took himself by surprise, allowing the words to escape. And a tear rolled down his left cheek.

"It's just… I don't know how to fix us right now."

Rose looked directly at him. Nate couldn't meet her eyes. He felt her gaze, but he turned to the glass of water beside him and reached out for it. He realised his hand was shaking as he grasped the icy glass. There was an urge to roll it against his forehead. Instead, he took a shaky sip and placed it back down.

"Thank you, Nate," said Dr Thomas, breaking through the stifling silence that hung heavily in the room. Nate lifted his eyes to look at the man opposite. Compared to how Nate felt, he looked so calm and assured. Somehow, he'd perfected a look of being relaxed yet authoritative. He wore a plain blue tie with the top shirt button undone, sleeves rolled up past his elbows. His thick dark brown hair was sculpted smoothly into place, sweeping back without a single strand going astray. In between writing on his notepad, he had a habit of keeping his fingers clasped together but moving his thumbs up and down sporadically.

Rose reached across the gap that had formed between

her and Nate on the sofa and placed her hand on his.

"Tell me, if you can, Nate, how you feel you might be able to help Rose."

"I was kinda hoping you could tell me how to help, if I'm honest, Doc." Nate offered a nervous laugh. It was met with silence and a sympathetic look, which he took to indicate the platform for speaking was still his.

He cleared his throat and used the extra moment to consider his words again.

"I just wish things were good between us again. We used to have a laugh. Those little moments from nothing — like Rose sneaking her chilly hands onto my back; or singing along together while we cooked dinner; tickling the soles of her feet because she says she hates it, but I know she loves it, really. Daft, simple stuff, you know? I don't mean we should forget the sad or the serious stuff. I just think… we had some great times and we've kind of stopped having them anymore. It's like they've all been squeezed out by the crap that's happened and we've forgotten how to have fun together. And I guess, maybe I could help by trying to make us focus on that again? Maybe try to get back a bit of the fun?"

He thought he had phrased it as a question. Something to which he could receive an appraisal or acknowledgement of his suggestion. Instead, a "Hmm" and the scribble of notes made Nate feel like he'd failed that test. His pathetic answer was being judged and critiqued. He wanted to do better.

"… The thing is," he went on, "it really breaks me up inside to see Rose hurting so much. She's the woman I love, and I'd do anything for her but, actually… I feel helpless. I can see how much she's torturing herself. But it's torturing us all around her, too. She's on this downward spiral, being sucked further and further down, and I don't know how to help. I want to make her feel better. I want us to be closer again. But nothing I ever say or do seems to help. I don't know if it's just what she's been through with the accident or if there's something else. But I want her to know that I'm here and I want to make it better."

Dr Thomas finished scribbling before looking up and responding. "That's great, Nate. It's important that you can open up too. Rose is right there. You can tell her how you feel."

Nate felt his face flush. He realised he had been talking about Rose as if she wasn't right there on the same sofa. He had laid bare his feelings in the best way he could. Now, he realised he'd directed it at the wrong person. His wife was the bystander listening in.

He turned towards Rose and placed a hand awkwardly on hers. He looked straight into her eyes but glanced back down again before he spoke, like an embarrassed teenager. "I know I don't say this stuff as often as you want to hear it. You know I'm here for you, though. It's like the happy times we used to have are gone. I just sometimes wish we could turn the clock back."

Dr Thomas studied them and tapped the end of his pen on his pad. He hesitated before speaking. "I wouldn't normally rush into this after merely a couple of sessions, but the more I speak to you both, the more I'm convinced you could be ideal candidates for the early stages of a medical trial that I'm involved with."

"Medical? There's nothing physically wrong with me!" Nate said. He sat up a little straighter.

"Hear me out," the doctor said. "Like I say, I know it sounds sudden, but the window for accepting new candidates closes soon."

He paused again, and his eyes bored into Nate. "What if I told you we could help you focus on those happier times in a way that's totally new? That we could use your own memories to not just remind you of what you have lost but to inspire you to rekindle that happiness."

Nate looked at Rose, whose face showed no more understanding than he felt himself. They waited for Dr Thomas to continue.

"What if I told you we could use new technology to delve into those memories and give them renewed clarity and emphasis, to help bring them back into focus? It's only a trial, but imagine being able to relive the best memories of your relationship here on screen. Taking your memories, digitally recording them and viewing them back, together. It is something my research team, and I have made a reality."

"Wait, are you saying you can actually do that?" asked Nate.

"Essentially, yes."

"That's insane!"

"On the contrary, it is merely a step along the way towards something many scientists have been working on for years."

"A step? Towards what?"

"The ultimate goal for some researchers is to produce a complete emulation of the human brain. There's quite an academic focus on it, known as 'Whole Brain Emulation'. It has been a lifetime's work for some of my professional colleagues. It's a formidable, complex problem, but many people are convinced we will achieve it one day. Eventually, it could allow us to back-up our entire memory digitally."

"Surely that's not possible," said Rose, aghast.

"Well, not yet. Scanning of the entire neural tissue is still currently invasive and potentially destructive."

"Sounds painful," said Nate.

"Fortunately, it is not something to consider; we are years away from that level of sophistication. The goal is getting nearer, though, and we have to start somewhere. Developing this technology is the next step. Testing it on healthy brains first is key to unlocking its potential. The possibilities for it helping amnesia and dementia patients are groundbreaking."

"So, tell me again what you're saying we could do," said Rose.

"In simple terms, the therapy available to us right now would involve you being connected to some specialist equipment while we explore some of your existing happiest memories. It's an area of research I have been involved with for several years. My position on the research team would allow me to sign you up for the trial. It would be the first time we have used this technology outside of our research centre. You taking part would be hugely beneficial to the research, and I can assure you it's perfectly safe. It's non-invasive apart from an element of chemical stimulant involved which just serves to focus the brain."

"Chemical stimulant? As in drugs? I'm not sure that's what I signed up for," Nate said.

"The stimulant is partly to relax you and partly to allow your brain to home in on the things you're recalling. We can see right down to the molecular level which part of the brain is firing neurotransmitters and isolate them for the upload feed. Think of it like a digital signal being sent to your tv. It's all just data and code but on the screen, you get to see channels and pictures. It's like that, only the data-codes from your brain become movie files on here." Dr Thomas proudly tapped the laptop on the desk to his right. "You can then watch the memories back like a film.

See how you each remember things. Appreciate the tiny details you might otherwise gloss over or never articulate."

Nate looked to Rose for back-up.

"Would we need to go to hospital?" she asked.

"No, we can do it all here in my office," the doctor reassured her. "My licence to run a home practice extends to my research."

"It sounds really interesting," she said.

Nate's brow creased as she spoke. "Why can't we just look at old photos, watch home movies, talk about our memories? It seems excessive."

"Have you ever talked about a memory that you shared with someone else and realised you both remember it slightly differently?" Dr Thomas lent forward on his elbows.

Nate nodded.

"This therapy eliminates any bias or distortion that naturally occurs in all of our memories. It allows you to see things as they happened in that moment, not how you remember them now; see them in that same light. It also allows you to observe the other person's intimate subtleties of attraction. The minuscule indicators such as direction of gaze and focus that could only have been seen through their eyes, not a camera. Do you understand how that might be helpful in a situation such as yours?"

"I guess so," said Nate hesitantly.

"Could it help me remember the accident?" asked Rose.

Her body unfolded, and she sat forward.

"Technically, yes, but I'm afraid it's not currently within the parameters of the trial permissions." Dr Thomas narrowed his eyes. "As it's in the early stages, we are focusing on couples and happy memories until we can gain more data for use with trauma and amnesia."

"Who would know?" Rose's eyes were wide. "I'll sign something that says you're not responsible for any problems. Please, I'm desperate to know what happened."

Dr Thomas sat back in his chair and crossed his legs. He examined Rose's face, then tapped the pen against his chin. "Ok. If you both take part in the trial, then we can view the accident memory as an aside. But, I must stress that I can't give you data on the effects under those conditions, Rose. It would need to be done entirely at your own risk."

"I understand. Thank you so much." Rose looked at Nate and smiled. Nate's face made no movement.

Dr Thomas clearly sensed the disparity between the way they had both received his pitch. He looked at his watch, then closed the cover on his notepad.

"Listen, why don't you take an information pack and both have a read," he said, handing Nate a paper folder filled with documents, leaflets and forms. "It will answer most of your inevitable questions, I'm sure. Let's talk further next time."

4

Rose

Rose reached forward and turned down the radio. Nate's propensity for loud music had not dwindled with age. It was a staple of working in garages all his life, but Rose craved peace with growing urgency. Most of her days involved feeling overwhelmed, but today was off the chart. She still hated being in the car — any car. Her feet pushed at non-existent brake pedals while she sat in the passenger seat. Her fingers gripped the seat so tightly the tips turned white.

She watched as lights appeared in homely windows as they drove back towards Halewood Heath. The warm glow enveloped the people inside with an aura of cosiness that contrasted with the chilly car. In the slow-moving traffic, she saw snippets of domestic scenarios: couples debriefing after a busy day, parents in kitchens preparing dinner, children in living rooms watching cartoons. Every window enhanced the sense of longing that welled within her. Longing to feel normal again, to be calm and content. More than anything, she ached to go back to a time when she was safe in the glowing light of her mum's care.

"What do you think?" asked Rose, her stare fixed through the car window.

"About what?"

"About everything that's just happened!" Rose's cheeks felt warm again as she turned to face her husband.

"Yeah, it was fine," said Nate.

Rose rested her head against the cold car window and drummed her fingers on the door.

"Stop it," said Nate through his teeth. "What's the matter?"

"I guess I was just hoping you'd have a bit more to say about it," said Rose. "Today was a huge deal for us, Nate. Do you think it's going to help? You started to open up at the end. I didn't expect you to get emotional."

"It's not like I don't feel anything," said Nate. "I just never know what to say. Whatever I say seems wrong and when I say nothing that's wrong too."

"I thought what you said was nice."

Nate moved his hand from the gearstick to Rose's thigh. She felt a longed-for surge of comfort and inhaled to quash any more tears. Her head was banging and tiredness throbbed behind her eyes. She was done for today. She tucked the folder that Dr Thomas had given them into her bag and saw Nate's eyes glance towards it. She would need to read the information thoroughly, but barring any scary revelations, she wanted to go ahead with the memory therapy. Nate, however, would need persuading. It wasn't an argument for now. Despite her frustration, she had got everything out of him tonight she was going to. She was grateful he had stepped out of his comfort zone for her. All she could hope for was a quiet evening with no arguments.

*

Rose was woken the next morning by the noise of the front door slamming shut. She flipped over to find the bed empty and a perfumed humidity escaping through the open door of the ensuite. Nate must have already showered and left for work despite it being Saturday. Rose wished he would have woken her to say goodbye. Burying her face in his pillow, she inhaled the smell. Without raising her head, she felt around for her phone on the bedside table. She turned her head to see the screen and began her morning routine of checking messages, emails and the news.

She sent a quick text to her sister, Alannah, to cancel their brunch date, then opened her text conversation with Nate. It spanned back years and varied from heartfelt messages of love to random items that needed picking up from the supermarket. The latter had become prevalent long before her mother's death.

'Nice of you to say goodbye!'

She added a winky face to feign lightheartedness. Within seconds, she saw he had read the message but no sign of Nate typing. She pulled a childish face at the phone and tossed it dismissively across the room.

Half an hour later, the noise of vibrating wood woke her again. She sat up and saw her phone, which had landed on the dressing-table. Rose's heart-rate increased as she checked to see who it was. There had been sporadic silent phone calls for almost a year. No caller ID and no voice at the other end once she'd answered. It made her jumpy every time the phone rang. This wasn't one of them, though. Alannah was ringing. Rose couldn't let her think she was still in bed — it wasn't worth the lecture. Being several years older than Rose, Alannah had the tendency to believe she always knew what was best for her little sister — a trait that had become stronger since their mother's death. She rose quickly and cleared her throat, answering the phone with a breezy tone.

"Hey, Sis, you ok? Ringing to tell me about another late-night booty call?"

"Shut up," laughed Alannah, "that only happened once!"

"Yeah, but I know what you're like when you have a new fella — can't stay away, even at 2 am."

"Well, you can't blame me for being a romantic."

"Romance? Is that what you call it?"

"Shh, enough now, Miss Monogamy."

"That's Mrs Monogamy to you!" Rose corrected the title but flinched momentarily at the implication of the word.

"For fuck's sake. Actually, since you stood me up for brunch, I rang to see how yesterday went."

"Oh! Yeah, it was good, I think. It's still only the second session. He's a good listener, although I think it will take a while for Nate to warm to him…" Rose's voice faded as she opened her dressing-table drawer and rummaged through the contents.

"Why, what's the problem?" asked Alannah.

"You know what Nate's like," said Rose. "He's just not a talker." She slammed the drawer shut.

"OK, so it's not a problem with Adi?" asked Alannah.

"No, I don't think so. Just Nate being Nate. Like trying to get blood out of a stone. Why? Does it bother you? I didn't realise you were still friends with him or anything."

"Oh, I'm not, we're just friends on Facebook. Haven't really seen him since we left school. I know other people who've used him for therapy and said he's good. But I didn't want my recommendation to look bad if Nate wasn't happy with him."

There was a pause as Rose checked the floor around her bed.

"You OK?" asked Alannah.

"Yeah, sorry," said Rose, snapping back to focus. "I just can't find my sodding hairbrush. I swear there's a black hole in this house where things go missing." She stopped searching and settled back to the conversation. "I don't remember him from school — Adi. I remember some of the boys you were friends with, but his face wasn't familiar. Anyway, Dr Thomas…" Rose emphasised his full title, "… seems very good at his job. He actually recommended a treatment that's still being trialled, but it sounds amazing."

"What, like drugs?" asked Alannah. "I thought couple's therapy was about talking through your problems and stuff?"

"It's not drugs," said Rose. "It's a new memory therapy, to help us remember the good times we've had together. Dr Thomas has been working with a group of scientists and psychologists to develop some technique that allows you to view your memories more clearly. I don't understand all the jargon and science, but it sounds amazing. Apparently you can download your memories and see things you can't even remember forgetting! You view it all on a screen. He's quite a big deal in his field, your friend. I've looked him up online. I never realised you moved in such academic circles?"

"Haha!" said Alannah sarcastically. "Rose, this whole memory therapy thing sounds creepy and invasive!"

"It's not invasive at all. We just talk through the memories and he records them digitally so that we can watch them back together."

"OK, maybe not physically invasive, but certainly emotionally. I thought you were trying to get over your problems, not rake them all up and watch them at the cinema."

"It's not about watching back awful memories," said Rose. She felt embarrassed and confused by the discrepancy between her reaction and those of Nate and Alannah. She knew she was grabbing onto the idea out of desperation. Nothing else had worked — not the previous counselling sessions nor the antidepressants she had been taking since her mother's death. She had exhausted all ways to fix herself, and now her marriage was at stake as well. How could Nate and Alannah not realise how important this was? After all their pleas for her to get out of bed each day, not give up. This new hope might lift the blanket of gloom and shake her awake. Was that not worth the risk?

"We can focus on the amazing memories we have; when Nate and I were happy, had the energy for each other, for our relationship. And it's not only that, Lana, don't you see? If we do this, I can watch back the accident and see what happened! See what went wrong."

"Are you sure it's a good idea? This isn't what I was expecting it to involve. I didn't want you reliving the accident or having your brain tapped into, I just wanted you and Nate to be OK!"

"We can enter the trial now," said Rose, ignoring her sister's negativity. "They're looking for volunteers to try it out and Dr Thomas said that we would be perfect candidates."

"And Nate's agreed to this?" The pitch of Alannah's voice became higher.

"Not yet," Rose said. "But he's just as committed as me to getting our relationship back on track."

"And is this the answer to that? Or are you using it purely to find out what happened in the accident?"

Rose paused. "Maybe that's part of it, but it's the perfect way to kill two birds with one stone. I get my answers and Nate and I go back to how we were. It's a win-win. Finding out what caused the accident will help me move on and remembering the good times will remind us both of the foundation that we built our relationship on."

"But you can do that without this brain therapy thing! You can talk about your memories or look at photos. It sounds like you're asking a lot from Nate in order to help you remember the accident."

"It's not just about me. Nate and I haven't been right for a while, and he is just as much to blame for our problems as I am."

"Don't get defensive." Alannah sounded concerned. "I wasn't implying you were to blame for any of it. None of this is anyone's fault."

"The accident was. I was driving," Rose said sharply.

"Please, let's not start this again. No one was to blame, you've got to stop doing this to yourself."

"Do you not want to know what happened?" Rose wasn't getting sucked into the cyclical argument that united Nate and Alannah against her. "I mean, she was your mum too. Aren't you desperate to know the truth?"

"That's not fair. Of course I am, but I can live with just knowing it was a terrible accident. I know you, Sis. You would never have done anything stupid or dangerous, and I love you. I can't bear seeing you beat yourself up day in, day out. We need to learn to move on."

Rose had told her sister, more times than she could count, how desperate she was to clear the muddy waters within which her memory of the accident was submerged. She felt angry that Alannah couldn't see the connection. This could help her find closure.

The sisters' relationship was prone to trials. As teenagers, jealousy had marred the closeness of telling each other everything when Alannah dated Rose's best friend, George. The years afterwards had been rocky, with Rose losing her closest ally to a sister who would dump him just two months later. Rose and George had never fully rekindled their friendship, but Rose often thought of him.

By the time Rose had returned from university, qualified and excited to start her career as a teacher, teenage rifts had healed. Alannah, who had gone straight from school to a job, was still living with their mother and the three of them had become a tight-knit trio. Saturday mornings held a regular brunch date at Harvey's Bistro on the road out towards Matlock, a tradition the sisters had attempted to keep up in the aftermath of losing their mum. Without her, though, the odd week had been forgotten or cancelled and today was amongst them.

The same pattern had emerged with Rose making excuses not to go. Alannah knew that the only real obstacle was Rose's anxiety and had made it her mission to push her sister to try harder. Even though Rose knew it came from a good place, the pressure to 'move on' had made her even more desperate for space.

"Babe, this is such a bad idea! You've experienced trauma. You need help but—"

"I've had help, Lana! Three different counsellors, a support group, antidepressants, yoga, hypnotherapy… nothing works. I still feel as shitty as I did a year ago. This could be the key."

"I know, I know," said Alannah, softer now. "Sorry. I didn't mean to sound unsupportive. Please, just promise me you'll give this a lot more thought before you jump in."

"OK. I promise."

"Right, well, get back into bed. Don't think I don't know your sleepy voice," Alannah resumed her playful tone.

"Fine, you caught me but it's Saturday and Nate's at work so I just needed to chill."

"Go! Chill! I love you and I will see you next Saturday for brunch, OK?"

"OK. Love you too. Bye, Sis."

Rose smiled. Alannah drove her mad sometimes, but she was relentlessly her champion. Without her, the last year would have been unbearable. Rose reminded herself that Alannah had lost her mum as well, and that she needed to step up the sisterly love a bit more. Her mum would take comfort in the knowledge they were supporting each other.

She climbed back into bed and opened her messages again: still nothing from Nate, one from her ex-colleague, Scott, sharing some silly meme that she would ignore and one from her friend, Helen. Helen had been a pillar of strength for Rose in the accident's aftermath. She had shown up with lasagnes and casseroles; checked in with Rose daily. With her, Rose felt no obligation to tidy up or pretend to be OK. If anyone was going to understand Rose's desire to do the memory therapy, it would be her. It wasn't just that; Helen was a nurse. She knew about things like therapies and trials. Rose trusted her to give an honest opinion of the drugs involved and the potential pros and cons. Keen to gauge her friend's thoughts on whether it seemed like the madness Nate and Alannah were making out, she composed a text to arrange a catch up later in the day. She smiled as the reply came through.

'BRING WINE!'

∗

The cupboards in Rose and Nate's kitchen were sparsely stocked. The garage had been really busy so Nate had been working late and Rose, determined to get herself together, insisted that the responsibility of food shopping should fall to her. But as days came and went, so did the excuses not to leave the house. Nate tried his best to be understanding, but Rose felt guilty for the frustration she assumed he was feeling at having to pick up dinner one meal at a time on his way home from work.

Today, however, the motivation to buy wine to take to Helen's was spurring her on. The therapy gave her something to tell her friend about, and more than that it gave her hope. Was this the beginning of her road to recovery?

Rose grabbed her keys and took a deep breath as she left the house. She looked at her car parked on the road. What a step it would be to get in it and drive to the supermarket. She wasn't there yet, but walking to the off licence on Station Road was a positive start.

As she walked, she tried to ignore the light-headed

feeling that came with daylight and fresh air, both things she had only felt in short sharp bursts recently. She smiled at the lady coming out of the butcher's laden with a toddler and several bags. She listened as they walked past her in the opposite direction and their footsteps faded. New footsteps emerged instead, heavier, slower. She turned around, but no one was there. She crossed the road and turned left towards the off licence. A mantra spun around her head like a chant: go in, buy the wine, go home. It was so simple, yet success seemed so far away.

Rose turned again. Nothing. The footsteps were further behind now, but remained sure and steady. She could have sworn they stopped as she turned. How could she let anxiety control her like this? It was daylight in a safe area. She was simply going into a shop — not the right time for fight or flight, and yet she could feel it creeping in. With every step, she grew more sure that someone was following her, watching her. Her lungs worked over time and before she knew it, her feet kicked in. She realiscd she was speeding up, breaking into a run, and it was beyond her control. Running faster, her eyes froze ahead. At the corner, she faced a decision — right, towards home through quiet streets or left, away from her house but with the safety of shops and lots of people. She could call Nate from there. As she considered her options, the urge to check behind her was too much. She turned her head and gazed at the empty pavement behind her. No one was there.

She began to run again, but her feet moved forward quicker than her head and she felt the thud of contact.

"Sorry!" said a voice. "Oh! Rose!"

Rose looked up and saw James, half a foot taller, staring at her.

"Oh my God, J!" Rose hugged her ex-boyfriend, clinging on for longer than a simple greeting.

"Hey, are you OK? What's up?" James furrowed his brow and held eye-contact with Rose.

"Yeah, no, I just... I'm not sure," panted Rose. She pointed behind her and was about to speak before humiliation developed. "Sorry, yeah, I'm fine."

"You're not fine," said James. He had always been able to read her like a book. "Come on, let's get a coffee." He put his arm around her shoulder and guided her to the cafe nearby. She had no energy or desire to argue.

*

Rose sat in the corner booth with her back to the wall. While James went to order the coffees, she took a moment to compose herself and a message to Helen cancelling their plans. She was safe with James.

5

Nate

The Verve's Bitter Sweet Symphony was blaring out from the grease-covered radio in the corner. It competed with the hum of machinery and the buzz of workshop banter. The workshop side of the garage had ample space for working on two cars side by side. It was a local business that had been operating for at least twenty years. Some of the metal racks of shelving had probably been there since it first opened up, too. The corrugated metal sheets for both roof and walls meant the place was permanently cold.

"Chuck us the half-inch torque, will you, Gaz?" Nate called out to his best mate.

"Don't think that's how you speak to the boss, pal," Gaz said as the metal tool clattered on the concrete floor not far from Nate's feet.

"Oh, listen to this big man, Andy," Nate shouted to the only other mechanic with them. "Don't be letting the power go to your head or anything, ay, Gaz? You're only in charge on Saturday mornings!"

The pair had worked there for several years, although

Gaz for slightly longer than Nate. Andy was a young apprentice who said little but joined in occasionally with the constant wisecracks. Gaz had helped Nate to get the job when he was looking for somewhere new — and in the best of humour, he liked to keep Nate reminded of his marginally more senior employee ranking. He walked over to where Nate was exploring under the bonnet of an ailing Fiat as its engine coughed and juddered.

"Remember why you get all the crap jobs, pal. Don't worry, though, one day you might be able to match my magic touch. Till then, I'm ready for a brew if you're making."

"I thought we gave Andy all the crap jobs?" Nate joked. "Does it look like I'm making?"

"Alright, alright. Tell ya what — I'll flick the kettle on if you sit your grumpy arse over there and tell me if things are any better with you and that missus of yours. You'll be alright for a bit won't ya, Andy?"

Andy looked up and nodded. Nate sighed as he straightened up a little and rested both hands on the car bonnet.

"Jeez, Gaz, you're no agony aunt are you? This heap ain't going anywhere fast, though, is it? Grab the biscuits and you can solve all my other problems instead."

The mechanics' kitchen area was a makeshift addition in one corner of the building, separated by a grubby internal door. The boss got his hands dirty occasionally, but usually concentrated on buying and selling from his desk. These days he was off at an auction as often as he was in the garage. A reception area connected the boss's office and the workshop. Linda worked on the phones there and sat at the front desk. She was always up for a laugh with the mechanics but was older and a lot less flirty than the previous receptionist, Nina.

"So you went along with this couple's counselling, then?" Gaz asked.

"Well, I figured if it has a chance of helping us, then why not? It's been a pretty rough year you know — since the accident and all that. I think it's knocked us for six, so maybe we need a bit of help to get sorted. It's not something I ever thought we'd be doing. Just trying what we can. She's still proper torn up, to be honest."

Three digestives later, Nate had given him the bare bones about the visit to Dr Thomas.

"Shit! Fair play to you, pal. That's rough, though. D'you think it's gonna make any difference, then?"

"I dunno, mate. The guy's got some pretty wacko ideas. Wasn't my kind of thing from the start, and this is definitely not what I was expecting. If it helps Rose, then it's worth it, though, ain't it? She needs to open up to someone about it all. I don't know what to say to her half the time."

"Must be bloody hard to come to terms with — driving the car when your own mother's killed."

"She blames herself, mate."

"It's no surprise, though, ay? Wouldn't we all?"

"But for how long? It was an accident. How long's it supposed to take to get over? When do we get to move on?"

"Look, it's tough, pal, but you've just got to give it…"

"Give it time? Don't tell me. That's what everyone says — 'give it time'. But no one tells you how much! Where's the rules on that? Am I being a dick for trying to put it behind us instead of letting it rule everything? Don't we have to put the effort in to move on, rather than just be stuck in the misery? Is that me being a selfish idiot? Cos I just don't want every waking moment to be about that crash."

"She lost her mum, pal. There're no rules on how long that takes to get over. And if she blames herself, it's even harder."

"I know, I know. OK, no need to say it. I am being a dick."

He took a final swig from his mug, then got to his feet. "That Fiat ain't gonna fix itself, is it?" he said and headed back under the bonnet.

*

"Pretty young lass in reception asking for you, Nate.

Linda's jealous — it's not even your missus." Gaz winked as he stuck his head through the workshop door not long later.

Nate looked up, waiting for any more information, but none was forthcoming. Wiping his hands on an oily rag didn't make them any less black, so he stuffed it into his pocket and rubbed his palms against the legs of his blue overalls. He walked through the door into the office side of the building and Gaz gave him a friendly punch as he passed. "Careful, it's the sister-in-law," he whispered in his ear.

"Alannah," Nate said as he emerged through the interconnecting door to where Linda looked up from her computer. He manoeuvred from behind the counter around to the opposite side where Rose's sister was standing, twirling her keys around her finger. "What are you doing here?"

She smiled at him as he came around to the customer side of the counter.

"I'll be taking a look at that Fiat for you, then, pal," Gaz called out from the doorway with another wink.

Nate walked Alannah out through the front office door to the yard full of cars. A couple of them were in for repair; one was an M.O.T. fail that was waiting on a customer's return call. Next to that, Nate recognised Alannah's powder blue VW Beetle.

"I thought I could hear it making a kind of rattling

noise as I drove this morning," she said, pointing towards the car.

"Oh, right?" Nate met her eyes for a moment. "Do you want to pop the lid and start her up? I'll have a listen."

Alannah did as he'd asked. Nate propped open the bonnet and took advantage of its shield while his sister-in-law sat behind the wheel. He listened and poked around, but nothing seemed amiss.

"Was it just when you were driving or as soon as you started it up?"

"Erm… I think I just noticed it while I was waiting at the lights earlier."

"Sounds alright to me," he called over the noise of the engine. Alannah turned the key and killed the sound. She got out and leaned against the car.

"Really? Ah thanks, Nate. Probably just me being paranoid, then. I'll trust your expert knowledge." She flashed him a wide smile.

"No probs…" The silence lingered for a moment. "Well, keep an eye on it and let me know if it seems to keep happening. I might need to take it for a drive. Was it just that, then, or—"

"How's Rose been this week?" Her question was loaded, but with what, he couldn't tell.

"Oh, you know." Nate shrugged. This was exactly what he didn't want to get into.

"She mentioned to me about that memory therapy

idea," Alannah prodded.

"Right. Did she?" Nate felt cornered.

"Yeah, she seemed keen but, I'm not sure. What do you think?"

He didn't want this conversation. Not at the garage, and not with his wife's sister. But he did sense the expression of caution that he could relate to.

"Well, I'm not sure either, if I'm honest. Wasn't it you that put this counselling idea in her head in the first place? It's not my thing. Just feels like this might be a step too far to me."

"Exactly! Counselling, yeah. The two of you talking, fine. This brain therapy trial, though? I get Rose might want to do it. I just think it's risky trying to rake over memories in her head like that. That's not what your therapy was supposed to be about was it? You're her husband — do you think that's what she needs?"

It irked Nate, Alannah knowing so much — first about the relationship problems, now about this development. The only silver lining was it seemed like she was on his wavelength here.

"No, I don't suppose it is but—"

"Exactly," Alannah said to seal their agreed consensus. "Listen, thanks for looking at the car, Nate. I appreciate it. I'll see you when you two come over next week, hey?"

She waved and gave him the gleaming smile again as she got back into the car and drove out of the yard.

Nate retrieved the oily rag from his pocket and wiped his hands as he watched her leave.

*

After work he drove, as he did most Saturday afternoons, to his parents' house. It usually involved a bottle of beer with his dad, while his mum frequently asked if she could get him a biscuit or a sandwich or some cake.

"Honestly, Mum, I'm fine," he said, waving away an assortment of chocolate bars in a plastic container. He sat with his dad at the kitchen table, who was still in his gardening clothes — jeans which had oval patches of soil on both knees and matching-coloured streaks down each thigh where he had wiped dirty hands. The old man had taken to wearing a flat cap and often had the same sleeveless fishing jacket over his jumper. Given that the bloke had never been fishing in his life and used to claim hats didn't suit him, Nate took delight in ribbing him about both.

"Carry on, Son," his father said — after the interruption — pulling out a pack of extra strong mints from one of about a dozen pockets in his jacket. "What were you saying? The memories can be recorded digitally? On what, a DVD?"

"Well, I don't think it's like getting a souvenir copy!" Nate laughed, waving away the offer of a mint. "I'm not sure if I feel it's a bit… I dunno… like an invasion of privacy."

"I think it sounds incredible," his father said with considerably more enthusiasm than Nate was expecting.

"Really?" he asked.

"Well yeah, don't you think it's amazing what they can do nowadays?"

"I guess so."

"I mean, no offence, it's a bit wasted on your love life. The pair of you can't see what you've got in front of your eyes. You're bloody great together, you and Rose. You don't need to see a video of your own memories to know that."

"I thought you were just telling me it sounds incredible?"

"Yeah, but I mean for other things. If this works, just think what it could mean for court trials, the justice system, for interrogating criminal suspects."

"Oh, trust you, Dad. You don't stop thinking like a copper no matter how long you're retired, do you?"

Nate's father had served over thirty years in the police force before taking his pension in his mid-fifties. He'd always remained a constable through his career, never choosing to progress to a sergeant or any other role. He doled out his overused phrase about joining the force to catch the bad guys if anyone questioned a lack of ambition. That was usually followed by 'you don't catch criminals sitting behind a desk'.

Nate admired him. He'd always admired his father's work ethic, his moral compass, his integrity. He knew he was lucky to get on well with both his parents. And he valued their opinions. He hadn't been expecting the perspective offered by his dad in this case — although he realised now he should have suspected it would be the first thought his father had.

"I'm not saying it replaces good old-fashioned policing," he went on, "but imagine someone not coughing up info when they're being questioned. You could put 'em through this. It'd be like reading their mind. Even better than a lie-detector."

"I think you'd have some problems with consent and human rights, there, Dad. You can't just strap someone in and read their mind. Me and Rose would be willing participants if we agreed to it — there's a difference."

"Fair point, Son, fair point. That's half the problem nowadays as well. Too much focus on the criminal's human rights instead of the victim's. Maybe it could be compulsory in serious cases, though, you know? The killers who refuse to confess what they did with a body, assault cases, organised crime."

"I hadn't really thought about any of that," Nate admitted.

"They've tried stuff like this before, though, you know?"

"Like what?"

"These drugs and interrogations and whatnot. They reckon the American police used to use the stuff in the thirties — truth serums and all that. And in the war, the drugs they used for anaesthetic turned out to be pretty good at getting soldiers to talk and say what had happened to them."

"I do wonder how you remember some of this stuff, Dad. Anyway, we're not talking truth serums. Just a drug that is some kind of stimulant, but it's the technology that's the real advancement here, apparently."

"What a chance for you to be involved in trialling something like this, though. It could be huge in the future if this technology really works. Might take a long while for it to become admissible in criminal court…" His dad was becoming quite animated and excited at the prospects he was imagining. Although the ideas sounded fascinating, it did nothing to convince Nate that it was something he should get involved with for relationship issues. He agreed with his dad that he and Rose just needed to recognise what was in front of their eyes — each other.

"I don't think you're getting the idea of the purpose, Dad."

"I'm just saying, it has all kinds of possibilities. Mind you, it's a can of worms too. Can you control what's being recorded? What about memories you're not keen to share?" he pondered aloud. Sitting back in his chair, he folded his arms and stuck out his bottom lip to show he was sceptical.

"Well, we've not looked into it all yet and I haven't agreed to anything," Nate said. He felt his father's apparent reluctance seeping into him, too.

"You never know, though, when it makes the news as the next big thing for making a prosecution stick, you could look back thinking you were involved before most people had heard of it. I'd give it a go, just to experience it."

Maybe the man sensed himself swaying Nate's deliberation too negatively. Maybe he just thought better of providing a more balanced view. It wasn't leaving Nate feeling much clearer about the situation that was already clogging up his brain.

"Trust you, Dad! I think I'd rather just wait to see it on the news," he said.

6

Rose

Rose could hear the alarm going off but couldn't quite rouse herself. Nate was still snoring next to her, and the heating was clunking. She listened to the beeping for a few moments before the warm brush of Nate's arm summoned her from wherever her mind had wandered off — she couldn't remember now. He reached across her forehead and turned off her alarm.

"Morning," he whispered and kissed her gently on the head. Since their last appointment, he had been attempting to be more affectionate. Rose felt guilty for her cynicism in thinking he was just trying to avoid going forwards with the memory therapy.

"Hey." Rose still had her eyes shut.

"You all set for today?" asked Nate.

"Course, no big deal."

"I'll make us a cuppa." Nate got out of bed and wafted the covers, exposing Rose to the chilly morning air.

"Fuck off, it's freezing!" Rose wrapped herself up again.

"All the more reason to get in the shower!" called Nate as he disappeared downstairs.

"All the more reason to stay in bed," grumped Rose, checking her phone. There was the predictable text from Scott. These texts had become a regular occurrence. More often than not, it was a drunken message saying how much he missed working with Rose or inviting her to join them for the next staff night out. Rose never replied. She had vowed to distance herself from him after the pair of them became close at work. Rose knew he wanted more than her marriage vows would permit. If she ignored him for long enough, he would eventually get the message — the last thing she needed was an awkward conversation. Today needed all of her focus.

Rose had been helping Alannah with sorting some of their mum's belongings. Alannah had never left home. With no long-term relationships to plunge her into the world of cohabitation, she never had the incentive to move out. Rose had always felt a tiny pang of jealousy at the time Alannah and their mum got to spend together. She often visited for film nights and barbecues, but she missed the inane chatter at breakfast or the hugs from her mum before she went to sleep. It had been a hard tug to move out. Had it not been for the excitement of a new relationship and the urgency for Nate to move out of the flat he shared with his ex-fiancée, Rose believed that particular step would have been far more drawn out. She had certainly dragged her heels when James suggested they move in together. In the end, it had sealed their fate when he presented her with an ultimatum. They had parted amicably, agreeing that they'd become more like friends than lovers. Staying at her mum's had always had the stronger draw... until she met Nate.

Their mum's bedroom remained exactly as she had left it. Alannah had admitted to sitting in there and talking to her in the evenings, but she hadn't been able to bring herself to pack away any of the clothes. Rose had promised they would do it together today, and she had run out of excuses to put it off. Nate had taken the day off work to help them and borrowed Gaz's van so he could deliver any bits to charity shops and second-hand furniture stores.

Rose threw the covers back and counted to three before prising her head off the pillow. She threw her pyjamas onto the laundry basket in the ensuite and started up the shower, before noticing that the bathroom window was open. Had that been open all night? As she shut it, a movement through the frosted glass caught her eye. The garden backed onto farmland on the outskirts of the village, and it had never occurred to either her or Nate to get a blind fitted. It was unlikely that anyone could see in from the fields over the garden wall. Occasionally, though, Rose jolted at a movement from outside. A tree branch in the wind or an animal in the garden, maybe. Nevertheless, she had recently felt more exposed.

She took a shower and got dressed in comfy leggings and a baggy jumper. She borrowed Nate's comb, screwed her hair into a messy bun and climbed back into bed. Nate had left tea and toast for her on the bedside table. He would find it there cold hours later. He called up the stairs and Rose heard the sounds of the van engine.

Minutes later, Rose slumped into the front seat and curled up with her hood pulled over her face, the heaters blowing warm air at full force. She leaned her head on the window and snoozed as Nate drove the three miles to her old home.

*

Rose opened the front door and called inside to announce her arrival. Even though she no longer lived there, she had always felt comfortable to walk in. But now she paused for an answer before entering. It was different with only Alannah living there. Rose never knew what she could walk into or whether she still had the right to do so. She did legally own half the house, though — as Nate had recently reminded her, again.

The sisters had spent a few evenings since the accident discussing what to do with the house. They had both grown up there; it was home. The thought of selling it to strangers broke Rose's heart, but the alternative wasn't ideal either. Alannah couldn't afford to buy out Rose's share. However, with a mortgage that wouldn't stretch them too much, Nate and Rose were in a position to move in and buy Alannah's half from her. Aside from the awkwardness of kicking Alannah out, Rose didn't know if she could bear living in the house without her mum there. She was bombarded by a nostalgia that knocked her for six every time she visited, and she didn't know if it would ever soften.

They had made no decisions, but Nate had voiced his feelings to Rose that she shouldn't let Alannah stay there without at least paying rent. Today would bring yet another discussion that Rose wasn't ready to have about where to go next with the legal stuff. Nate usually instigated these, and Rose didn't have the energy to argue with him. She knew how quickly calm conversations had turned to arguments in the recent months. Therefore, both sisters avoided the topic but for different reasons — Alannah because she didn't want to leave the house and Rose because money was the furthest thing from her mind.

Rose was exhausted by the thought of more paperwork. After her mum's death, despite endless emails, phone calls and more visits to various offices than she could bear, letters still arrived. On a couple of occasions, envelopes had landed addressed to The Deceased Mrs Elaine Dawson. Nate had brushed it off with humour by asking whether they should forward it on for her. Rose had managed a little laugh before sneaking off to throw up. It still caught her in the gut like a boot. Her mother was deceased because of her. If she hadn't been driving, her mum would have been around to open those envelopes, to swear about the rise in bills, to giggle at the various misspellings of her name.

The familiar sound of Alannah's voice shouted for Rose and Nate to come in. She came running down the stairs and greeted Rose with a hug.

"Alright, gorgeous?" She winked at Nate and ruffled his hair. "Tea, anyone?"

Nate gave a coy eye roll with a brief smile. "Yep — tea would be good, cheers."

Rose had found coming to the house hard since the accident. Stepping through the front door was fine. She could even cope with the photo of her, Alannah and Mum that greeted her in the rustic hallway. It was the minor details that made her chest feel tight: the shoes missing from the rack; the garage full of half-finished art projects that would never be complete; the messier kitchen than Mum would have tolerated. It was these smaller things that spiked her tear ducts. Worst of all, though, was the row of tea mugs ready to accept their fill. Mum had always lined them up in the same order: Rose's to the left, no sugar; Mum's, one sugar; then Alannah's and Nate's each with two sugars. Rose couldn't handle Mum's mug being the only one left in the cupboard now. The sight made her light-headed and desperate to get on with the job in hand before running back to her safe space where the energy to be OK wasn't required.

"Shall we get on?" she said.

"Sure!"

Alannah was chirpy, and Rose hated it. It made her feel like she wasn't coping as well as her sister. Alannah had spent a year living in the house. She was used to the reminders in which it was dowsed. She had felt all the pangs of grief a hundred times and adjusted. Rose had rarely visited since the accident, and every handwritten note was a sharp dig in her chest. How could someone be so full of life one minute and not even exist the next? She had lost her safety net, her comfort in any storm, the security of the one person who had looked after her for her entire life. Adulthood had never seemed daunting until now, and she never realised how much she had relied on her mum. Without her, every decision seemed harder, every achievement less valid, every piece of news pointless.

"Do you want me to start in the garage?" asked Nate.

"If you don't mind that would be amazing," said Alannah. "Rose and I can get cracking with the bedroom."

"You OK?" said Nate, his palm on the back of Rose's neck.

"Yep," said Rose without looking him in the eye. She

started towards the stairs and Nate gently pulled her back. He placed his index finger under her chin and raised her eyes to meet his.

"She'd be so proud of you, you know," he said.

Rose buried her head in his shoulder and sobbed. "She'd be telling me to pull myself together."

"No. She'd be telling you not to put your tea down there without a coaster," said Alannah, scooping up the mug. "Come on, Sis, let's get this done."

Rose laughed and wiped her eyes, following Alannah up to their mother's bedroom.

"Two secs," said Alannah, popping Rose's tea on a little crocheted square on the bedside table. "Just need to nip and show Nate my system in the garage. You stay here and get started, won't be long."

Mum's room was neat and airy with crisp white sheets on the bed. Rose had never understood how she kept her sheets looking so fresh all the time. She wished she had inherited her mum's work ethic for ironing and folding laundry. Rose was the first to admit that her housework skills left a lot to be desired. She sat on the bed and smoothed over the sheets with her hand.

"Where do we even start?" she said out loud. This was the only place she felt like her mum might be listening.

She looked across to the chunky wooden dressing-table and visualised her mum sitting on the stool looking into the mirror. She had watched her doing her makeup so many times as a child. Even into her teenage years, she had sat in that same spot on the bed talking about friends, fashion, schoolwork and the latest argument with Alannah.

Rose made her way to the stool and stared into the same mirror that had captured her mother's image thousands of times before. 'If only mirrors had memories,' she thought.

Mum loved perfume and collected colourful glass bottles in different shapes and sizes. She had picked them up from all over the world and barely a birthday or Mother's Day went past without her receiving one from her girls. Of course, she had her favourites, and into those, she decanted her everyday perfume, her special occasion perfume, and the perfume Rose's dad had given her on their wedding day. She never wore that anymore, just kept the last few millilitres in a bottle to smell when she wanted to be reminded of him. Rose's dad had died of cancer when she was just two and Alannah five. Growing up, Rose was sure she remembered him, but the few images she had were very similar to those in the photos her mum had kept in pride of place around the house. Rose accepted the possibility that her memories were in fact of the photos and not of the man himself.

Alannah walked in as Rose was sniffing one of the perfume bottles.

"Don't do it to yourself," she said.

"It's comforting," said Rose in a quiet breath.

Alannah perched on the bed, and they remained in silence for a few moments.

"Is that Nigel?" asked Rose, looking out the window. "I didn't know he still came."

Alannah pulled back the curtain and peered at the blanket of gold and yellow leaves in the back garden. Outside, a serious-looking man was raking the lawn. He was in his late fifties with tanned skin from a lifetime spent outdoors. Nigel had been helping their mother with the garden since Alannah and Rose were children. He had never been a man of many words, but their mum had been fond of him.

"God, yeah," said Alannah. "You know what I'm like with gardening. Can't be arsed. I'd much rather pay someone to keep on top of things, and the garden was getting so overgrown. He worked for Mum for so long, it seemed like a no-brainer. I called him back about a month ago. He's been a godsend. Wish he'd smile a bit more, though!"

Rose laughed and wrote a label for a box of unopened toiletries, destined for the charity shop. "Don't think I'd smile much if I had to freeze my tits off in other people's gardens all day."

Rose went to the wardrobe and sighed. "I guess we've put this off long enough."

"I don't know what to do with it all," said Alannah, appearing at Rose's side. "I can't bear the thought of someone else in Mum's clothes." Rose put her arm around her big sister and pulled her into her shoulder. Alannah sniffed and took Rose's hand.

"Let's just get it done," said Rose. "Maybe it will help to not have it hanging over us."

Ever since their appointment with Dr Thomas, Rose had become obsessed with focusing on the happiness of the past. Life had become a list of things to endure before she could flip a switch and get back to normal. First on the list was getting her mum's stuff sorted. Once they'd done that, she could focus on remembering why she had crashed the car. It was a much more achievable to-do list now that Dr Thomas had suggested the memory therapy and Rose felt heartened by the prospect of clarity and closure.

As she stared into the old pine wardrobe, Rose imagined her mum getting ready to leave the house on the morning of the accident. Picking her outfit; putting on her everyday perfume; making the bed and replacing the plump cushions that finished it off. She would have taken a few minutes choosing which scarf to wear. Mum felt the cold and had a myriad of scarves, mostly given to her by Rose and Alannah for Christmas or birthdays. The predictability of the presents she received was a standing joke in their house. Even on sunny days, Mum had always worn something around her neck.

Rose realised she was holding a dusty pink cashmere

scarf to her cheek. A small circle of darker pink had formed and Rose wiped her eyes with her sleeve. The light-headed feeling circled again, and she sat down.

"Do you want to keep that one?" asked Alannah.

"I think so," said Rose, her eyes blurring.

"Would you mind if I kept the turquoise one with the golden leaves on it?" asked Alannah. "I gave it to her for Christmas a few years ago."

Rose felt a wave of nausea coming over her. She tried to refocus her eyes, but the room was spinning and out of sync. Despite being sat down, she felt the need to steady herself with her hands.

"Sorry," she said as she ran out of the bedroom towards the bathroom across the corridor.

Behind a locked door, Rose was no longer on show. She felt safer hidden from the humiliation of being overcome in front of other people. Sitting on the floor with her back against the bath, she closed her eyes and faced the ceiling. She monitored each breath. In and out for the count of three, just like the doctor had told her. After repeating this a few times, she got to her knees and rested her elbows on the toilet seat. She ran her hands through her hair and closed her eyes to stop the room spinning.

There it was, waiting behind her eyelids, the image of her mother's face which was never far away. Her eyes open and staring straight ahead, a trickle of blood running from the corner of her mouth, her cheeks clammy and discoloured. The emergency lights flashing around her, and there, under her head, the turquoise scarf with the golden leaves. Rose had placed it there for her — one last comfort before her last breath. She wished that her mum was there now as the one giving comfort. She had always known how to make Rose feel better when she felt sick as a child — a towel to rest her head on, a stroke of the forehead.

A knock at the door summoned Rose's attention.

"You OK?" asked Alannah.

"Yep. Fine. Just needed a sec,"

Rose could now hear the depth of Nate's voice join Alannah's in a whispered conversation.

"I'm fine, you guys," she called again.

"Did I say something wrong?" Alannah's voice was wobbling.

Rose could hear Nate comforting her sister. Broken sentences emanated from the staircase — "… happens all the time…" and "… not your fault…"

She got to her feet and unbolted the door, resting her head on the doorframe.

"Seriously, I'm fine." said Rose, emerging into the corridor. "Sorry, babe. No, you didn't say anything wrong, just felt dizzy."

Alannah handed Rose a glass of water with a brief smile.

"You can't have that scarf, though, Sis, sorry. It's not

here. Mum was wearing it. You know."

7

Nate

The information given to them by Dr Thomas lay on the glass coffee table in the lounge next to where Nate rested his crossed feet. Yesterday, the same folder had appeared on the kitchen worktop and the day before it was on the hall table. He knew that Rose was leaving it around on purpose for him to come across, but had chosen not to take the bait. He wondered if she didn't realise how obvious she was being about it. Or whether she knew but didn't care.

They had talked briefly about the memory therapy. Twice, in fact. Each time, Nate felt the tug of apprehension grow stronger. His father's voice plagued him, convincing him it was a brilliant concept — just meant for much more important matters than their love life; he had Alannah's voice proclaiming what a bad idea it was to rake over the past. Both stoked his initial instinct that it seemed a risky exercise and wouldn't bring anything positive. Mixed with those views, he pictured Gaz laughing at him for the whole thing. He'd agreed to the idea of couple's therapy, albeit advocated by Rose. Admittedly, he'd seen the potential benefit, but what he pictured was the pair of them talking things through; finding some clarity, rekindling what was great about their relationship a year ago. This went way beyond that. He pictured the scene from *A Clockwork Orange* where the guy was strapped in a chair with his eyes clamped open for some primitive psychological aversion therapy. Nate's irrational response was to ignore the issue completely, screw it into a ball and throw it to the back of his mind.

For a few days, the folder had been the elephant in the room. A zing of tension built between them everywhere their paths crossed. Now, due for their next appointment, the subject needed addressing. Nate had simply decided it wouldn't be him to broach it.

"Lift up your legs," said Rose as she flicked a duster around the coffee table. She picked up the folder, skirted the duster across the glass surface and dropped the paper-clipped stack of pages back down a little closer to Nate's legs than they had previously laid. The table had been dusted and polished the day before. And probably the day before that. Nate had stopped questioning his wife's manic cleaning, which had gone through relentless phases in the previous few months. The only times it stopped were the periods that flipped to the opposite end of the scale — when she seemed not to have the energy to do anything at all, let alone housework. If he offered to help, it was like whatever he did wasn't good enough; if he told her she was going over the top, he was told he didn't understand. So, he obediently lifted his legs, held them in the air, and dropped them back down on the table.

Nate felt the scrutiny of his wife's eyes boring into him. He raised his own gaze from his phone and smiled half-heartedly. They hadn't argued. They hadn't properly talked either.

"Have you seen my lilac and grey scarf?" Rose had put down the duster and was rooting through pockets of coats on the hooks by the door.

"No, have you checked the car?"

"Yeah, it's not there. It's gone. I swear someone must have taken it. I know I left it here."

"Honey, we've been through this…"

"Yeah, I know — you think I'm going mad. You think I've just lost something else. I swear, though, Nate—"

"I'm not saying either of those things. Just that there's probably a logical explanation."

"Are you getting changed for the appointment?" Rose asked as she rummaged through the dresser drawers, murmuring expletives as she searched.

"What's wrong with this t-shirt?"

"Just looks a bit scruffy with those jeans, don't you think? Doesn't really give a good impression."

"Right. I didn't realise we were needing to give a good impression. Who are we trying to impress?" Nate baulked a little at his own words. They sounded more facetious than he had intended. Rose sat down on the armchair opposite him, taking up only the edge of the seat and leaning towards him.

"Do you think we should talk about what we're going to say to Dr Thomas?" she asked, tip-toeing into the subject.

"I s'pose so." Nate shut down his phone and put it in his pocket.

"Have you looked at the documents any more?" Rose asked.

"Not really had a chance." He knew Rose was weighing up his response. She wouldn't believe the excuse any more than he did.

"This memory therapy sounds really interesting. Have a look at page five in that first set of information," she said. Nate picked up the folder and thumbed through the first few pages as Rose continued. "It says we'll be in this deeply relaxed state because of the drugs. The therapist will guide us through the memories of some of our happiest times. While we talk about them, the digital extraction takes place and downloads the thoughts and images to this computer file. It records everything, not just what you say, picking up things you don't even realise you remember! It's pretty amazing stuff by the sounds of it."

Nate had read it. He'd talked to his dad and briefly to Gaz about it. He knew how keen Rose was, so there seemed little point in talking to her because it wouldn't be a reasoned debate. She wanted to do it. Yet his brain felt peppered with doubt and distrust, like bullets sprayed by a tommy gun. Did he want to be wired to a machine? Have to take the drugs required? Could it cause him any damage? Was it safe? Would it even work? Would he be in control? These questions plagued him. His reaction — bury his head. He knew it and cursed himself for it.

As he skimmed the pages, a section leapt out at him that hadn't done previously. Two words sharpened in focus — 'wedding day'. He read more carefully.

'The deeply relaxed state will enable subjects to verbalise their memories with subconscious recollection. Subjects typically find they can describe elements of their memories that they may have thought to be forgotten or consciously suppressed. The ability to recollect happy or momentous occasions such as the birth of a child, a wedding day or a birthday party is enhanced during the therapy. Associated memories not verbalised are also extracted and downloaded to the digital memory files.'

Shit. The wedding day. He had never told Rose what happened that morning. He hadn't meant to keep it from her, but it was hardly something he could have spewed out at the church or reception. After that, there was never a good time — or reason — to bring it up. She was bound to talk about the wedding day as one of their happy memories. There was no way they'd be able to avoid it, given the purpose of the therapy. What if he blurted out the details in this 'deeply relaxed state'? What if he didn't say it out loud, but it got captured as part of his memory, anyway? Could he stop it from happening? Stop thinking about it or picturing it? Would he have any control over it?

"Nate, are you listening to me?" The words from Rose jolted him from his thoughts. "It sounds amazing, doesn't it?"

"It sounds… meddling," Nate offered.

"Meddling?"

"You know, like someone's going to be prying into our memories. Poking around. It's weird, really."

"I get that — but it's about reconnecting with the times when we were happier. Remembering them so we can get them back again. Helen thinks it could be really helpful for us. She once had a patient on the brink of divorce who changed her mind after a night of waiting around in A&E with her husband. Nothing to do but reminisce. This technology sounds amazing — we can get an insight into how we've each remembered some of our favourite times. And the accident too — this could be a chance to remember things from that day that my mind hasn't let me until now. "

"Yeah, I get that part, honey, but—"

"But, what? Do you want to do this or not, Nate? You've put off talking about it for days. You've barely spoken to me at all. We're supposed to be leaving for the appointment in half an hour. Just say what you want to say, will you?"

Nate rubbed his hands over his face and through his hair. After a long breath in, he let out a trail of thoughts. "This whole 'therapy session' business, you know it's not my thing. I've gone along with it and I can get on board with most of that stuff, if it helps you. All this about digitally uploading your memories, though, some doctor invading our private thoughts, deeply relaxed bloody states… it's not me. I'm just not sure…"

"Honey, you know how much this means to me — how important it could be for us! I can't do it unless you're there too. You know the conditions of the trial. It's for couples. They need shared memories to compare for accuracy. I need you there," she pleaded.

"Yeah, I know but, honey, I just… I can't—"

"OK," said Rose. Her voice was trembling and her face looked panicky. "I get it, I really do. I just… I don't know what else—" Her eyes were wide and full of tears. It was the face of someone beyond desperation. "You stay here, then. I'm going to—" She took a flustered deep breath and, grabbing her bag and keys, ran out of the door. It slammed so hard behind her that Nate felt the table shudder beneath his feet.

He sucked the air in through his teeth. "That could have gone better," he said to himself. He stood up, clenching his fists as he pondered his next move. Rose had made hers, though. The engine of the Mini revved, and the gears crunched as she reversed, then tyres squealed and she was gone.

Nate paced the lounge. Rose rarely drove herself anywhere since the accident, especially on her own. It was a telling indicator of how upset she was that she was willing to get behind the wheel. Had she gone to the appointment on her own, anyway? If not, where the hell else would she go? It worried Nate how distracted she might be by the argument ringing in her ears. His stomach knotted at the thought of her driving in that state. The sound of the tyres squealing stung his ears.

More than ever, he was torn by opposing thoughts about the whole situation. He wanted to put things right with Rose. It wasn't just about today or the last few days. He'd struggled to say the right things while she grieved. He could still put things right. Yet the prospect of this memory therapy bothered him. Rose was blinkered, obsessed with the memory of the accident. That was a dangerous avenue to explore. Wasn't it all full of dangerous avenues to explore, though?

He beat a fist on the back of the sofa as he sank back down onto the seat cushion. A silver-framed photo of them on their wedding day sat on the side, right in his eyeline. Looking back at him from next to the table lamp, their smiles beamed through a shower of confetti. He wanted to see Rose smile again like in that photograph. But it was his former self in the image that he addressed with his silent thoughts. Your memories are your own. Even when you share them, you're only sharing a version of them. In your head, you can edit out the bits that don't fit the narrative. You can't do that if someone else is scanning them, saving them, downloading them... whatever was being done with them.

Could he get Rose to see any other side to this apart from her blinkered view? Perhaps not; perhaps it didn't matter. She needed the chance to try the therapy. Perhaps the benefit for her — for them — outweighed his reservations. His dad was right about one thing: they were great together. Maybe they just needed reminding, and this was a justifiable opportunity. He glanced back at the wedding photo. If he didn't give this a go, maybe there wouldn't be another chance to get that happiness back.

First, he needed to know that she was safe.

"Shit!" he said to the empty house.

It didn't take long to throw on a chequered shirt over his t-shirt and swap his jeans for a pair of chinos. He took a quick look in the mirror and ran his hand down his cheeks and chin, feeling the bristle of stubble growth. His face was rarely clean-shaven these days, so he reasoned that this counted as more of a deliberate beard than just scruffy unrazored negligence. He grabbed his car keys, jacket and gloves, and headed out of the door.

As he started the engine of his own car, one dilemma tortured him. Tell Rose about Nicola or leave it to chance in the memory therapy process?

He pulled away and turned left at the top of the road, knowing this was the obvious route out of their estate but not yet sure where to head after that. He didn't have to worry for long. Within a few hundred metres, he spotted Rose's silver Mini parked under the shade of a tree. He drove past, then swung the car around and rolled into the space directly in front of her car so they were facing each other. He saw her still sitting inside. Her shoulders bobbed up and down, head bowed and tissue in her hand. She hadn't made it even half a mile from their house. Nate looked at his wife from his car to hers. He needed to tell her that he loved her. And that he was sorry.

Turning his key to kill the engine brought silence. He opened his door. The movement caught Rose's attention, and she looked up through bleary eyes.

Nate climbed into the passenger seat of the Mini and leaned across to Rose.

"Nice shirt," she sniffed with a half smile. "How did you find me?"

"I didn't need to look far. I'm sorry, honey."

"Sorry for what? It's me that's been awful to live with, obsessing over this therapy. I'm so sorry, Nate, I just don't know how to get better." Rose sobbed heavily and Nate was listening now, really listening.

"No! You don't say sorry, honey. You've done nothing wrong." Nate put a hand on each of her cheeks and looked deep into her eyes. "It's me who should be sorry for making this so difficult, for not being supportive. It still seems weird, but I can't blame you for wanting this so badly. I can see that now. I just need to ask: have you really thought it through? Could there not be a downside to having your memories harvested? What if there's stuff that you didn't want to remember?"

"I need to understand what happened that day. If it's bad, so be it. This is my only hope."

"So, this is about the accident, not about us?" asked Nate.

"It's both."

Nate reached down for Rose's hand. With his thumb, he toyed with the wedding band on her finger. "If you're set on it, then we'll do it together," he said.

Rose flung her arms around him. "Really? Oh my God, thank you! You have no idea what this—"

"But there's something I want to get off my chest first." Nate interrupted before Rose could get too excited. "I should have told you sooner." He felt her stiffen. Her eyes searched his face for a clue as to what was coming next. "It's about our wedding day."

"Our wedding day?" Rose echoed in surprise.

"Not the wedding as such. But before. The morning."

"What about it? You're worrying me."

"It doesn't need to be a big deal. I mean, it's not a big deal at all. It's something and nothing. But this talk of remembering our wedding day as one of our good times, it just raked this up a bit. Like I said, I should have told you before…"

"Will you spit it out, whatever it is?" Rose's puffy eyes were now focused on him. Creases stretched across her forehead. Nate cleared his throat.

"You remember Nicola?"

"What? Why the hell are you mentioning Nicola? Of course I fucking remember her."

"OK, OK, just listen. This is why I didn't say anything."

"What's your ex got to do with our wedding day, Nate?"

"Nothing. I mean, this is what I'm telling you, but she has nothing to do with the wedding day. She just turned up that morning."

"She turned up on the morning of our wedding? Turned up where?"

"At Gaz's, where I'd stayed the night before."

"Did you see her the night before?"

"No, no, no. Just listen. I hadn't heard from her for months. Not since all that crap had happened, and she finally got the message. There'd been nothing. Then, the morning of the wedding, she just turned up out of the blue."

By 'all that crap', they both knew he was referring to Nicola's inability to accept them splitting up. Nate had been the one to end the relationship. It had just fizzled out, and he knew it would have been a mistake for them to have stayed together. He'd never been unfaithful; neither had she as far as he knew. But he met Rose soon afterwards, and Nicola was adamant that something must have been going on longer. She would follow them when they went out, turn up at Rose's house, make drunken phone calls at ridiculous hours. She made life difficult for months. Over time, Nate had forgiven her because he knew the sweet, fragile girl that he'd once loved. Rose only ever knew the bitter version of her — and there had been little resembling forgiveness from his wife.

"For what? Why would she turn up to see her ex-fiancé on the morning of his wedding?"

"I dunno, just to talk, I s'pose…"

"Talk about what, for fuck's sake?"

"Well, I suppose she was just making sure I was doing the right thing."

"Jesus!"

"Which I was, obviously. I let her say her piece, but there was nothing to it. Nothing happened. She said what she wanted to say, and I told her she shouldn't be there and she went. That's it. It just… I just didn't want to spoil anything. For you, I mean, at the time — about the day."

"Oh, but you can spoil it for me now because I haven't had enough shit to deal with in the last 12 months with Mum and the accident, silent phone calls, things going missing?"

"No, nothing needs to be spoilt. It's good that I'm telling you, right? I didn't know she was going to turn up. God knows how she even knew I was there. I didn't do anything — just told her to go."

"After you had a cosy chat. On our wedding day. And then you lied to me about it."

"I didn't lie. It wasn't a cosy chat. Look, I can't do anything about it now. I'm just telling you to be straight. It was nothing. But it happened. That's all."

"So, hang on. Why now? Why are you telling me now? Because you think you're gonna get found out when we do the memory therapy?"

"It's not about getting 'found out'. I did nothing wrong. I just thought it would be good to be straight with you before we go through with it."

"It would have been good to be bloody straight with me at the time, Nate." She turned her head away from him and looked out of the driver's side window.

Silence filled the car. Rose turned back. The adrenaline of anger dissipated and her eyes became teary. She held his gaze for a moment before speaking.

"I get why you've told me now. You should have told me before. We can't have much more of a conversation about it this minute, can we? Are we going to this appointment or not?"

"Do you still want me to?"

"Of course."

"Right, then let's do this together. And right now, let's get you driving a little further too. Look, I'll get back in the Toyota and take it steady. You follow. I'll be there looking out for you the whole way."

8

A Confession

I'm sorry to see you having to put up with such sadness. It's a ripple effect. I wish it didn't have to take this path, that these weren't the consequences. I know I need to be patient for things to happen at the right time.

I've tried so many times before to show you how I feel, I've lost count. I only want to make you realise what I can offer you — if you give us a chance. It's so hard seeing you with someone else who isn't right for you. You two aren't meant to be together. Surely you see that?

Such a waste.

But I can be patient. I always have been.

I can feel it in the core of my soul that if you can just get through all this stuff hanging like a noose around your neck, there's a life for us. You'll see what I can still offer you instead.

I am being as patient as I can be.

9

Rose

Rose was conscious of her face on arriving at the therapist's home-office. On the worst of days, when her eyes were puffy and tinged with red, she felt exposed. She nipped into the loo and splashed her face to relieve it from the swollen track marks left behind by a morning of tears. Her blotchy cheeks bore the tribulations of the day so far — the argument, the revelation from Nate, and then the rare ordeal of driving even a short journey. She applied some concealer to the dark circles that betrayed her exhaustion and she ruffled her hair. A fake smile in the mirror made all the difference.

Dr Thomas tilted his head and gave Rose a closed smile as he gestured towards the overstuffed leather sofa.

'Who am I kidding?' thought Rose, sweeping her hair back and then over her face again.

Rose took the same seat as last time, and Nate followed suit. The room was exactly as they had left it, a strange hybrid of clinical precision and home comforts. The tissues had been refilled and the water glasses refreshed to the same level — here was a man who liked order and routine. Rose noted that this thoughtfulness and attention to detail were precisely the qualities she sought in someone who would be poking around in her subconscious.

"So," he said. "How has this week been?"

Rose and Nate looked at each other, waiting for the other to begin.

"Um, OK." Rose took the lead.

Noting the pause, Dr Thomas said, "How has the communication been between you?"

Rose appreciated the guiding question. "Um. I feel like Nate's been making more of an effort to be affectionate and noticing when I need a bit of support. We had to clear some stuff out at Mum's and he was a huge help. I had another anxiety attack, but he looked after me and helped to calm me down."

"That's encouraging to hear," said Dr Thomas.

"It's been a tough week, though, and I think maybe we could have communicated better. Especially around things like, well, big decisions." She knew she was being passive aggressive, but it was all the kindness she could muster after Nate's week of ignoring one of the biggest decisions of their lives.

"Ah!" Dr Thomas made a note and shut his book to offer them his full attention. "Can I assume you're talking about the memory therapy?"

"How did you guess?" said Nate.

Rose felt a pang of uncertainty as she looked at her

husband. She had been so happy out in the car when he had agreed to go ahead, but hearing his tone now, she had lost confidence in his agreement. She knew he was only doing it for her. There was no hiding from the fact that he wouldn't even be considering this unless she had pushed. She knew he had felt bullied, emotionally blackmailed and at the time she had felt justified in being angry with him for being so reluctant. Surely this was the least he owed her? After the lie about Nicola, the months of being emotionally distant at the worst time in her life.

She told herself that, had the tables been turned, she would do it for him — but would she? After all, she wasn't entirely innocent. There were secrets in her past she would hate Nate to see — Scott for starters! She hadn't always discouraged his attention; she'd flirted with him, let things get too far. There had been conversations she knew full well had crossed a line, even if she hadn't physically cheated. Cosy chats, endless texting and drinks after work; always the last two standing at closing time. It had all built up to one moment where things had got too close for comfort one Christmas. The entire episode had been a fleeting moment of weakness that she had put a stop to after an evening of soul-searching with Helen. She had not let the urges get the better of her. Nonetheless, she knew that the truth would hurt Nate. How would she react if those memories were at risk of being exposed? And they were, weren't they? The prospect hadn't entered her head.

Now she was thinking of what she might reveal — and worse, what might be revealed by Nate.

She couldn't dwell on that. She needed to do this. They both did, and she just had to hope that they wouldn't regret it. Despite his inability to express how he felt, she knew, somehow, that Nate loved her and he wanted to save their marriage. Finding out what had caused the accident would solve everything. She would have the closure to move on and be free to focus on the happy memories of the past, on Nate, on their future. She was doing this for both of them. It was the only option left, even if she was being selfish and desperate. She had no choice if she was going to regain control of her mental health, of her marriage. It would make them or break them, but the alternative gave no hope.

"Have you had time to look through the information I gave you?" asked Dr Thomas. "It's an interesting line of research, I hope you'll agree."

"It's a lot to get your head around," said Nate.

"It's fascinating!" Rose interjected. "I can't believe they have the technology to actually record your memories, it's incredible! I can't wait to see the results!"

"So you've decided to go ahead, then?" asked Dr Thomas. He smiled, opening his notebook again to retrieve two pieces of paper from the back.

"Yes, we've decided," said Rose, sitting forward in her seat.

"I have some questions, though," Nate's tone was firm.

"That's only natural," said Dr Thomas. "But I can assure you, Nate, if you're committed to getting past this… communication stalemate, then I can't recommend this enough. Sometimes relationships fall into a rut. It's easy to take each other for granted. The effort to perform thoughtful gestures or to open up emotionally — or, indeed, physically — can become too much when both parties are distracted with separate lives. It can leave couples feeling distant and numb. Particularly in this case when trauma is involved. Rose has diverted her energy to the survival aspect of her emotional existence. She's subconsciously cut herself off from the world around her, it's a form of self-defence. Without perseverance in communication from you, Nate, the walls are growing taller and stronger."

"I'm sorry, I'm trying but—"

"Nate, please hear me out. No one is blaming you. It's not about blame. We're working through all of this together. Focus on the solution, not the problem."

Rose's stomach sank as she heard the doctor's words. She knew Nate would be inwardly rolling his eyes.

Dr Thomas continued, "This therapy has the potential to bypass the need for those communications that make you feel so uncomfortable, Nate. It will allow Rose to witness for herself the memories you hold dear. Seeing with such clarity the role you have both played in each other's happiest moments will reignite the spark that has dwindled with time and open you both up to focus on these positive shared experiences. It's the greatest of compromises to achieve a common goal whilst allowing for different levels of emotional capacity and expression."

Rose turned to Nate and smiled. She took his hand and gripped it tight. She felt her face brighten and the heaviness in her shoulders lighten for a moment. This was their chance, and Nate would see it too once it was done. How could he not?

"And that all sounds great," said Nate. Rose sensed scepticism. "But how does the risk compare to the reward and all that? I mean, what are the risks? It still sounds quite invasive, you know? Have there been any problems, side-effects, you know, in past patients?"

Nate's questions sent a small wave of realisation through Rose. She had considered none of the risks because she didn't care. The worst thing imaginable had already happened: she'd lost her mum, and it was her fault. She couldn't perceive anything that came from the memory therapy being worse than everything she had endured in the last year. Only now did it occur to her that the same was not true for Nate. This was an ordeal for him, and his motivation to go ahead was not in the same ballpark as hers.

Dr Thomas placed his notebook and pen on the small table next to him and crossed his legs. "All valid questions,

Nate. Firstly, you can rest assured that it's perfectly safe. The treatment has been in trials at Uttoxeter University for a while now, and the results have been extremely promising. All the case studies and results are in the pack." Dr Thomas talked through the stats and details as they flicked through the documents together.

Nate reached for his phone and opened the notes app. Rose turned her head to read the words he was typing.

'Uttoxeter Uni, case studies.'

No doubt a prompt for further in-depth Googling later. She knew that he'd already trawled several sites relating to the types of study referred to. She caught him looking at them on his phone in bed. It was the only indicator that he was even considering it at all.

"The procedure is non-invasive," Dr Thomas continued. "It involves creating a brain-computer interface or 'BCI'. It means your brain and the computer can talk to each other via the wires I place on your head. I will inject a drug called Benzopentalin into your arm, which will become effective within minutes. The drug works by suppressing your inhibitions, relaxing you whilst stimulating the neurotransmitters involved in memory recollection. When under the influence of the drug, your thoughts become extremely detailed and vivid. You won't be able to fabricate or manipulate any of your memories. I will use information you give me about some joyful events in your past — for example, birthdays or your wedding day to stimulate memories and the computer will pick up data as the neurons fire. It will even record events you do not talk about out loud within a certain time frame before and after the memory taking place."

"Um, what's the time frame?" asked Nate.

"It can vary," said Dr Thomas. "Usually only a few hours, but subjects have been known to record memories from up to a day on either side of the specific event. It all depends on what images are being linked and then processed by your subconscious in response to the stimulus."

Nate and Rose exchanged glances, and biting her lip, Rose looked down towards her wedding ring.

"Of others who have been through the treatment, only around 25% have reported side-effects and they have all been mild and short-lived. They can include things like headaches, nausea and dizziness."

"Is it normal for the headaches and dizziness to set in before you've even started?" asked Nate with an awkward laugh.

Dr Thomas gave a forced, uncomfortable chuckle and cleared his throat again. "Does that all seem clear?" he asked.

"Absolutely." Rose smiled. She had read the information folder from cover to cover and devoured every word, whether or not she understood it. It didn't matter.

Nate shifted in his seat and gave Rose a sideways glance.

"If you're sure you'd like to go ahead, then may I ask you to complete these short consent forms?" Dr Thomas lifted the two pieces of paper that he had taken from a leather folder and placed them each on a clipboard that he had ready within arm's reach. Identical pens were attached at the sides and the bottom parts of the forms had already been completed in small, tidy handwriting.

"You were confident," said Nate. Rose nudged him in the ribs with her elbow. He was doing what he always did — trying to cover discomfort with humour.

"Always best to be prepared." Dr Thomas smiled and retrieved the forms once the couple had signed. Nate took much longer than Rose as he read each line. Rose sat impatiently, desperate for the inked moniker to bind the decision; no going back now.

With the signed sheets of paper tucked into the back of his folder, he opened his diary and flicked through a couple of pages.

"OK, so we're looking at next week for the first session. We can use our usual starting time, but you will need to prepare to be here for several hours. I have cleared the entire afternoon. You will need to choose three significant events that you have experienced together. They must be happy memories, so have a think about which moments you would like to revisit. Your wedding day, the day you met, any time when you shared a positive experience. Please bring along any photographs you have of the events, and it might be worthwhile writing down the key features of what you remember. The treatment will of course pick out all the details with great clarity, but I need a starting point. Then besides those, if it is something you still want to explore, Rose, we will also visit the day of the accident. Does that all sound OK?"

"Sounds great!" said Rose.

"Yep, OK." said Nate.

Dr Thomas handed them some leaflets. "These give you more information on how to prepare for your procedure. Rose, I have to ask, is there any chance that you could be pregnant?"

Rose shook her head as a wave of guilt washed over her. They had talked about a baby just before the accident. She knew Nate wanted to try again, but was grateful he had not yet mentioned it. She couldn't imagine being ready for that any time soon.

"No," she said, aware that Nate was looking at her. "Definitely not."

"Right, then I shall see you next week," said Dr Thomas with an uncharacteristic grin. "Don't forget the photos!"

"Thank you so much," beamed Rose.

"Cheers," said Nate. He placed his hand on the small

of Rose's back and guided her into the hall towards the exit out onto the driveway.

"Right, see you at home, then?" said Rose over the beep of her Mini unlocking.

"OK, I just need to nip to the garage first. I need to check an invoice for a parts order. Will you be alright driving?"

"I think I actually will," Rose answered after a moment of hesitation.

"I know you will. You'll be fine. You did great earlier. Be back in a bit," said Nate as Rose kissed him on the cheek.

As he went to close the car door, he was stopped by Rose's hand. She focused on his face. "Thank you," she said strongly and sincerely.

Nate kissed the air between them and smiled before banging the door shut. Rose watched him drive away and noticed how good he looked in that shirt.

She took out her phone and got comfy in the driver's seat of her car. She texted Helen.

'Fancy a coffee? I have news.'

Helen came straight back.

'Is the Pope Catholic?'

Rose smiled. She had told Helen all about the memory therapy, and her friend had reacted more positively than anyone else she had spoken to. As a nurse, Helen's knowledge of other medical trials had been a big comfort to Rose, and she had loved seeing the interest on her friend's face as she read all the information.

According to Helen, the research looked promising, and the case studies encouraging. Rose was excited to get started on picking the events they would focus on and knew that Helen would be enthusiastic in a discussion about it.

As she drove cautiously home, she realised she was smiling. It was rare that she ever felt calm in a car anymore. It made her feel hopeful and brave enough to pull into the garage to pick up some milk for coffee.

"Hey you." A voice came from behind a pile of cereal boxes waiting to be shelved.

"Scott! Hi!" Rose was surprised.

"You look great — as always!" Scott rested his elbow on the shelf containing peanut butter.

Rose smiled. "Haven't seen you for a while. How have you been?"

"Yeah, great thanks. Did you get my text last week? Got that leadership position at work and a decent little pay rise. Have just moved into the new housing development near Elizabeth Park. Great to be on the property ladder at last."

"That's cool," said Rose. "Lovely to—"

Scott interjected before she could end the conversation.

"How's… Nick, is it?"

"Nate." Rose forced another smile.

"God, sorry, yeah, of course. How's Nate?"

"He's great, yeah, really good thanks."

"Listen, Rose. I was so sorry to hear about you still having a tough time. It was such an awful tragedy about your mum. I'm here for you if you want a chat or a drink sometime?"

"Thanks," said Rose. "Yeah, it's been a tough year. I'll keep it in mind. I—"

"It's not been the same at work since you left either. If you ever think about wanting to do a day or two — supply cover maybe — I can put in a good word. Say that I've seen you and you're on the mend. Be great to have you around again."

"Thanks, erm… I don't think I'm ready yet. Sorry, I'm meeting a friend so I need to get going, but it was lovely to see you."

"Absolutely. Take care." Scott smiled and ran his hand through his hair before taking out his phone and heading for the drinks fridge.

Rose paid for her milk and made a quick exit. She looked back over her shoulder as she walked across the car park and saw him watching her go. He smiled and waved. She pulled her jacket tighter and hurried to the car.

*

Rose arrived home to find Helen sitting in her car outside their house.

"That was quick!" Rose got out and headed towards the front door.

"I'd just finished with a patient when you texted," said Helen. "They only live round the corner from here."

"The lovely lady?"

"Nope, a cheeky old man who calls me Sandra. I get all the fun jobs!"

"Ha! Sorry to keep you waiting, just needed to grab some milk," said Rose. "Bumped into Scott. It was super awkward."

"Oh God, is he still texting you?" asked Helen.

"At least once a week," said Rose with a groan.

Helen rolled her eyes. "Put the kettle on, then. I need coffee and a good gossip."

Rose paused as she looked down towards the flower bed under the lounge window. Some of the pansies looked squished like they had been trodden on.

"Next door's cat again?" asked Helen.

Rose paused. "Yeah, probably," said. She tried the front door — locked.

Rose let them both in and made the coffee before running upstairs to the spare bedroom. A breeze wafted across the landing and she realised the bathroom window was open again. She wished Nate would leave it shut.

"So what's your news?" Helen asked as she threw her

coat onto the arm of the sofa. She settled down into the seat and exhaled as she relaxed.

Rose marched back into the room with two big fabric boxes. They were patterned with fading flowers. Neither lid fit as the contents threatened to exceed the boxes' capacities.

"We're going to give the memory therapy a try," grinned Rose. As she plonked the boxes onto the coffee table, a thin layer of dust from the lids danced into the air.

"Oh, wow! How did you persuade Nate?" Helen asked, shuffling forward on the sofa to inspect the boxes that Rose was opening.

"To be honest, I'm still not sure he's convinced. He's at the garage now; made up a lame excuse to go into work, so hopefully that means he'll be talking it through with Gaz. I think a big part of his concern was a secret he's been keeping. Did you know Nicola showed up on the morning of our wedding?"

"She did what? Where?"

Rose filled Helen in on the revelation she had only just become privy to herself. With mugs of coffee in hand, they exchanged words of shock about the audacity of Nate's ex. Rose felt better for being able to process the news out loud with someone who understood her frustrations and the need to vent.

"Have you had any more weird phone calls lately?" asked Helen.

"Not for a while now. Hopefully, whoever it is has got bored and started getting their kicks elsewhere. Anyway, enough of the freaky stuff." She slid from the sofa to the floor, then pulled one box down next to her. "Fancy helping me find some photos to use for the memory therapy?"

10

Nate

"What are you doing here on your day off?" Gaz asked.

Nate stood at the open metal shutters of the garage, looking in. Andy was still working on the job Nate had asked him to do yesterday — nothing to do with any of the motors waiting for attention, just sorting out a ridiculous amount of tools and odd parts. Between them, they should have been able to keep a tidier workshop, but as Andy was the most junior mechanic, it was easy to allocate these jobs to him. It was expected of the apprentices to get the crappy jobs. Gaz was standing underneath a Ford Mondeo, raised on the vehicle lift, clutching a length of exhaust in his hand. Nate dug his hands into his pockets and rocked on his heels, nodding his head towards the internal door that connected the workshop to the office. It felt odd to be at work but wearing his shirt and trousers, rather than a t-shirt, jeans or overalls. He raised his voice to be louder than the radio.

"Just checking if those parts had arrived that we ordered yesterday," he called back over the sound of Oasis declaring, '*Some Might Say.*'

"And have they?"

"Oh, erm… haven't been through to check with Linda yet," said Nate. Gaz raised an eyebrow before propping the silver pipe up against a toolbox and strolling over towards the vehicle entrance where Nate was standing.

"Right. Well, while you're here, I s'pose you could tell me how that appointment's gone this afternoon. You did decide to go, didn't you?"

"Yeah, I went. Nearly bloody didn't, though."

Gaz waited for a second. He wiped one greasy hand down his overalls and then tried to catch Nate unawares with the other hand. Nate pulled his cheek away just in time to dodge an oily stripe from ear to chin.

"Come on, pal. I was ready for a break. Sounds like we might need a brew. Nice shirt, by the way."

They walked across the workshop and through to the small kitchen area in the corner. Nate leaned against a battered worktop, peppered with coffee ring stains from previous days, while the kettle boiled. Gaz dropped tea bags into a pair of almost-clean mugs and rinsed a spoon under the tap. Nate started by telling him about Rose storming out of the house before they were due to leave for their session.

"So, why was she so pissed off with you — and why hadn't you just gone along with it, anyway?" Gaz asked.

"I already told you what I thought about all that

memory stuff. Plugging us into a computer or something. Just wasn't sure about it from the start, was I? Still not convinced now, if I'm honest."

"Yeah, did sound a bit weird."

"Well, there was Alannah the other day who didn't like the sound of it — and it was her that Rose got the idea for the sessions from in the first place. My dad thinks the whole idea is bloody fascinating, but says it's wasted on us. Then I started reading some more about it after Rose left the info under my nose enough times. Turns out we've gotta be talking about things from the past and what happened. Our memory gets read by the computer and uploaded into cyberspace — and we have no control over what's being recorded."

"Bloody hell, mate."

"Yeah, and that's not even the whole thing. We've gotta be talking about stuff like what we remember about special occasions you know, like the *wedding day*?" Nate phrased it as a question, hoping Gaz would get the gist of where he was leading.

"Oh," said Gaz, stirring a couple of sugars into his mug. "Ohh!" he said again with sudden realisation, "the wedding day."

"Exactly!" Nate acknowledged.

"Bit worried all that business from the morning with you-know-who is going to come spilling out, then?"

"Well, not now," said Nate. "I've gone and told her

already, haven't I? Just in case it did."

Nate saw Gaz's eyes widen. He knew his mate wouldn't have been expecting that development. It was something Nate had locked away for three years. With every passing anniversary, it became buried further and therefore harder and harder to dig out and present to his wife as something that didn't matter. This was the problem with baring all your memories with limited control. Even the ones that didn't matter, might suddenly matter.

"You what? You've told her about Nic coming round?" Gaz said.

"I had to, didn't I? Better telling her now than her finding out, anyway."

"Better not tellin' her at all, I'd have thought."

"Yeah, well, look how well that plan's turned out in the end!"

Both men gulped a mouthful of tea. Gaz shook his head a little. "How did she take it, then? Rose. She's let you live, I see. What did she say?"

Nate thought about Rose's initial reaction in the car: signs of rage at first, then the silence. Then they'd had to go in for the appointment. He hadn't deliberately chosen the time when there would be little chance to react. It just ended up that way. Maybe not a bad thing either. He just wasn't sure how Rose was feeling about it now.

"Well, you can probably guess," he told Gaz, without going into detail. "She wasn't bloody happy, but we didn't have much time to talk about it."

"So, you've signed up for this thing now, then? Some doctor's going to be spying into your brain and showing all your other secrets to your wife. Is that wise, pal?"

"It's not exactly like that, Gaz! Jeez! Trust you to think it's all about bloody secrets. With a bit of luck, it'll mean being able to watch back some of the good times, you know? Remember when we were all younger, no worries, less shit going on."

"Yeah, I remember you when you were younger, pal. I'm not sure you want to be revealing all that either," said Gaz with a wink and a deep, throaty laugh.

"Bloody hell, good job I'm not coming to you for reassurance isn't it?" Nate paced the small kitchen area. He drummed his fingers on the worktop before turning to face Gaz again and leaning against the side, folding his arms.

"Look, I'm just not sure whether you're trying to convince me or yourself!" Gaz said.

"I know," Nate admitted. "Neither am I. I reckon she wants to use it to remember the accident as much as anything else. She's still got it in her head that she's gonna dig something up from her memory about it all."

Gaz gulped another mouthful of tea. He'd sat down on the shabby two-seater sofa that was squeezed into the corner. A pile of well-thumbed car and bike magazines were splayed across the other seat. He rested his cup down on them while still holding onto the handle and clicked his tongue in his mouth as he thought.

"What else has she said about it — the accident — something new?"

"No, nothing like that. She keeps saying she still feels like there's a missing piece. Like, she's blanked a bit out or she doesn't remember it properly." Nate's mind wandered back to the events of the accident as it occasionally did, to his car ending up in the crumpled heap.

"Do you think something else might come out about that day, pal?"

"No," Nate responded. "Course not. She had an accident. There's nothing to 'come out'. It could just as easily have been me. I should have been driving after all. The car was fine — you know that. It was in here that week."

Gaz muttered a vague agreement just as Andy walked in. They silenced the conversation for an awkward moment as both of them watched Andy pour himself a mug of tea and walk out with it. Gaz took another slurp of his own drink and looked down at the magazines. Nate could tell he wanted to speak and wondered why the reluctance.

"Listen, I've never asked you before, but do you think maybe she was driving too fast?" Gaz asked.

"No. Maybe. I don't know. How the hell would I know? But what difference does it make now, mate? What's gonna be achieved by raking it back up when she's still trying to get over it. Alannah's probably right."

"Her sister? That's the second time you've mentioned her. What's she got to do with it? Is that why she was here the other day?"

"Like I said, she thinks it's a bad idea. Half of me thinks she's damn right and the other half thinks Rose just needs to do it anyway to get it out of her system."

"But you're worried how it's gonna turn out?"

"Can you tell?" Nate gave a wry smile. The conversation drifted elsewhere. Nate felt the vibration of his phone alerting him to a text. He looked at the screen but put it away again to respond to later. By the time he swallowed the final dregs of his tea, the swirl of uncertainty in his mind and the events of the afternoon were giving him a headache. He had committed himself, and to some extent, that brought the path ahead into focus. Regardless of whether he was sure about it, their signatures were on the forms now.

"I'd better get back to it, then. Some of us have got work to do," said Gaz. He slapped Nate on the back as he exited the kitchen back into the workshop. Nate heard him shouting at Andy, his words fading as he went. "You still not finished sorting that toolbox, kid? Bloody hell, it's not like we've got half a dozen cars waiting to get done…"

Nate put his empty mug with a pile of others. He'd needed some time to cool off after the appointment, let it all sink in. Other than his mum and dad, Gaz was the only person who he felt he could talk to about it. What he really needed next was to head back to face Rose. But on the way, it was about time he called his mum. Before he left, one more thing nagged at him. He crossed through the workshop and into the office.

"Alright, Linda? Just need to check on a couple of old files," he said.

"Oh, I didn't think you were in. Chap here waiting said he knows you."

Nate hadn't even noticed James sitting in the customer waiting area. He wondered if he'd forgotten he was going to be coming in. Nothing registered as he strode over towards his wife's ex-boyfriend. Not that he thought of him as the 'ex-boyfriend' now. James was a good friend to them both, and Nate had always found him a decent bloke.

"Alright, mate. Were you here to see me?" Nate asked.

"Oh, not as such. Phoned last week to book the car in. Assumed you'd be here but didn't matter. You and Rose OK?"

"Yeah, well, you know. Could be worse. We're getting there."

"Mmm. Bumped into her the other day, actually. I guess she told you. Just grabbed a coffee. She was a bit freaked out ——paranoid she was being followed or something?"

Nate cast his mind back over the preceding days. He

had no recollection of Rose mentioning a coffee with James. No mention of being followed either. He thought she'd got over those paranoid feelings of being watched and thinking things were going missing.

"She might have mentioned it, I'm not sure. It's been a bit chaotic to be honest. Lot going on. Appreciate you looking out for her, though, thanks." James nodded as Nate patted him on the arm. "Listen, I've just gotta grab some paperwork. Let's get a beer one night, shall we? Or come over. I'll let Rose know."

"Sure. Will do," said James. "Take care of her, mate."

Nate smiled as he left the waiting area and headed back around the counter to the back wall of the reception.

Opening the bottom drawer of a filing cabinet, he thumbed through grubby plastic wallets and documents from twelve months ago. When he came to the one which had his old make, model and registration number printed on, he pulled it out and folded it into his back pocket.

"See you soon, then, James," he called across the counter, waving. "Make sure you knock off the friends and family discount for him, Linda."

Nate made his way back to the workshop.

"Thanks for the chat, mate," he shouted at Gaz as he walked through and out onto the forecourt.

"Did you check on that parts order you needed, pal?" Gaz called after him.

"Oh, yeah, erm, all sorted," said Nate as he opened the

car door and climbed inside. He took his phone from his back pocket and read the message again that he'd not responded to earlier.

'Walked dog over big park today. Why can't other people clean up after their dogs? Drives me mad. How was your appt love? Mum X'

He smiled. She always signed off her messages as if his phone wouldn't reveal who she was. And her unwitting priority of topics brought him back to simple realities — first the crucial dog fouling news; then the query about the groundbreaking therapy, which may or may not affect the sanity of his wife and the stability of their marriage. Annoying about the dog mess, though.

The smile brought on by the relatively insignificant message had already softened the edges of his worry, even if just a little.

He started the engine and waited a few seconds for the dashboard to indicate it had connected with the bluetooth of his phone. Then he tapped on the call icon by his mum's name.

He'd already pulled out of the garage parking area and set off up the hill by the time she answered on the sixth ring.

"Hi, Mum. Just catching you while I'm driving home. You OK?"

"Always busy or driving somewhere, you, Nathan.

That's what your nan always says. Only time you can fit in a chat with your mother, is it?"

He pictured her, most likely sat on the sofa, half-finished knitting on one side of her; Alfie the King Charles cavalier snuggled up on the other side. The TV would have a quiz show on, but she wouldn't be able to see it well enough because her glasses would be up on her head. Dad would be puzzling over a crossword. It was a picture of contentment. She and his dad had been married for over 40 years and they still held hands whenever they were out walking together.

"You know I can always fit in a chat with you, Mum. How's Dad doing?"

"We're alright. Same old, same old. Doctor says I've got to watch my cholesterol again and your dad's been having trouble with his knee. Thinks he's twenty years younger than he is and tried to clean out the fish pond yesterday. I told him not to spend too long kneeling on the cold floor…"

Nate zoned out as he waited at a junction to turn right, then sat behind a bus that was picking up passengers. His mother had finished the list of ailments and moved on to who she'd bumped into whilst walking the dog — both today and on yesterday's trip.

"… well, I hadn't seen her for years, not since she used to run that market stall with all the dollhouse furniture. Anyway, enough of me. Tell me about what's happening with you and Rose. Have you agreed on what you're doing with this therapy?"

Nate took a breath and then filled in his mum with enough detail to give her a flavour of what they were committing to but not enough detail, he hoped, to worry her.

"So, I thought about what Dad said the other day and we're gonna give the trial a go to see what happens." He tried to sound chirpy about it. He continued behind the same bus which had stopped twice to let passengers on and off, neither time allowing him an opportunity to get safely around it.

"It sounds very clever, darling. Very clever and very complicated. Your father was quite excited about it when you left on Saturday. But, I wonder, have you thought about whether some memories might be better left as private? Even from those closest to us? I sure as heck wouldn't want your dad reading all my thoughts. Especially not when the Sunday football team's on the bottom field with their tight shorts on—"

"Oh, Mum!" said Nate. He was equally amused by his mum's schoolgirl lusting as he was appalled at it. "Enough, please! Listen, I know what you're saying. But we need to give this a try. For Rose."

He spotted his chance to overtake and swung the car across the road to get past the bus. At the same time, the double decker belched out a plume of smoke and also pulled away. Seemingly from nowhere, a BMW came around the bend on the opposite side, heading directly towards him.

"Shit!"

He braked hard and swung the steering wheel in the other direction to file back in behind the bus. Narrowly, he avoided colliding with either vehicle. The horn of the BMW was held down as the car passed, and Nate just caught the hand gesture aimed at him from the angry driver.

"What on earth was that?" he heard his mother screech as he recovered his own composure.

"Nothing, Mum. It's fine. Just an impatient driver. I'd better go anyway, I'm nearly home. Thanks for the chat. Tell Dad I said, 'Hi'."

Nate hung up. He straightened his arms and pushed himself back into the seat, exhaling slowly. That felt like a close call. Yet it occurred to him it was nothing compared to what Rose went through with her accident. His pounding heart and dry mouth came from reimagining the events of her accident all over again. Of course she'd do anything she could to get over it. If this therapy had a chance of helping, it had to be worthwhile.

Nate was sure now. To stand by his wife's side through this was enough to outweigh the initial reluctance about the process. He just hoped she would forgive the wedding day secret that he'd stashed away until now.

Two streets later, he pulled up outside their house. He spent a moment collecting his thoughts before heading inside. He'd planned what to say if Rose was still frosty. Yet, as soon as he pushed open the front door, he sensed there might be reconciliation in the air.

The cherry scent of his wife's favourite candles blended with the sound of Otis Redding's *Sittin' on the Dock of the Bay*. It was one of their favourites. He assumed it was not a coincidence that the song had begun just before he arrived in the hallway. Nate kicked off his shoes and walked through to the lounge. He dropped his keys on the table next to the phone.

Rose was sitting on the floor. Her hair was loosely tied up in a way that she'd call messy, but he thought was adorable. She was wearing the love-heart pyjamas he'd bought her last Valentine's Day, and she had a glass of red wine in hand. All around her were piles of photographs.

As he strolled over with a smile, he caught glimpses of holidays, day trips and family gatherings. Glossy 6 x 4 inch reminders of the many memories they had shared. Although it was becoming old-fashioned, Rose had a thing for getting their digital photos printed. Some were in frames around the house, some made into scrapbook albums — which she had a true gift for being able to turn into little works of art — and the rest lived in fabric boxes, usually stored in the spare room but which had now been virtually emptied across the lounge's laminate floor. He sat next to her on the white sheepskin rug.

"Hey, you," he said to her.

"Hey, back at you."

Everything else he planned to say drifted from his mind. Rose poured him a glass of Merlot and topped up her own. Their favourite chilled playlist moved from Otis to Etta to Aretha. For the next hour, they became absorbed together in memories as photos reminded them of times they knew well and times they had almost forgotten.

They laughed about their poor ski skills in France; indulged in a winter wonderland of romance in Bruges; and recounted one family gathering after another. Each memory prompted and aided by a photo. They didn't even need any drugs or technology.

It was all going so well. Any animosity from earlier in the day had slipped sip by sip from Nate's mind. Then they came to the wedding album. Rose lifted open the thick velvet cover.

As she pressed her fingers on their embossed names which adorned the cover, the landline phone rang, jolting them both from the spell.

"I'll get it," Nate offered. "Just in case, you know…"

He got up from the floor and walked over to the table, snatching up the receiver.

"Hello?" He listened but there was no reply. There was a noise that suggested someone was there. A breath? Just some background hum? He pressed the receiver into his ear, trying to pick up any clue as to who was on the other end. "Hello?"

The line went dead, and the call cut off. Nate muttered as he deposited the receiver back on the base with too much force.

Something about the mood had changed as he rejoined Rose on the living room floor. They looked, silently as she flicked through the photos. Rose stopped and ran her fingers down the picture of herself, taken from behind but smiling into the mirror of her mum's dressing-table as she sat having her bridal makeup done.

The previous warm glow of the room now felt like it had been pierced with a chill.

11

Rose

"Were you thinking about her?"

"Who? When?"

"When you were standing in the church waiting for me. When we were saying our vows? I dunno, just during the day in general. Were you thinking about Nicola?" Rose wasn't angry or upset. She was gazing at the photo and speaking softly.

"Of course, I wasn't. It was our wedding day. God, Rose, when I saw you walking down the aisle, you know, in that dress, there was no way I was thinking about anything else other than spending the rest of my life with you." He paused, pensive. "And ripping the dress off you afterwards of course."

Rose didn't take the bait. She was not letting him just sweep this under the carpet with humour designed to lighten the tone. Nate shuffled a little closer to her on the floor and kissed her neck.

"Hey, I love you," he whispered in her ear.

Rose didn't move.

"You know I haven't done anything wrong here, right?"

Nate snuggled up to her shoulder. He was almost laughing. "Please, don't get hung up on this. She's a psycho — which is why I split up with her. I'm sorry I didn't tell you, but it was so insignificant to me that once the wedding started, I just wiped it from my mind. You didn't need to know. I actually felt sorry for her."

"So you admit you felt something!"

Nate sat up straight and the playlist came to an untimely end. "That's not what I meant and you know it. She was a mess, and I told her to get lost. I had no control over the situation other than to do the right thing and not give her the time of day. I've done nothing wrong here, Rose, and you're acting as if I cheated on you or something."

"You didn't tell me, Nate! If there was really nothing to it, then why didn't you just tell me and we could have laughed it off together? Now I just feel humiliated that she got to take a part of our wedding day for herself, and you've played right into her hands by keeping it a secret. The whole point of being married is that you tell each other everything and trust each other. You've only told me now because you thought it might be exposed without your control."

Nate moved away from her. He shifted his head back with eyebrows raised, then moved from the floor to the sofa. Rose felt cross with both of them. Her, for not being able to hold her tongue and ruining another lovely evening with her insecurities and temper; him, for not grovelling hard enough. Even when he was in the wrong, he couldn't be bothered to comfort her.

"Trust?" said Nate. Rose saw something change in his eyes. It was a familiar flicker that showed he had crossed the line into anger. "You want to talk to me about trust? I've told you that nothing happened — you don't believe me. Where's your trust now? You want me to have some quack download my memories so that you can watch them back. Do you know what an invasion of my privacy that is? Do you have any idea what you're asking? It's insane, Rose. Marriage isn't about telling each other *everything*! How many other couples do you know who would literally share *every* aspect of their inner thoughts with each other like that? Cos that's what you're asking me to do — give you the most intimate thing imaginable and turn it into a computer file. And I am actually letting you, I'm willing to do it, for *you* and you're telling me you can't bloody trust me?"

Rose's eyes were no match for the surge of emotions welling behind them. They buckled.

"And of course, now you cry right on cue so that I look like the arsehole in all this." Nate stood and walked towards the door. As he approached it, he slammed the palm of his hand into the doorframe and spun around on his heels.

"I can't win here. I can never win. You know what? I'm

not doing this now."

Rose felt panic rising within her as he turned around once more and headed out to the kitchen. An instant regret for letting the words fly out before she had considered the consequences. Her brain scrambled, wishing she could take them back, but it was like trying to catch water. What did he mean? Had he changed his mind about the therapy? She'd gone too far, talked him out of it. She should have focused on the bigger picture, not let her petty jealousy get in the way. Wiping her tears with her sleeve, she stood to follow him.

"Don't say that, please, Nate. I'm sorry, I shouldn't have pushed. I don't know what's wrong with me, I just feel so insecure. You and Alannah are all I've got left and I can't handle you keeping things from me. I'm so scared of losing you. Please don't walk away, please!" She reached for his arm and found it.

Nate paused. He didn't turn around.

"I know. I just need some space. Do what you need to do. Pick whichever photos you like."

Rose was beyond words. Her throat felt hot and tight, her chest was aching, sobs escaped like blood from an artery, thick and unpredictable. She watched Nate walk across the kitchen, popping up his hood and swiping his keys and headphones in one swift movement. She watched the back of him and she realised how familiar his form was. Even with his hood up, she would know him anywhere. Memories circled — conversations she'd had with Alannah after they had first met. The things she found attractive in him that were so important at the time — his broad shoulders, his dark tousled hair, his height, the way he looked in jeans. These tiny things that singled him out to her back then seemed so insignificant now, yet so conspicuous because they remained. If that physical attraction was still there, how had all the other qualities she loved been so diluted with time and familiarity. Why didn't she still giggle at his jokes? Where was the depth of fondness she used to feel when she talked about him? How had her feelings for him become so buried beneath the rubble of routine, responsibilities and tragedy, when he was still the same man she had fallen in love with and been inseparable from six years ago? What had changed to make them so distant now? She realised it was her. Now, she needed more than someone she fancied, more than someone who made her laugh. She needed someone she could rely upon to be her champion, to be gentle with her fragile state, to be on her side without question. She had once felt like he was all of those things, but back when she didn't need him to be. Now she did, and he was walking away.

*

"Hey, what's wrong?" Alannah's voice was comforting. Rose realised how often she had phoned her sister in tears over the last year.

"Is it me, Alannah? Have I tipped over the edge and turned into a massive drain on everyone? I just seem to make everyone miserable." Rose's voice was gaining velocity and volume; she realised she was losing control of the sobs that she had quashed long enough to dial.

"Whoa, slow down. No! Absolutely not to all the above. What's happened? Actually, scrap that, tell me in a bit, I'm coming over." Alannah hung up before Rose could argue.

Rose flopped on the sofa and felt her stomach sinking as she considered how pathetic she must seem to everyone around her. Falling out with Nate over something that happened years ago and Alannah once again was dropping everything to talk her out of a state. All of her anxieties pooled. Alannah was moving on with her life, she had a steady boyfriend and seemed to be coping really well. Nate wanted to move on too, but Rose was driving him away by pushing an idea that was supposed to help them. For the first time since Dr Thomas had suggested it, Rose doubted her faith in the memory therapy to help her marriage. Maybe doing this together wasn't the answer.

The front door sounded much quicker than Rose expected. She called for Alannah to let herself in and headed to the kitchen to drain the last bit of Merlot into a glass on the draining board.

"Never fear," said Alannah, plonking a fresh bottle onto the table.

"How did you get here so fast?"

"I was only up the road in The Willow Tree," Alannah said as she followed Rose back to the sofa.

"Oh God, you were out and I've ruined your night. What is wrong with me?" Rose drew her hands into the sleeves of the hoody she had pulled on, brought up her knees and buried her head.

"Sis, chill. It's not a big deal. I needed to escape anyway."

"Oh, trouble in paradise?"

"Not really, just a difference of opinion about something. He can be patronising, but I know I'm in the right."

Rose laughed. "Aren't you always, in your opinion?"

"Rude! I can't help being the font of all wisdom."

"Is this why you won't let us meet him?"

"No, it's not that. It's nothing personal. It's just that every time I bring someone home to meet you guys, I end up getting dumped." She laughed. "Not that I'm saying there's a correlation!"

"Charming." Rose sniffed with a meek smile.

"I just don't want to jinx it!"

Rose had never seen her looking quite so smitten and talking about things long term. She had often teased her sister about her string of short-lived boyfriends and one-night stands, but she realised this guy had been around for a while. Months had gone by without Rose even conscious of the fact that her sister was in her first proper relationship.

"I'm really happy for you," said Rose.

"I promise I will let you meet him soon," said Alannah, and she rubbed Rose's knee. "When I'm sure things are good and I'm not going to fuck them up like I always do."

"And then can we know his name?" teased Rose.

"Hmm, we'll see."

Rose felt her pulse slowing as she giggled with her sister. Her eyes dried and her argument with Nate seemed less alarming. Alannah had a calming influence that she had inherited from their mum and when the sisters were together, Rose could feel her there too.

"Right," said Alannah. She straightened her back and folded her arms. "What's happened? Where is Nate, why do you have all these photos out and why are you so sad? Do I need to kill him?"

Rose laughed. "No, you can hold off the hired assassin for now."

"Who said anything about an assassin? I have my bare hands!"

No matter what, Alannah was always there, her cheerleader, her champion. With zero information, she was on Rose's side. Would that still be the case when Rose told her she was taking part in the memory therapy?

"That bloody bitch Nicola," said Alannah after more tears and more wine. "What is her problem? How dare she!"

"I know, I was fuming," said Rose. "But it's not Nicola who I'm cross with, it's Nate for not telling me. But now I think maybe I overreacted and drove him away. He's right, he was prepared to do the memory therapy, and I'd rather he told me now than watch it on the screen with no warning."

"This is the problem, though, babe." Alannah was cautious. "Don't you think that going ahead with all this memory stuff is dangerous. How do you know you won't see something that'll make things even worse? I hate to think of you and Nate falling out over something from the past. There must be better ways for you to move on together and get back to how you were. Maybe by focusing on the future instead of the past. I mean, look!"

Alannah picked up another photo from their wedding day. Nate held Rose by the hand as they prepared to walk back up the aisle — a married couple. Rose was acknowledging some cherished faces in the pews. Nate, however, looked only at Rose. In the black and white hue, their eyes sparkled and their faces beamed without the distracting detail of colour. It was a moment captured on paper; the image was fixed, but the feelings it prompted were moulded and adjusted by those who were remembering. Did it matter if those memories were different? Did it matter if the feelings conjured altered between people, moods, years? Surely this was enough.

"You're right, but it's not just about me and Nate, though, is it?" Rose said.

"Which brings me to my next point." Alannah set her glass on the coffee table. "Babe, I really don't think you should use this to watch back the crash. I mean, shit, Rose, have you not been through enough without seeing it over and over again? It wasn't your fault. It could well have been Nate driving. The police ruled it an accident. Why can't you just accept that and try to move on? You could use your time with Dr Thomas to help you look to the future and help you find coping methods for all of this."

"Lana, I can't move past anything until I find out why I crashed that car. I owe it to Mum."

"There's no way Mum would be on board with this, babe! She would hate you to be torturing yourself like this. She wasn't like you, she didn't need to know all the details of everything. She was OK with letting things lie if it meant that it brought peace."

"But she deserves the truth, Alannah! I can't find peace until I've got to the bottom of it for her… for me. If Nate had just gone as planned…" Her voice trailed off and she stared through the patio door into the darkness that had engulfed the garden.

"How can I persuade you not to do this, Rose?"

Alannah's voice was desperate.

"You can't."

A small thud from upstairs stopped them in their tracks, and Alannah pulled a fake-scared face.

"You got ghosts?" she joked.

"Ha, probably just the heating," said Rose, the light-headed feeling of adrenaline in her system betraying the confidence in her voice. Fight or flight was just a hindrance when you couldn't do either. She knew she was letting her imagination run away with her, but she also knew that she wouldn't be going upstairs on her own until Nate was back.

*

A few hours later, Rose was woken by the swoosh of curtains closing. As the wooden hooks swept across the rail, the thick blackout curtains snuffed out the orange streetlight glow. She froze with fear as her eyes adjusted to the sudden darkness and the figure in front of her became clear. Nate was laying a blanket over Alannah who was asleep, curled up at the other end of the sofa.

"What time is it?" Rose asked him in hushed tones. He jumped, not realising she was awake.

"Gone midnight." Nate held his hand out as he whispered back to Rose. "You coming?"

She took Nate's hand, and he led her up the stairs in silence. Rose's head was banging and her eyes felt sore. The bed was turned down on her side and she climbed in, already in her pyjamas. Nate tucked the covers up around her and climbed onto his side, fully clothed. Rose felt the warmth of his body as he wrapped his arm around her and the intense relief of comfort as her head rested on his chest. He held her as their breathing became synchronised and said, "I'm sorry."

"I'm sorry too," said Rose. "Let's forget all this memory stuff; don't do it if you don't want to. I was being unreasonable. It's too much. But I need to remember the accident, Nate. I'll persuade Dr Thomas to let me do it on my own and no one is going to talk me out of it."

"I know," said Nate. "I'm not going to try. We do this — all of it — and we do it together. I have nothing to hide from you, honey. I love you."

Rose's voice broke as a meek, "Thank you", spilled from her lips.

"But I will change my mind if you start crying and get my side of the bed wet," said Nate.

Rose giggled, and Nate inhaled a contented breath.

"You're wearing the perfume I bought you," he said.

"No, I don't have perfume on today,"

"Oh, I thought I smelt it."

12

A Confession

I t's a special feeling being in someone else's bedroom. You feel a closeness to them you never get through conversation alone. The things people keep in their bedrooms are known to so few. And these things change. People change. New relationships, new influences — they all bring about changes that we don't notice ourselves until we step away. Like our taste in clothes… or fragrance.

I've been thinking about rooms and homes. They hold the essence of what makes a person tick. From there, we can see into their world. If only rooms had eyes and ears… the stories they could tell.

You two are not right together, you know. Don't let the occasional moment make you think otherwise. Half-hearted apologies and insincere declarations of love. Those moments are not real. Anyone can make promises to one another in the warmth of a moment like that. But when the cold light of day hits and that moment has dissolved, what is left? Do those promises remain? Or are they just stripped back to mere words that can just as easily be forgotten? I've seen how unhappy you are in the long term. I've watched those bright promises fade in front of my eyes. The truth can't be glossed over with empty words. They always dissolve when the clouds come back. Always.

Don't worry, though. I've set things in motion now.

We have history, you and I. It means something.

I will watch everything unravel.

13

Nate

The doorbell rang on the morning of their appointment — *the* appointment. The one where the procedure would take place to harvest their memories and record them as videos to watch back. Nate's sleep the night before had been fitful. He knew that Rose's had been worse.

"That'll be Lana at last. I'm just finishing my hair and I'll be down in a minute," said Rose, suggesting that Nate should get the door.

Alannah had agreed to drive them after Dr Thomas had recommended neither of them got behind the wheel following the session. The effect of the drugs involved would still leave them groggy and impair their driving ability.

He pocketed his phone, on which he'd been thumbing through mundane Facebook posts of everyone else doing ordinary things. He checked the mirror in the hallway as he passed it and smoothed his fingers down the stubble around his chin. Dark patches under his eyes belied his usual claim of being able to sleep through anything. There was redness in his eyes that made him look and feel older.

"Hey," he said as coolly as he could muster when opening the door to his sister-in-law.

"Hey, handsome, you OK? Sorry I wasn't here any earlier."

"It's fine. Rose is still upstairs getting ready."

"Oh, good. I've got you to myself for a bit, then." Alannah smiled, brushing past him and dropping her handbag on the floor. The contrast of her airy manner sent his own apprehension further down the scale.

Nate laughed nervously and cast an eye up the stairs. He followed as she led through to the lounge.

"Everything OK with you, then?" he mustered.

"Yeah, just the car playing up again. Nigel offered to take a quick look. He says it might need a new belt or pump?"

"Nigel? Since when did old Nigel know anything about motors."

"Well, I don't know, do I? The only belts and pumps I know about are in my wardrobe, not under the bonnet of a car. I just know it's still making a dodgy noise and Nigel was there to take a look."

"Well, bring it back over the garage again this week if you're still worried. Maybe I should have taken it for a drive myself to listen. Me or Gaz will check it properly."

"Never mind Gaz, I'll expect your undivided attention, Natey-boy. And on the car too." She winked.

They reached the sofa and Alannah took off her coat, threw herself down, then patted her palm on the space beside her as an invitation for Nate to occupy it. She was wearing the wide elasticated neck of her top pulled down to reveal two bare shoulders. The bottom of it hung loosely over a tight-fitting pair of dark blue jeans. Stepping out of her shoes as she walked in left her feet also bare, showing off crimson-painted toenails.

The last time he'd seen her was just under a week ago when she'd slept in that very spot after he'd covered her up with a blanket. Nate hovered for a moment as images of that night came back to him. Then he sat to the side of Alannah, resisting the spot to which she had invited him. His body position mirrored hers, twisting to face each other from opposite ends of the sofa — one foot pulled up off the floor and tucked underneath the other leg.

"So how have you guys been this week?" she asked.

"It's been nice, yeah, good," said Nate.

"Wow! Nice *and* good. Nate, you're really gushing about it," Alannah teased.

"Oh, get lost, you know what I mean," Nate countered, relaxing a little. "It's been… positive."

"Well, that is good. I'm glad to hear it."

Alannah kept her eyes fixed on him, and Nate tried to decipher whether her words were genuine. Of course they were, he told himself. He acknowledged his own tendency to give his imagination far too much freedom. It was an innocent exchange. If there was anything ulterior encapsulated in that doe-eyed flutter, it was him projecting it there.

Alannah tilted her head and smiled. Nate jolted himself from his thoughts and felt momentarily embarrassed as if they had been readable across his forehead.

"So." Alannah broke the spell. "What happened that night last week when I ended up here on your couch. Where did you get to?"

"Oh, I just walked for a bit. Needed to cool down, you know. I'm sure Rose filled you in on all the details."

"She may well have done, but I was asking for your side of it."

He wasn't sure whether he wanted to delve into these details with her — least of all right now. But his guard was down and he reeled off more than he'd have measured out, had he better controlled his tongue.

"It had gone so well up to the wedding album, then we got into that whole thing about Nicola. I just wanted to diffuse it. That's when I went out," he finished.

"Ah, the unhinged crazy ball of bitch that is Nicola. What did you ever see in her?"

Did that warrant an actual answer? The line of questioning didn't sit comfortably with Nate, but he didn't know why. *He* could be disparaging about her. If he was talking to Rose, it was part of his role to put down his ex. That was their shared dutiful gratification as a couple. But the dynamic was different when talking to Alannah. And it was another step entirely for Alannah to be the one being so derogatory. He didn't feel like playing the game of insulting his ex-fiancée just for someone else's indulgence.

To whom should his allegiance be in this case, he wondered. After all, he'd proposed to Nicola once upon a time. His memories of her weren't all bad. They had three or four years of pretty good times before it went sour. And where were those memories stored? In a place where the imminent therapy could probe? Did one image leap to another and is that something that would be recorded? These thoughts had prevented him from answering Alannah's question — whether or not it had been rhetorical. He shrugged in an effort to kill that particular direction of conversation. His effort failed.

"Did you know she turned up on Rose's hen night?"

"What? Nicola did? Rose never told me that!"

"Rose never knew. Still doesn't." Alannah lowered her volume.

"What the fuck!? Are you serious?"

"Yep. I saw her in the club when I went to the bar. I recognised her. She was looking to cause trouble, I knew it. So I got her out of there. Me and Helen. Rose never knew a thing. We didn't want to spoil her night."

"And you never thought to tell me either?" asked Nate.

"No. I *chose* not to tell either of you. Because it was better, wasn't it? Better that neither of you knew. Better that her jealous, spiteful presence didn't get in the way of you making new happy memories. You see what I'm getting at, Nate?"

"I think so, but—"

"Don't you see? It's about not clouding memories unnecessarily. You do realise — none of our memories are absolute truth? They're just our version of events. The bits we know about, the bits we happened to notice or focus on. The bits we choose to filter in or out."

"If you're still trying to talk us out of the therapy, don't you think it's too late for that already?"

Alannah put her hand on his knee and looked him in the eyes again. "There's nothing that's going to come out of this therapy that shouldn't come out, is there?"

Nate tried to meet her stare, but he'd never been confident with eye-contact. His gaze drifted up and right before answering.

"Why would it? This is about us connecting over our happy memories. Me and Rose," he said. Alannah's arresting brown eyes searched his expression. She had the confidence to embrace the silence, while he felt the urge to fill it. "Rose needs this. We both need it and we need to give it a go together, to save everything that's good about us. That matters to me. A lot. More than anything."

"That's good," Alannah said curtly. Her hand reached to her gold necklace, teasing it from one side to the other across her collarbone.

Now, Nate felt like he was finding his own confidence and, at last, he could control the conversation.

"I had to calm Rose in the middle of last night when she woke up crying and sweating. Screaming 'Mum'. Reliving her nightmare. Still blaming herself. And it's not an uncommon occurrence. Whatever comes of this, she has to feel she has explored this option to satisfy this thing that gnaws away at her. If something about that accident is locked away in her memory, then I owe it to her to help release it. We're definitely doing this, you know."

Alannah sank back into the cushions as she took in the scene Nate was describing, but he wasn't finished.

"I don't know if it will work for us as a couple, or do anything for Rose's grief. But now it's presented itself, there's no way she'll miss the chance to try it. And I see that. Maybe I didn't at first, but I see it now. And that's why I'm by her side all the way now. I'm there for her. We have to do this."

"OK, I get it," Alannah said. She allowed her necklace to fall from her grasp and folded her arms. If she'd arrived with any genuine hope or intention of putting a spanner in the works, then Nate felt right now he'd prevented it. As much as Rose had turned to her sister for comfort these last few months, shutting him out in the process, he now felt like it was him and Rose again. He'd nailed his colours to her mast. He was the one who was there for her. Hopefully, she knew that too, now.

"What are you two gossiping about? Should I be worried?" Rose glided into the room, fastening the strap of her watch as she moved. The sight of her was more striking to Nate than it had been for a long time. Her hair, her outfit, her glow. She was prepared for her mission. There was no sign of doubt. Nate felt her energy and fed from it.

"Nothing much. Just how big today is for us. You look great, honey," Nate got to his feet.

"Ah, thanks. You don't scrub up too bad yourself." She smiled at him before averting her gaze towards Alannah. "Thanks again for this, Sis. We really appreciate you driving us."

"No probs, babe, you know I'm here for you." Alannah grinned.

"I think I'm ready, then," said Rose. "Let's get moving, shall we?"

14

Rose

Rose's palms were sweating, bending the photos within her grip. Four photographs: three that evoked the most wonderful memories in her marriage and one captured by a passer-by on the worst day of her life. Aware of the damage her anxiety was doing, she released them from her grasp and lay them flat on the arm of the brown leather sofa. The space that normally dwelled between her and Nate had diminished. Rose felt like they sat there now as a united front. Them against the rust that was threatening their future together, no longer willing to let it seep into cracks and penetrate the foundations of their once happy lives. All relationships had baggage, it was down to the people involved to decide whether they could carry it and they wouldn't know until they tried.

No one had spoken for longer than Rose found comfortable. She hovered over the tipping point between spontaneous chat and obvious desperation to fill the silence. As the moment came and went, she felt compelled to giggle as Nate caught her eye. He raised his eyebrows in the playful way he used to when they were sharing a joke. For a second, she felt like a schoolgirl again, pulling faces at George across the Year 11 classroom, full of adrenaline at the thought of their maths teacher, Mrs Haskins, catching them at any minute. Nate's eyes rolled as Dr Thomas pulled yet another piece of paper from his briefcase and meticulously wrote in the empty boxes. His glasses lowered slightly on his nose as he cross-examined the details he had just written with those on a previous form.

"Quite a lot of paperwork there, Doc!" Rose knew that if anyone's urge to break the silence was going to get the better of them, it would be Nate's.

"Indeed…" Dr Thomas spoke slowly as he checked over the boxes on the current form. The dragging out of the word suggested he was not yet ready to have his concentration broken. "Yes, one can never be too careful with the finer details," he said finally. "Consent is always a priority in this job."

"Absolutely," said Rose. "We completely understand."

"Right," said Dr Thomas. "I trust that you've read all the information I gave you? Your online psychological evaluations have both been cleared, and I'm happy that you will both cope well with the procedure. Have you completed the medical questionnaire I gave you?"

"Yep, don't worry, Doc. There's no way I'm letting you prod around in here without checking the small print."

Nate gestured towards his head as he handed over the pair of forms they had filled in at home. "The bit where it talks about, you know, not really being with it because of the drugs. This is all... confidential, right? I just feel uncomfortable, like with stuff being recorded when I'm not aware of what I'm saying."

"Rest assured, Nate, that nothing said within these four walls will leave them. And anything considered too... intimate... will not form part of the viewing session. Patient confidentiality is extremely important to me."

Dr Thomas's words seemed to put Nate at ease.

"OK, so I need a few moments to review your medical forms," he said. "Then there are just a couple more routine questions for you to answer before I can administer the Benzopentalin." His eyes pored over the forms. Rose felt nervous, like she was sitting an exam or being questioned by the police again. The doctor had already confirmed it was safe to take the drug on top of her antidepressants but she couldn't help feeling anxious that this opportunity could be ripped from her grasp at the last minute.

"Right, I think we're all set," said Dr Thomas. "Did you bring the photographs?"

"Yes," said Rose, spreading three of the four photos out on the desk.

Dr Thomas stared at the images laid out before him and paused for a moment. "Good," he said as he examined them for longer than Rose was expecting. None of the photos were the original. Rose had been paranoid about losing them, and so had insisted on printing copies. The cheap printer paper didn't do justice to the richness of detail that was held by the professionally processed ones safe in her memory box at home. But the essence of each picture was preserved, and the smiles of contentment contained within the memories were clear.

Rose had found it difficult to choose. In the days after making up from their big argument, Nate had been far more open to chatting things through with kindness and enthusiasm. He had still left Rose to make the final decision, but Rose no longer felt this a spiteful act. Wherever he had gone and whatever he had done after storming out of the house that night, he had come back with a very different attitude. Rose had wondered, but not asked, what — or who — had persuaded him to be more supportive. The couple had spent several evenings with a bottle of wine and a home-cooked meal reminiscing over all the possibilities at their disposal. Rose had remembered some precious times in her life, and she wondered if this was all part of the therapy process. Maybe it wasn't about watching the memories at all but in fact about having this period of discussion around a plethora of moments that had brought the couple joy. Nate too had commented on how much he had enjoyed the process and how good it had been to laugh with his wife again.

Dr Thomas gathered up the photos and walked over to the medicine cabinet.

"I… I wasn't sure if this is any help," said Rose. "But I brought this photo as well. You said to bring photos, but I wasn't sure if that was just for the happy stuff. I didn't know if you needed a prompt for each event and I know this isn't a memory as such, as I can't remember it, but—" Rose knew she was gabbling. She always did this when she felt insecure. "Well, it's here if you need it, but if you don't, then I'll just put it back in my bag. Thought it wouldn't hurt to bring it just in case."

Dr Thomas sat back down and gave her his full attention. "That's very helpful, thank you, Rose," he said kindly. He took the flimsy piece of paper from her and examined the image. It wasn't a pleasant sight to present, and the doctor baulked as he looked. It comprised a cut-out of a newspaper article dated nearly one year earlier. The headline read, *'One Dead and Three Injured in Weekend Crash.'* A grainy photo underneath showed the image of a black Volvo 4x4 upturned onto its roof at the side of an A-road. The car was badly smashed with the passenger side wrapped around a tree in the embankment. Two other cars were in lesser states of devastation but damaged beyond repair on the grass nearby. Police cars book-ended the scene and cones had been laid out to stop the traffic from encroaching on the recovery efforts. It was an image Rose had studied at length, much to Nate's discouragement. She had always believed that this photo, taken by an eyewitness — the only physical evidence she had left of the crash — would be the key to unlocking her memory of what went wrong that day. Maybe there was still a chance that it would be.

With Rose content she had done the right thing, Dr Thomas returned to the medicine cabinet, which he opened and locked again with a set of keys that he kept in his trouser pocket. They were attached to a teddy bear keyring that was one half of a set of two. A cuddly teddy seemed incongruous to the personality demonstrated to them so far by Dr Thomas. Rose wondered if a wife or a child had gifted it to him.

Dr Thomas donned some latex gloves and tore open a white and green packet that contained a syringe. He removed the lid and jabbed it into a glass bottle of clear liquid. He carefully measured a dose and turned back to the couple opposite him.

"Right, who would like to go first?" he asked.

"I will," said Rose. "I'm the one who has pushed for this, it's only right that I go first."

Nate looked like he was about to protest, but Rose was already out of her seat and rolling up her sleeve. She couldn't risk any more time passing, she needed this to happen now.

"I'll administer the injection and then attach the electrodes while we wait for the Benzopentalin to take effect. It will take roughly three to five minutes and then we can begin." Dr Thomas led her over to a big chair which sat behind a curtain in the corner of the room. Rose's stomach knotted with anxiety and she hoped she could get through this without having a panic attack. She focused on her breathing and found a fixed point on the wall to concentrate on as she settled into the chair.

Routine questions out of the way, Dr Thomas rubbed the outside of her upper arm with an alcohol wipe. "OK, sharp scratch," he said.

Rose closed her eyes. She had always done this when receiving an injection, ever since she was a child. She gripped the arm of the chair as she winced at the prick of the needle. Dr Thomas asked if she would mind removing her hairband and he helped her to smooth down her wavy hair. She felt comforted by how gentle he was being with his touch.

He positioned a large machine above her head that was attached to a stand. It reminded Rose of the drying hoods you get in hairdressers. Coloured wires with electrodes on the end protruded from the centre tube. Dr Thomas opened a case that contained a cap covered in circular discs and placed it over Rose's head. She felt relieved that there was no mirror, like in the hairdressers, to make her feel even more self-conscious. The doctor took the wires and attached one to each of the discs before manoeuvring the machine so the tube sat directly above Rose's head. He pressed a button and Rose noticed a red light appear on the machine at her side.

"Comfortable?" asked Dr Thomas as Rose tried her best to sit back and relax. She nodded, and he moved to a table next to her where his laptop was already set up.

Rose heard the clicking of the keyboard and the whirring of the electrical equipment that she was entangled in. She was facing away from Nate, but she could hear him fidgeting on the squeaky leather sofa.

"It doesn't hurt," she said. As the words came out, they seemed louder and more muffled than usual, as if she was wearing headphones. The familiar sound of her own voice was distorted, and she knew the drug was taking effect. As she spoke, she felt lighter, as if she were a few large sips into a glass of wine. The muscles in her face eased and the nerves in her tummy loosened.

"Whoa, it feels weird." She giggled as her vision became blurry. She was conscious of every word she spoke and thought perhaps she was slurring. Rose had never been a big drinker and always knew her limits. It was rare that she relinquished control to the point of being blind drunk, and so the more the effect of the drug intensified, the more she felt concerned for what she might say. The feeling was short-lived, however, and she quickly began to embrace, even enjoy the sensation. The room spun into a dreamlike landscape of pastel colours and blurred lines. Sounds became minimal, and she soon forgot Nate was even there. The wall ahead faded as her eyes closed and a warm purple glow descended behind her eyelids. Dr Thomas's voice floated through the thick sensation in her ears and she became transfixed by his every word.

"Can you hear me, Rose?"

"Yes." The 's' seemed to linger for ages.

"When is your birthday?"

"25th of July."

"What is your favourite colour?"

"Green."

"And how many siblings do you have?"

"One sister."

"That's excellent, Rose. Well done." Dr Thomas's voice was deep and comforting. In her drug-induced state of relaxation, she trusted him implicitly. All thoughts of Nate in the room vanished, and any remnants of self-consciousness dissolved into the mist.

"OK, Rose. I can see an image in this first photograph." Dr Thomas spoke slowly, gently and clearly. "The image is of you sitting on a seat and in your hand is a large glass of what looks like lager. The seat is outside; it looks like a town square behind you with shops and an ancient-looking building in the background. You are smiling. Can you tell me more about this memory, Rose?"

Rose described a day she had spent with Nate in Bruges just before their second Christmas as a couple. She spoke about the beautiful hotel they had stayed in, the contentment she had felt as they explored the river by boat and the city on foot. The lights of the town square, the bustle of the marketplace, the awe she had felt at the view from the top of the bell tower. Nate had bought her a bracelet from one of the market stalls before they had eaten dinner in a tiny backstreet restaurant, the enticing smell from the chocolatier next door too tempting to resist afterwards. She described the enormous drinking vessels from which they had enjoyed the local beers that evening before wandering back through the narrow streets to the hotel with vast windows looking out over the river. With no hesitation and a drug-induced confidence, Rose described the way they had hardly been able to keep their hands off each other as they fell through the door of the hotel room.

Before she could go any further, a voice entered her thoughts. It was Nate whispering to Dr Thomas, "We don't need to record the next bit." Then Dr Thomas's voice reassuring Nate.

Although Rose had stopped speaking, Nate's interjection wasn't strong enough to penetrate the memory that was unravelling vividly in her mind and the images of them making love on the floor of the hotel room. Unaware of the depth and detail of data being recorded through the stark clinical equipment to which she was hooked up, her mind could not have been further away, engulfed in a memory that felt as real as the day she had experienced it. She could sense the cold, hard tiles against her back; hear Nate's voice whispering in her ear; feel his fingertips brushing down her stomach, and she realised goosebumps were developing in real-time. Rose had never felt so relaxed, so focused on a thought that she believed she could have reached out and touched anything within it. The feelings she had for Nate on that evening were rushing through her like they had been bound behind a locked door for the last year, released in a flurry of urgency — no concern for who might watch this back in the coming weeks.

She'd barely been in the chair a few minutes but the treatment was working. The days spent choosing photos and reminiscing were now being enhanced by this wonderfully vivid memory. She felt close to Nate again, and happiness was trickling in. It was all still there; it had not been lost, it just needed to be reawakened. If this was the case for such long-faded emotions, maybe it could also be so for memories beaten down by trauma.

Prompted by Nate's intervention, Dr Thomas moved onto the next photograph and Rose talked for ages about their wedding day. The words drew out of her like a string of colourful handkerchiefs in a magic trick. Each one sparked another train of thought, leading to a myriad of memories burning in the darkness. As one was shared, another ignited with equal brightness as if being experienced first time around. She relived every detail of the day through vivid description and emotional recollection, the words less significant than the joy and passion evoked in Rose during the process. With only the occasional prompt from Dr Thomas, Rose had described her wedding day with the detail of an author.

Finally, she relived a garden party and barbecue at her mum's house where all the people most precious to her had gathered to celebrate her 27th birthday. She had picked the memory because it featured her mum, Alannah, Nate, her closest friends and favourite colleagues. It had been a precious day, organised as a surprise for her by Nate and one that had made her feel truly loved and spoiled.

With the happy memories recorded, Dr Thomas cleared his throat.

"Rose, do you feel able to move onto this fourth and final memory? It is not a happy one and may invoke some deep emotions." His voice gave Rose confidence. This was why she was here, and the memories she had just recounted bolstered her. She felt stronger than ever, and her faith in the love and support of her husband was freshly renewed, not to mention the drugs flowing through her body that squashed any hesitation or inhibitions. She was ready.

Dr Thomas described the scene in the photograph, being careful, as he had with the others, not to make assumptions about the images or put words in Rose's mouth.

"I want you to take your mind back to the start of this day," he said softly. "What led to this car ending up here?"

Rose could see the photograph in her mind. She mentally clasped the image despite her thoughts racing. She tried to find the clarity that had formed with the other three memories. The words did not flow as quickly as they had previously, though — this memory would not be harvested that easily.

As if sensing her struggle, Dr Thomas interjected. "Tell me about leaving the house that morning, Rose."

"It was a Saturday, so my alarm wasn't set. Nate was already up, getting ready to pick up a conservatory sofa that Mum had bought on a local selling site. He was pissed off about it because Alannah was supposed to be going but had bailed a few days earlier. I woke up because Nate's phone rang. It was work, an emergency breakdown that needed recovery. I can't remember why Gaz couldn't go. It was Nate's day off, but we needed the overtime so I told Nate to go to work and I would pick up the sofa. He agreed to leave me his car as it was bigger than mine. I had a shower and then chatted briefly to Mum on the phone while I got dressed. I just wanted to tell her what time I'd be round with the sofa, but when she found out I was going instead of Nate, she asked if she could tag along. She had heard about a little Saturday morning market in the village where we were collecting from. I was glad of the company, so I said I'd pick her up on the way. I remember getting into the car and turning on the engine quickly to get the heater going. It was freezing and my hands were hurting, but I'd lost my gloves. I remember taking down the air freshener from the rearview mirror. Nate was always putting new ones in from work, and I hated the smell. It gave me a headache, so I put it in the glove compartment. I saw Nate's gloves in there that he uses for work, so I put them on until the car warmed up. I pulled out of the space on the road by our house but stalled. I wasn't used to driving Nate's car, and the clutch always felt weird. Mum's is only 10 minutes away, and I remember driving through the gate that leads to her house. You have to swing out into the road first because it's a sharp turn and some bricks from the gateway had fallen away in a storm earlier in the week. Nigel, my mum's gardener, was in the garage mixing up some cement to fix them and he waved as he saw me."

Rose could hear the gravel beneath the tyres as she drove towards the house, the beep of the horn as she pulled Nate's 4x4 up in front of the door. And there she was, clear as day! "Mum," whispered Rose as she visualised her mother appearing from the house wearing her light grey jacket and the turquoise scarf with golden leaves on it. Rose inhaled deeply as she remembered her mum climbing into the car and the waft of her 'everyday' perfume filling the car.

Rose wished that this wasn't just a memory; that she had some control over what happened next. She would have taken her mum to the safety of the living room, tea in hand, and talked about nothing in particular for the entire day — not driven anywhere. She would have hugged her so intensely that her mother's shape and warmth would forever be etched on Rose's arms. And she would have told her she loved her, more than any mere words could ever have conveyed. It was rooted in every cell; infused into every vein; sewn into the fabric of her being. Rose had never appreciated the concept until it was too late; until her mum was lost and so too was a piece of herself.

But no amount of effort could change the following events. Rose had done some reading about memories amid her frustration. She knew the human brain was flawed in its accuracy of recollection, capable of altering memories to such great extent that the owner could believe with all sincerity that what they were recalling was true. Even seconds later, a memory could be altered, giving different people, different perceptions of the same event. It could also go even further and erase the memories of events so horrific that no one would want to remember. She knew there was still lots to be learned, but this therapy was groundbreaking. It had all been there in the information provided by Dr Thomas — scientists had discovered that the alterations and even deletions of memory are not permanent. This drug could help them reach past the corrupted data, restoring everything to its accurate foundation by sifting through the haze and recording the original files. It was like viewing things on a camera, not a brain prone to human fallibility. No amount of trauma or repression could distort the details that were appearing in Rose's mind, and Dr Thomas had told her that even the details she didn't see during the harvesting process would be transferred within the computer files to be converted into pictures.

Rose had anything but control. Like a moth being drawn in by light, her mind was following the events of that day. She didn't leave the car, nor did she hug her mum or tell her she loved her. She had simply smiled and given her a greeting like any other not known to be the last.

Rose talked through the details of pulling back out of the drive, of hearing a clunk that she assumed was the access hole cover the fallen bricks had disturbed. She could hear the gears crunching as the car left the junction near her mum's house. The soles of her feet were reminding themselves of the right amount of pressure, the slightly bigger distance between brake and accelerator pedals in the unfamiliar car.

"We drove out to get onto the A6 towards Bakewell. I was tired because I'd been up late the night before, catching up on some marking. I hadn't intended to be up that early," she said. "I remember I was telling Mum about an issue with one of the kids in my class at work and how it was stressing me out. It had been a busy week and I think I just complained the whole way out of town. I never even asked her how she was."

Rose could feel the familiar thickness forming in her throat but was surprised at how freely the words continued to flow. The usual urge to stop speaking and protect herself from an embarrassing barrage of sob-ridden words was not there. No inhibitions. She spoke through the tears. She didn't suppress the onslaught of emotion as she berated herself for not being kinder to her mum, for not knowing what was to come, for not driving more slowly.

"We pulled onto the inside lane and I put my foot down. I remember feeling a bit more comfortable with the car. Despite the cold, it was sunny. We had the radio on and Mum was being her usual wonderful self, reassuring me I was doing a good job. She offered to make dinner for me and Nate that evening as a thank you for helping her out. I was feeling relaxed and became excited at the idea of a home-cooked meal with a glass of wine." More tears broke rank, and the haze behind Rose's eyelids turned from purple to orangey-red. The words stopped flowing so liberally, while muddled thoughts seeped into the clear stream she had experienced until now.

Dr Thomas prompted her. "What happened next,

Rose?"

"I can't remember." Rose's tone was brimming with all the frustration that had built up over the last year. "Why can't I remember?" Rose became agitated. She tried to open her eyes but couldn't. Her eyelids were heavy like tar, her eyes stung, and she panicked as the drug-induced lethargy stopped her from rousing. The clarity of the images present in previous memories had been replaced with grainy, bitty flashes of colour and sound. She cried out and felt a hand on her arm. The voice of Dr Thomas floated over the greying shapes and she tried to stay still enough to hear what he was saying.

"Focus on your breathing, Rose, like you've been practising."

Rose inhaled deeply and started to count, but couldn't focus long enough to get to three. Traffic noises flooded her ears, and a tune played in her mind. The radio. Lyrics broke through until she recognised the song — *Dreams* by Fleetwood Mac. She had felt nauseous when it came on at the garage while she was visiting Nate about a month ago; she never put two and two together.

"Rose." Dr Thomas's voice broke through again. "Focus, Rose. What happened next?"

"The brakes!" Rose was distressed. "I tried to brake but nothing happened!"

A clattering of sound pounded in Rose's mind as she clawed at the cap on her head until Nate's voice could be heard saying, "Stop it! That's enough!"

Footsteps approached from behind her and she felt someone grab hold of her hands. She felt a release of pressure on her head as the cap was removed and Dr Thomas's voice calmly urged her to open her eyes. The lights of the room felt blinding as she rose from her trance, but there, squatting in front of her, was Nate, each of her hands in one of his. "It's OK, honey, I'm here. You're safe."

"Did you get enough?" Rose's voice was desperate. "I'm so sorry, I tried, I just couldn't remember any more. It's too hard." Tears seeped through the shoulder of Nate's shirt as he gripped her close.

"It's too soon to tell how clear it will be, Rose, but there is plenty of data," said Dr Thomas. "It will just take time to convert before we can see if it gives you the answers you need. You've done all you can. Well done."

Rose wiped her face with the sleeve of her top. "Fuck," she said, giving in to the exhaustion and letting some more casual tears finish their journey down to her chin. She sniffed and put her head in her hands. Nate rubbed her back, still crouched next to the chair.

The doctor helped Rose over to the sofa where he encouraged her to lie down for a little while. Rose could feel the heaviness on her eyelids as she fought the urge to sleep.

"Don't fight it," said Dr Thomas. "Sleep if you need

to."

He disappeared and returned with a glass of water. Rose took a few tiny sips and lay still for a little while.

She awoke twenty minutes later, and Nate hadn't moved from her side.

"Are you OK?" he asked.

"Fine," said Rose as she lifted her head and sat up. "Your turn," she said, feigning composure and having another sip of water.

Nate looked concerned.

"Take your time," said Dr Thomas. "We have all afternoon. I need time to set up ready for Nate and recalibrate the equipment. There's a coffee shop across the road by the park. When you feel able, I would be happy for you to have a little walk so long as you don't go far. Why don't you have a sugary drink and some fresh air before we continue?"

15

Nate

Rose walked unsteadily to the coffee shop that sat on a busy corner overlooking the park. Nate supported her, Rose's arm threaded through his. It gave him thoughts of guiding Gaz back to a taxi after he'd had a Saturday night skinful. More of the tender arm-linking and less of the football chanting, though.

She ambled to the bench in the corner of the park. Nate left her there while he nipped inside the cafe to order himself a flat white and Rose's favourite honeycomb iced cappuccino. On the bench, he squeezed her thigh as she talked. Rose put her hand on top of Nate's and interlocked their fingers. She tried to describe the feeling of experiencing the therapy.

She expressed feeling in control of what she was saying at first. The questions from Dr Thomas had been coherent; her answers began as measured. Yet somehow, early on, she had sensed the feeling evolving. She was still aware of what she was saying, but the words that came from her mouth had an element of surprise, like she was hearing them along with the other people in the room. Everything she had audibly articulated, she was picturing in her mind too. The images flickered and raced, though, and she speculated how much could have been recorded during the process.

"I feel like I braked, Nate." She recalled the accident memory. "I saw it happening as I heard the words coming out of my mouth. I felt my foot pushing the pedal. Does that mean that's what actually happened? If I felt it and I saw it in my memory does that mean that's how it was?"

"Try not to get worked up, honey." Nate tried to reassure her. "It's done now."

"But I was braking and pushing the pedal, and it didn't work. That's what I saw in my mind. That's how it flowed from my memory. Maybe I blocked that out until now. But that moment came back to me. The panic — I felt it again."

Nate put down his takeaway coffee cup on the bench beside him and rubbed Rose's hand. He gave her arm a gentle squeeze, but the right words of comfort were not coming naturally to him. Rose seemed to read doubt across his face.

"Do you think I could have imagined it? Could I have created some version of the memory to fill the gap?" she asked him, earnestly. Her eyes were searching him for an answer, or at least a crumb of reassurance. Nate didn't know what to think, let alone how to answer. His silence still floated between them. "It felt exactly like everything else I could remember from the day before the accident. It didn't feel made-up, it was just like the events that I already knew rolling on into the next scene but then… then it was like the lights went out again. I swear, Nate, I'm not making it up."

"I'm not saying you are. Not for one minute. It's just hard to get our heads around, isn't it? I guess we should wait and watch back what he recorded first?"

"I'm so sure of it, though. I wasn't distracted. It wasn't because I didn't feel used to your car. I needed to hit the brake, and that's what I did."

Nate didn't know how to answer. He was plagued by contrasting thoughts. They talked and finished their drinks before making their way back across the road for round two.

Back in the therapist's office, it was Nate's turn to experience the treatment. Until he sat in the chair, his thoughts had been entirely with Rose and helping her through her part. All too quickly, the reality caught up with him that he was now about to go through the same process. He hadn't considered the physical aspect of the preparation, even whilst seeing Rose experience it first.

He had given blood many times but still swallowed at the sight of the injection being prepared. He concentrated hard to avoid flinching as the needle entered his arm. He felt self-conscious at the fitting of the electrodes cap, then answered the same routine questions as his wife: naming his birthday, his favourite colour and the fact that, unlike her, he had no siblings.

He twitched in his seat and readjusted his arms by his sides while awaiting the first proper questions. As he did so, the sharpness of the room also seemed to readjust. He blinked repeatedly, trying to regain his own control over it. Instead, it felt like someone had a remote control button that was alternating his surroundings from fuzzy to sharp, then back to fuzzy again. Suddenly he was jolted by the soothing deep voice. He summoned the concentration to focus on the sound as he felt his eyelids becoming heavier.

"I'm going to start with this first photograph, if you're ready, Nate."

Nate cleared his dry throat but felt the answer emerge before he'd had time to form the words consciously.

"Yes, ready."

It was exactly what he'd intended to say, but it left his mouth before he had instructed it. The feeling was disconcerting, but he tried to focus on the doctor's words, as he would at a regular opticians check-up. It was like waiting to be asked which line of letters he could read out from the meaningless sign on the wall. Here, there were no letters to focus on, just the images in his head. He closed his eyes and felt his chest rise with a deep intake of air.

"Nate, I have a photograph here which I know you won't have much recollection of. I just want you to tell me anything that you do know. Your car is on its roof having left the road in a collision, but you weren't the one driving it. Can you tell me about this scene?"

"I wasn't driving. Rose was." Nate's answer flowed from him with the same limited level of control. His eyes were still closed, but his eyebrows rose and fell as he pictured the scene in his own mind. "It was supposed to be me. I got there afterwards. There were ambulances and police cars…"

Dr Thomas took advantage of the pause to redirect Nate's thoughts.

"Can you tell me anything about earlier in the day, Nate?"

"Yes. I told Rose I would pick up a sofa for her mum. On that morning, I had a call from work to collect a breakdown. Gaz was in charge at the garage, so he couldn't leave. I was the only other guy available who was insured on the truck. Overtime was always handy, so I woke Rose and said she could take my car to fit the sofa in. She checked with the seller that they could help load it for her. I left and took Rose's Mini to get to the garage. The next I heard from her was after the accident."

"OK, let's leave that one there. We can move on to happier memories. Take a moment to clear your mind, Nate."

Nate processed the words and wondered how he should clear his mind. If he was thinking of something else, was that not clearing it? If he was thinking of clearing his mind, did that count as clear? He had an odd tug-of-war going on between feeling loose and out of control versus hyper-aware and on edge.

"I want you to picture your memories from this next photograph," came the calm, assuring voice. A brief description followed of the photographed scene from the Christmas Bruges trip. Nate felt himself ease more smoothly into these events in his mind. Despite the cold surroundings of those December days, the pleasure evoked had a warming sensation inside him.

In response, Nate recalled the walks hand in hand with Rose around the beautiful old streets, the brewery tour and beer tasting, the market stalls and their fancy hotel.

The doctor then guided him into the second happy memory of their wedding day. The scene from the photograph in the church brought nothing of Nicola to mind. Instead, Nate spoke lovingly of how he'd melted inside at the sight of Rose walking down the aisle. He was absorbed in the contented recollection as Rose sat a few metres away and listened.

Nate felt loosely aware that for Rose, hearing him talk so romantically about their relationship would be a rare experience. He felt liberated by it yet also embarrassed to be so gushing in the presence of a stranger. It was teasing out a vulnerability in him, but he hoped his words would be having a positive effect on his wife.

Dr Thomas moved onto the last photograph and described the barbecue scene of Rose's surprise birthday party. Nate was now comfortably gliding through one joyful moment after another. Eyes closed but flickering under his eyelids, the corner of his mouth upturned in a smile as he spoke. He'd lost all awareness of his actual surroundings and was transported to Rose's mum's garden.

"Everyone had such a great time. Rose had gone through most of a bottle of Prosecco by herself. Beers flowed. There was laughing and games. We played that thing where we all had a celebrity name stuck to our foreheads. We had to ask questions to guess who we were. I was Freddie Mercury. I guessed it because Rose was tipsily singing *Don't Stop Me Now* as I asked my questions."

Dr Thomas closed his file and was preparing to bring the session to a close as Nate finished his last memories of the barbecue.

"I went inside to get the cake and grab another Budweiser from the fridge. Alannah was opening a new bottle of Prosecco to refill hers and Rose's glasses. She told me I'd done a wonderful job organising the party, and that I was such a perfect husband to her sister. We carried some of the empty bottles down to the recycling box in the cellar. We laughed at the loud clanging noise that echoed off the concrete walls as we dropped the glass bottles into the box. It was silly, but it gave us the giggles. Alannah stumbled a bit and put her hand on my chest.

Then she looked into my eyes and kissed me."

16

Rose

Rose felt winded. She was ready for Nicola to feature in Nate's memories of the wedding day. She had even prepared herself for other small secrets to unearth themselves as Nate fell under the spell of recollection. But this was far more than she was braced to endure; this was not a small secret, it was an unthinkable betrayal.

Rose felt the colour draining from her face and her legs tingled. She could see Dr Thomas sitting behind his laptop screen, his eyes looking straight towards her. Nate was facing the other way, still attached to the machine. She stood up and moved towards him.

"Please remain seated until I have finished the procedure, Rose. You need to allow time for the Benzopentalin to wear off." Dr Thomas's words were measured and calm — the antithesis of what Rose was feeling. Without a word, and as if she had not heard him, she walked past him and around the chair to where she could see Nate's face.

"What the fuck did you just say?"

Nate was still talking, but he had become agitated. He seemed unaware of Rose's physical presence, but it was clear he could hear her voice.

"It didn't mean… no! Alannah, please, tell her!" Nate's words were incoherent and his voice was gaining volume.

"Open your eyes!" demanded Rose. She knew how hard it was for her eyelids to fight against the weight of the drug, yet all empathy and patience had dissolved in the last minute or so.

Nate flinched in his seat, and his mouth moved with no sound.

"Open your eyes! What did you just say, Nate?"

"Rose, he needs time." Dr Thomas's words were gentle. "Why don't you take a seat and I'll get you some water?"

"I don't need any water." Rose was reminded of her mother's accident. She had lost count of the number of professionals who had offered her a drink of water. The kind police officer who had taken her into his arms at the scene; the doctor who had confirmed her mum's death at the hospital; the desk sergeant who had stared sympathetically as she waited to answer yet more inquiries from the police; funeral directors; grief counsellors. Why did everyone think water was the answer? Water doesn't dilute gut-wrenching grief. "What I need is for the one and only person it appears I can rely on, not to be fucking dead."

"Rose…" Dr Thomas's voice faded as she marched out

of his office, down the drive and, without looking, bolted across the road towards the park. A car horn beeped.

"Hey, you OK?" a man asked, rising from the bench where she and Nate had drunk coffee an hour earlier. He was about Rose's age and dressed in a shirt and chinos with a camel coloured overcoat.

Rose said nothing and brushed past him, heading towards a thick group of trees at the back of the green area.

"Suit yourself," he said under his breath.

Rose found herself on a bike trail leading into the trees and followed it until dense foliage surrounded her. She kicked a tree stump and threw a large piece of bark as far as she could towards a mass of brambles. Abruptly, she sat against the tree stump, pulled her knees up to her chest and cradled her head. A year ago she had a family — a faithful husband; a loyal sister; a loving mother. Now, all that she considered stable was being shaken to the core. She was alone. Her breaths became fast and erratic — deep inhalations came readily but refused to be released from her chest. She was panicking. Alone and panicking.

Her pocket vibrated. Nate was calling, but she rejected it. Her priority now was to get her breathing under control before she spun out. She went back to her tried and tested technique — breathe in for three, hold for three, out for three, hold for three. It had not worked earlier whilst she was in the chair, but it seemed to work now. Her chest loosened, her breathing slowed down and tears flowed. Rose closed her eyes and let the tears take over for a moment or two — sometimes that helped to release the pressure and allowed her to process her thoughts more clearly.

How could Alannah have kissed him? Her own sister. Could the memory have been false? Maybe it was a mistake. Nate knew no more than she did about the strength of the drug. Why would he risk coming here and not being able to control what he was saying if he had something to hide? He knew which memories were being analysed and he had, after all, come clean to Rose about Nicola. Why hadn't he done the same with events at the barbecue? Why would he not have told Rose that Alannah had kissed him if he'd done nothing wrong?

Maybe he thought he could overcome the drug and keep this secret safe. Or maybe it wasn't true. But what reason did he have to lie? Besides, the drug had limited their control. Rose had felt it herself whilst connected to the machine. Her thoughts had unravelled with little or no restraint afforded her. Would she have had the strength to fight the vivid reality of the memories and describe something that was untrue? She spent a few minutes contemplating and decided she could not have lied or withheld anything after being given the drug. He said Alannah kissed him; not the other way around. However, semantics were irrelevant. No matter who had kissed whom, someone she loved had betrayed her. Memories of George resurfaced. Was taking her husband just the next step up from her best friend?

Rose's thoughts became confused again, and doubt swirled around her mind. She folded her arms across her knees and buried her face deep into her jumper. Her phone beeped — a text from Scott.

"Fuck off!" she said to the screen as she forcefully deleted the message.

Rose heard the crunch of a twig as footsteps approached. Adrenaline pumped as her fight or flight kicked in but her body froze.

"Are you OK?" A deep voice came from between the trees.

Rose looked up, but it was not the face she expected.

"I'm so sorry," she said, caught by surprise and wiping her cheeks on a sleeve. "I didn't mean to be rude to you."

"Please, there's no need to apologise. You're clearly upset."

"I'm fine." Rose sniffed.

"What you've gone through in there today, Jesus, what you've gone through in the last year. Well, if it were me, I think I'd be tempted to swear at a few people too."

Rose managed a little laugh as Dr Thomas cleared a patch of dirt next to her. He folded up his jacket, laid it on the ground and sat himself down. She felt a little uneasy like she had misbehaved in front of a teacher. She considered that sitting on a dirty patch of ground was probably alien to this well-turned-out doctor.

"I just wanted to check you're OK," he said. "I hope you don't mind. It's just, that was quite unexpected."

"No, I don't mind," she said. "That's nice of you."

"I know I have to keep a professional distance in there, but I do care, Rose," he said. "You have experienced trauma, grief and betrayal all in a short amount of time and that is bound to take its toll. I can help you, Rose. If you come back and talk to me next week, we can talk through the pain and the confusion with or without Nate. We can do that every week until you feel like yourself again. The old Rose isn't lost, I saw that today. I don't need to watch those recordings back to see that parts of your happier days are trapped in there, desperate to overthrow the sorrow."

Rose listened as Dr Thomas, almost poetically, said everything she needed to hear. He was excellent at his job and she felt safe with him.

"Why me?" asked Rose. "What have I done to deserve all of this? I'm a good person. I might be self-absorbed sometimes, argumentative, neurotic, but I've never hurt anyone on purpose. What have I done to warrant this disaster of a year?"

"Nothing, Rose. You don't deserve it, no one does. That's not how life works. But you came to me at the right time. I promise we can work together and I can help you ride the storm."

"Has anyone ever told you, you're easy to talk to?"

"It's my job, Rose."

She reminded herself that Dr Thomas was not a friend. He was someone from whom she was hiring a service. It was his job to listen and care. She was paying him to be nice to her.

Rose's pocket vibrated again.

"You should talk to him," said Dr Thomas.

"Is he still in your office?" asked Rose.

"Your sister arrived shortly after you left."

"Oh God, of course she did." Rose buried her face in her arms again and groaned. "Well, at least they've had time to get their stories straight."

Dr Thomas stood up and brushed his trousers down. "I'll see you next week, Rose?" He posed it as a question rather than a statement. "If you want my professional opinion, I believe it is important we finish the treatment. You should come back next week to watch the memories back. You never know — maybe you and Nate can find a way through this."

As Dr Thomas walked back across the park, Rose's phone vibrated again. This time she pressed the green button and put the phone to her ear.

"Rose, thank God." Nate sounded groggy and was slurring. He also had a tone to his voice that Rose had rarely heard before. He sounded panicked. "Please, sweetheart, honey, you need to come home so we can talk properly. I promise, it meant nothing. I didn't know what I was saying. The memory wasn't meant to go that far into the evening. It's not what it seems. Please, come back and I'll make you believe me, I swear—"

"Words, Nate!" said Rose. "It's all just words, and even if I believe you, I'm furious that you didn't tell me. Why can't you just be honest with me?"

"She's your sister, Rose! I didn't want to be responsible for you guys falling out all over again. Listen, I know I've done nothing recently to make you think you can trust me, but I swear to God that every secret I've kept from you was to protect you, not me."

"Why do you always assume I'm too fragile to handle the truth? It's so arrogant to think that another woman looking at you would send me into the dark depths of despair. All of this anger is because of the lies, Nate. You're right, Alannah and I would have fallen out, but that's my business and my prerogative, you can't control that by lying to me."

"You're right, you're right, and I'm so sorry. Look, I'll tell her to go home and you and I can—"

"She's still there? Are you in the car with her?" Rose stood up and once again her legs took over.

"No, she's parked up on the road. I've told her we just need a minute."

"Have you told her I know?" Rose was becoming

breathless as her speed increased across the carefully mown cricket pitch at the centre of the park.

"Yes," said Nate.

Rose hung up the phone.

She approached the bench by the park for the third time that day. This time, the man said nothing. She stopped before crossing. She could see Alannah's VW Beetle parked on the opposite side of the road, a few metres down from Dr Thomas's. Outside the doctor's house, Nate was perched on the pavement, leaning against the neighbour's fence, phone in hand. It was clear to cross, yet Rose remained frozen on the pavement. She saw the change in Nate's face as he noticed her, and he attempted to stand up. He was wobbly on his feet, a side-effect of the drug that remained in his system, and he fell back against the fence. Rose launched across the road, but not towards Nate. She swerved him and headed straight for the driver's side of Alannah's car.

"Rose!" shouted Nate. "Let's just get home and talk about it there, yeah?" He was walking towards her, relying heavily on the fence to steady himself.

"Why wait?"

"Get out of the road, Rose, please. We don't need to do this in front of all these people."

"*We* don't need to do anything, Nate. This one is all mine."

Rose could see Alannah's dark hair scrunched into a

hair-clip. Her head rested against the window, oblivious to her sister marching towards the car.

"Get in!" Rose called to Nate.

"What?"

"Get in the bloody car, Nate."

She could hear Nate mutter under his breath. Rose was oblivious to the struggle he was having as he tried to increase his speed.

Alannah jolted her head as the palms of Rose's hands slammed against the driver's side window. Alannah looked flustered as Rose moved to strike the car again, this time denting the bonnet.

Rose reached the passenger side just as Nate reached the car and flopped himself between her and the car door.

"Please, Rose, I know you're angry. I'm so sorry, but let's just calm down first before you batter your sister."

"Battering people is not my style, Nate. You should know that. I'm all about the calm and collected conversation."

"Fine, before it becomes a slanging match, then. Can't we just talk first? I need you to hear my side before she spouts her bullshit."

"I've known her long enough to know when she's lying, she's not talking her way out of this one." Rose stopped dead and stared at Nate's face. "Shame I haven't developed the same sense when it comes to you. Guess I just always assumed you'd be on my side."

"I swear on my mum's life," said Nate. "The only reason I didn't tell you is because I *am* always on your side. I didn't want you to fall out with your sister again like you did in school."

"Wow, you're such a saint," Rose said sarcastically.

"You'll see when you watch it back," said Nate. "You can see for yourself. There's nothing else I can say."

"Right, well let's go, then," she said as she opened the door and pulled the passenger seat forward for him to clamber into the back.

Nate paused, seemingly unsure of what to do. He groaned and then did as he was directed. "Jesus Christ," he said as he fell into the back seat and put his seat belt on. He propped his elbow on the ledge and focused his gaze out of the window as he massaged his temple with his forefingers.

Rose slammed the passenger seat back into position and occupied it. For a few seconds after she closed the door, everything was still. Silence covered the interior of the car like a sheet of voile being dropped from above.

"Drive," said Rose.

"Rose... I..." Alannah had both hands on the wheel and her eyes looked down into her lap.

"Drive," Rose said, louder this time.

"Please, hear me out. Nate's told me what came out. I was really drunk and—"

"Drive!" Rose shouted.

Alannah began to cry. The gearbox emitted a grinding sound as she struggled to find reverse. With shaking hands, she slid the steering wheel through her tight grip and manoeuvred out of the space. Rose's face was fixed, staring sternly ahead. Small sobs affected Alannah's breathing as she drove through the familiar streets of their hometown. Rose felt irritated.

"Sorry, I'm confused about why you're crying, Alannah." Rose's tone was brusque.

"I'm so sorry, Rose, I didn't mean to give Nate that impression, I was just drunk and messing around. I don't even really remember—"

"Give him that impression? Do tell me what impression you intended to give him, Alannah. I mean, how many impressions can one get when someone sticks their tongue down your throat? This is what you do. You need to feel like you have some kind of power over men. But why Nate? Why the man I love?"

"That's not true, I was just having a laugh."

"Having a laugh?" Rose was incredulous. "Having a laugh is when you give someone a nickname or have a bit of banter with them, all of which I have ignored over the years because, despite your history with my friends, I genuinely believed that not even you would cross a line with my husband."

"I didn't mean to, I was so drunk, Rose, please, believe me. I don't have any feelings for Nate, I swear."

"Oh, I absolutely believe that, Alannah, because you don't have feelings for anyone. You don't care about anyone but yourself. It's not about feelings with you, it's about having fun. Having control over people, proving that you can take whatever you want whenever you want it and then just dropping them when you get bored."

"That's not fair," Alannah said.

"Isn't it? You did it with George. Of all the boys in that entire school, it wasn't good enough for you to just find one and date them. You had to pick the one boy who meant more to me than anyone. He was my best friend, and you chewed him up and spat him out without giving a shit what it would do to our friendship. I've seen you do it to countless other men. You're probably doing it to the poor bastard you're seeing now. Well, I hope he knows what he's got himself into. But I guess I'll never know because I'll never meet him."

"You will, Rose, I promise you will soon. It's complicated."

"I'm not interested, Alannah. I couldn't give a shit about meeting him. He could be Johnny bloody Depp for all I care. We're done."

Alannah paused as if searching for something to say.

"Please don't say that, Sis, I love you. Mum would want us to stick together."

"Stop the car." Rose was losing the control she had maintained so far.

"What? No, don't be ridiculous, we're nearly at yours, then we can talk."

"Stop. The. Car."

Alannah looked panic-stricken as she indicated and pulled up behind a line of parked cars along the road. Ahead of them a crossroads was getting busy as rush hour grew closer. The car behind beeped its horn at the last-minute change of course, and Alannah gestured impolitely as they overtook.

Rose got out and walked towards the pub at the crossroads. Alannah raced around the car to more beeps, having opened her door into oncoming traffic. She ran ahead of Rose and tried to stop her.

"How dare you?" Rose was breaking. "How dare you bring Mum into this? You can't use her death to emotionally blackmail me."

"That's not what I'm trying to do, Rose, I just meant she hates… *hated* it when we fight. Please, can we just talk. Give me five minutes, I'm begging you, that's all I ask."

"For what, Alannah? You think five minutes is all it will take to lie and manipulate your way out of this. Using Mum to catch me off-guard. It won't wash this time. You *always* do this. Selfish and thoughtless is one thing, but this goes beyond anything I thought even you were capable of. You tried to take the one thing that meant the most to me in the world just because you could. But it didn't work did it? Because Nate isn't the same as the other guys you wrap around your little finger. He's loyal and unlike you isn't hell-bent on fucking up his life for a bit of drunken fun."

Rose continued to walk, faster now towards the traffic lights. The sound of cars gathering grew louder and drowned out the clip-clop of Alannah's shoes behind her. Alannah caught up and Rose spun around. In the distance, Nate was now out of the car and pacing the pavement on his phone. He had eyes on the two sisters and looked concerned.

"Is that what he told you?" Alannah retaliated. "Well, more fool you, Rose. Do you honestly think he didn't enjoy it even just a tiny bit? Poor bloke has been stuck under the thumb since his early twenties with a wife who doesn't know how to just lighten up and have a laugh."

"Does your new boyfriend know what he's got himself into? Does he know that the only person Alannah cares about is Alannah? Hope he's prepared to just be dumped at the drop of a hat because nobody can rely on you. Not him, not me, not Mum."

"Now who's bringing Mum into it?" Alannah said childishly. Then, her tone changed as she processed the meaning behind Rose's words. "What's that supposed to mean?"

Rose knew she had struck a nerve. This had gone beyond the usual sisterly arguments they had got into plenty of times over the years.

"You let everyone down, Alannah. Mum put you up for

all those years…"

"I paid rent, Rose."

"Yes, but you didn't pay Mum for laundry services or cooking your meals every evening or picking you up at midnight when you were too drunk to get yourself home. She did everything for you and even on the day she died you let her down. She couldn't depend on you to pick up a sofa you had promised you would collect for her. It would have taken an hour, Alannah and you bailed on her and relied on me and Nate to get things sorted as usual. I bet you didn't even have a good reason. What was it, a pedicure?"

Alannah stopped. Rose was suddenly aware of how loudly they had been shouting. By the number of eyes on them from the bus stop and through car windows, it was obvious they had been making a scene.

"Don't you dare try to blame me for what happened to Mum." Alannah looked pale and shocked.

"I'm not blaming you. I'm blaming *me* because I was driving because Nate had to work and you had bailed out. Once again, I was the only one willing to put myself out to help, and I ended up with the death of our… beautiful, amazing mum on my shoulders. It's a burden I have to carry forever when I should have been at home. So tell me. You owe me that, at least. Where were you? What was so important that you couldn't go to pick up that sofa? What were you doing that was so much more crucial than answering your phone when your mother was dying on the roadside? So paramount that it took us *seven hours* to reach you to tell you she had died?"

"You have to stop blaming yourself, Rose. It's breaking my heart, it's breaking Nate's heart."

"You know nothing about Nate's heart, Alannah. You don't know him, you mean nothing to him and you will never speak to him again. Answer the question — where were you?"

Alannah sat down on the pavement with her back against the wall. A cyclist stopped to ask if she was alright and Rose abruptly sent him on his way.

"Well?" Rose was getting impatient, and she wanted an answer before Nate finished his phone call and felt compelled to drag her away.

"I was with someone. In a hotel."

"Who?"

"It's complicated." Alannah's eyes flashed towards Nate who had hung up and was now walking towards them.

"I'm sure," said Rose, rolling her eyes. "Why couldn't you have just gone after you'd picked the sofa up? It was first thing in the morning!"

"I said that, but then he suggested Nate's car would be better for it. It made more sense. Then we could get there early and make the most of the spa."

"How does this bloke, who we've never met, who we don't even know the name of, know what kind of car Nate drives? And who is he to be manipulating our family plans? Who does he think he is?"

"It wasn't like that… it's just his job is… complicated and he doesn't get much time off and—"

"Save it. I hope your dirty weekend was worth it. I hope *he's* worth it and you don't screw him up like every other bloke you've got your claws into."

"I told you this memory therapy was a bad idea!"

"Yes, of course. Blame the memory therapy. This has absolutely everything to do with that and *nothing* to do with the fact that you kissed my husband. Have a nice life, Alannah."

Rose turned and continued to walk away. Alannah remained sitting on pavement twirling her keys around her index finger. Rose could hear the steps of Nate, more steady on his feet now, running behind her, only stopping briefly to ask Alannah if she was OK to get home.

"Get lost, Nate." Alannah's voice carried and Rose gave a snort of derision.

As the footfall grew louder, Rose reached for the pedestrian crossing before feeling a hand on her shoulder. Nate guided her away from the traffic lights and towards the pub. Rose felt too angry to resist. She was happy for him to pull her aside and have a go at her for overreacting or being too harsh on her sister. She was perfectly wound up to come back at him with all the venom required to make herself feel better. She was too livid to care about the prospect of crying herself to sleep alone, having pushed Nate away… again.

But he didn't say a word — no lecture, no sympathy for her sister this time. He simply pulled her towards him and held her tight, walking them both to the corner of the pub car park. Rose was now numb. Too angry to cry; too tired to lash out. Her brain had shut itself down, unable to process any more emotions. She stared out to the road as she rested her head on Nate's chest in silence. It wasn't long before a horn sounded and the spattering of gravel under tyres announced the arrival of a blue van. It pulled up next to Nate and Rose.

"Someone call for a lift?"

"Thanks so much for coming, mate." Nate opened the door and helped Rose into the middle passenger seat of Gaz's van. Nate climbed into the window seat next to her and slammed the door.

"You alright, love?" Gaz's voice was warm and familiar.

"Nope," she said and rested her head on Gaz's shoulder, "but it's lovely to see you."

17

Nate

"I'd better not ask how the business went with the brain x-raying," said Gaz as he checked his rearview mirror and pulled away.

"It's not a brain x-ray, it's memory extraction, you muppet!" Nate responded. He shook his head but kept his gaze out of the passenger side window and felt his forehead throbbing.

"That whole Nicola thing came up, then, I guess?" ventured Gaz.

"No, actually," said Rose. "Turns out it was a different indiscretion that Nate's little memory bank was waiting to offer up — one with my sister instead."

The van jerked as Gaz's head swung to the side. Nate looked across at him with Rose squashed in between them.

"Shit. That's not what I was expecting." Gaz frowned as he quickly refocused his attention on the road ahead.

Nate's eyes switched towards Rose. Her arm was pushed up against him, with space at a premium between the three front seats of the van. Their thighs were touching too, but Rose's hands were balled in her lap and she looked straight ahead. Nate tried to decipher how she was feeling, but he couldn't read her expression for sure.

He deliberated on whether to break the silence that was germinating. Rubbing his temple, he reasoned with himself that he'd tried to be honest and upfront about Nicola before the therapy session. Surely that stood in his favour. But he knew that could also be perceived as rather hollow, given he was only being honest about something he'd kept secret for years. It would not win him a tremendous amount of sympathy.

Gaz was the one to break through the dead air. "Listen, then you pair — I'm no therapist. I'm sure you're paying the doc enough for him to sort your problems out. But, seeing as you're both stuck in here with me for the next ten minutes, let's hear it. Nate — mate — what the hell has gone on?"

Nate recounted the key details, uninterrupted. He knew Rose had just heard the story from his mouth during their session. Yet he also had the strange feeling of not knowing whether the details he was now regurgitating matched the way he had conveyed them in the doctor's office. The memory existed in his head, but it was as though the verbalisation of it was coming via two different channels of his brain. He knew he had talked about it earlier, but he couldn't be sure exactly what he had said. His head throbbed even more with the effort of trying to analyse it. He had to rely on the conviction that — given it was his own memory he was recalling — then there was only one version of it he could tell. What he was delivering was the truth.

"I swear, it was over in a second. I pushed her away." He finished the run-down of the events from his memory of that barbecue.

Rose turned to look at him.

"Look, I want to believe you. I think I do believe you. But I need some time to get my head around it all. My brain feels so overloaded with stuff right now, it's hard to even process anything. There's too much chaos going on in here," she tapped her palm against the side of her head. "There's something drawing me through the fog to this notion that you're being genuine but I've just unloaded all of my fury on Alannah and now I just need to be mad at you for a while, OK?"

Nate breathed a sigh of relief. It wasn't the perfect response, but it felt like the best he could hope for. He put his hand on top of Rose's and gave it a tender squeeze. "I can't say if the memory was extracted or recorded or whatever it is the doc can do. But if it was, then you'll see when it's played back. I'm telling you just how it happened."

"You still want to go back again, then? For another session?" Rose asked with a hint of surprise. It was the first moment during the whirlwind of recent events that Nate had even stopped to consider it. Even now, he didn't contemplate not going back. Despite his previous scepticism and despite what had unravelled, the least he wanted now was to see the results of the process. Even through morbid curiosity of what his brain would divulge without his full control. He was fairly confident the video would bring him some vindication. Fairly confident.

"May as well see it through now," Nate responded. "I want to see the videos played back since we've come this far."

"There you go," Gaz chimed in. "One session in Gaz's cab and the pair of you are talking to each other again. This therapy business is easy pickings. That'll be a hundred quid an hour, thanks and an extra tenner for the lift home."

Nate and Rose both gave a snort of laughter.

"Oh, and an extra twenty if I'm even getting you laughing," said Gaz.

"Alright, mate, don't push your luck," said Nate. "Tell you what, though, I wouldn't turn down a couple of paracetamol right now, if you extend to dishing out pain relief."

"Your head aching as well?" Rose asked.

"Been throbbing since we came out of the doc's. How about you?"

"Yeah, mine too. Don't know whether it's the drugs, the headgear from the session or just the sheer overload on my brain. Feels like it's gonna pop."

"You might have found my limit there, guys," said Gaz. "You're welcome to have a rummage in the glove-box. See if there's an open pack. You think you got something to worry about, both suffering like that? Is that supposed to happen?"

Nate pondered it for a moment as he reached into the compartment in front of him. Then he paused and patted his jeans pocket as if another thought had struck him.

"Have you got my gloves?" he asked Rose.

"Nope."

"Shit, I must have left them in your sister's car." He turned his attention back to the hunt for pills and shoved aside half a pack of mints, a few loose CDs and an assortment of junk but couldn't put his fingers on anything resembling a pack of paracetamol. He hadn't thought seriously about whether the headache was evidence of anything to worry about — he hadn't had time to consider that either. Now, Gaz had planted the thought.

"It's weird — both of us feeling rough, don't you reckon?" he directed his query to Rose.

"Not really. I'm sure the stuff Dr Thomas gave us to read mentioned potential side-effects, especially straight afterwards. And on top of the process, we've hardly had a minute to calm down from it."

Her response lacked the conviction she may have intended. Nate sensed she was trying to persuade herself as much as she was him.

"If this therapy is still pretty new, who knows what the effect might be, though, eh?" Gaz ventured.

"Oh, cheers, mate, your happy interventions didn't last long did they? Give us something else to worry about, why don't you?" Nate delivered his retort with a dose of sarcasm — at least, he intended to. He wasn't sure if it came out tinged with the genuine concern he now had.

"Nah, I'm sure it's fine, really." Gaz backtracked. "You said you'd checked it all out. It's legit and whatnot, right?"

"Dr Thomas was totally open with us. It's all still at a trial stage. We've seen the literature, though. And you can look up the studies online at Uttoxeter University. He's listed on their webpage. There's not much info made public yet because it's still being developed I guess. We read up, though, didn't we, Nate?"

Again, Nate felt like Rose was seeking reassurance rather than offering it. The niggling worry of what they'd got into pounded him with every throb of his temple.

"Let's just get back and get a couple of tablets and chill out for a bit, shall we? I reckon we'll be fine later." He wondered if he sounded more convincing to Rose than she did to him.

Gaz indicated and turned left off the main road towards Halewood Heath.

"Oh, that reminds me," he said nodding at the pub they passed. "I saw your sister in the pub last weekend. I don't mean The Willow Tree. Over in that new place near the retail park."

"Lucky you," said Rose.

"Yeah, I know it's probably not the best time to mention her. It just came back to me, though. She was with her fella, right?"

"Oh, typical, you've seen him as well," Rose butted in. "I s'pose everyone will have done before she introduces him to her family. Not that I'm even bothered any more. I pity the bloke, to be honest. I hope I never see him."

"Alright, yeah, I get what you think of her right now. That's not the thing that came back to me, though. It's about the fella. I thought at the time I'd seen him before. I just couldn't think where. But I've just realised where I've seen him."

"Go on, then, spit it out," said Nate.

Gaz glanced at him and seemed to reflect on whether he wanted to say it after all. Nate and Rose both waited expectantly.

"Well." Gaz cleared his throat. "I don't know if this is relevant to anything, but I swear I saw her fella months ago with someone else you know."

Nate kept looking and raised his eyebrows to urge the final bit of information out of Gaz.

"I saw him with your ex, Nicola."

*

Nate's mind was reeling as he drove to his mum's the following day. It was Saturday and he would ordinarily have been in work again. However, he'd thrown up during the evening and not been able to shake off the headache since leaving the therapy session. His head felt like hot needles were being poked inside his skull. Yet the thing plaguing his brain the most was Gaz's disconcerting observation.

Maybe it was nothing. Just a coincidence, Nate had reasoned. Rose dismissed it in her anger as typical of both Alannah and Nicola. She wasn't Nic's biggest fan, and right now, Alannah seemed an equally hostile target. To Nate, it still seemed odd — even if it was just a coincidence. The same bloke being with his ex and now his sister-in-law — the intrigue tugged him.

These thoughts distracted him and the shit-storm of events over the preceding 24 hours as he sat at the kitchen table with his mum.

"It can't be right making you sick and giving you a headache, Nathan," she said with more than a hint of worry. He'd focused on the side-effects to tell her about, rather than the details of the revelations when she'd asked about how the session went.

"Well, we'll see. Don't worry too much. I feel better

today. I guess you've got to expect some kind of reaction with electrodes wired up to your brain!"

He hadn't meant to be so blunt about it and straight away realised he should have softened it a bit for his mum. He saw her wince a little and shake her head as she took in the information.

"Are you glad you went through with it? Is it going to help?"

That was the ultimate question, of course. The bottom line was exactly that — would it help? It was clear Rose wanted it to help with her recollection of the accident. The original point was helping them to rekindle their marriage. So far, it seemed the answer to that question was stretched to both ends of the scale. Yes — going through the photos together, recalling the happy memories as they did so, hearing Rose talk about them whilst in the chair — all those moments felt like a gentle positive nudge in the right direction. However, the process had already led to him dragging back up the incident with Nicola beforehand, and now this one with Alannah. No way did it feel like those revelations were helping matters. He didn't know whether it was bringing him and Rose together or driving them further apart. It had certainly forced a sudden wedge between the sisters.

"I honestly don't know, Mum. We haven't even got to the main bit of the process. I'll let you know after that! One thing's for sure, though — there's a lot more than you might think to making a digital copy of your memories."

"I'll remember that when your dad gets on my nerves, forgetting what I've told him an hour ago."

"What's that, love?" his dad said right on cue, as he came in from the garden.

"Oh, nothing, dear," she said. "Did you cover up the garden furniture like I asked while you were out there?"

"Damn," his dad cursed before turning around and heading back out the door.

18

Rose

The following morning, Helen didn't leave Rose much choice in the matter when she shouted, "Can I come in?" She was already through the kitchen door and on her way to fill up the kettle. "Where's Nate?" she called from the kitchen to Rose who, having just got out of bed, was locked in the bathroom staring blankly at herself in the mirror. She had bloodshot eyes with dark circles underneath them. The remnants of the headache which she had been trying to ignore since the memory extraction were still there, although to a lesser extent than the previous day.

"He's at the garage helping Gaz."

"On a Sunday?"

"It's not for work, it's for Gaz's side project."

"Oh, the Skyline?"

"Wow, you pay way more attention than me," said Rose, massaging her temples. "Yeah, something about a prop shaft."

"Right, well, I'm glad he's not here because now we can talk about him."

Rose could hear the clinking of mugs being put on the side and a spoon being dropped into one of them. She put her face close to the mirror and examined her skin. No amount of makeup would help.

"Sugar?" called Helen.

"Yes, please!" The toothbrush hanging from her mouth distorted Rose's words as she bundled her hair up into a messy bun. 'I need it today,' she thought. Two minutes later she emerged from the bathroom in yoga pants, a strappy top and a half-zipped up hoodie. She headed downstairs to find a smiling Helen placing two mugs down on the coffee table. Helen plumped a sofa cushion and patted the seat, inviting Rose to sit down beside her.

"Oh, guess who I saw in the Willow Tree last Friday night," said Helen as she turned the mug to give Rose the handle. Rose looked at her blankly. "George!"

"George from school? My George?" Rose hadn't seen or heard from her old best friend for years. After falling out over Alannah, it had taken until graduation to smooth things over, and they had grown apart in adulthood. George wasn't on social media, and Rose often thought about him and wondered if he was still living locally.

"The very same," said Helen. "I didn't speak to him, he looked like he was waiting for someone. He looks good."

"Seems like the place to be," said Rose. "Alannah was in there last Friday too. Did you see her?"

"No. It was rammed, though, I didn't stay long. Right,

tell me everything," said Helen with a kind look. She always had time for anyone, and she genuinely cared. Rose felt lucky to have her as a friend.

Rose spent the next 45 minutes recounting the events of the previous few days. Helen listened sympathetically as her friend vented about every detail and surprise revelation.

"My head's still not right," said Rose. "And Nate threw up twice when we got home."

"To be honest, I'm not surprised that you've both had stress reactions. You've been through so much in the last year and now this tension in your marriage and the memory therapy. The last thing you needed was to be let down so badly by Alannah. I'm so sorry, Rose, what an awful thing to discover!"

"Do you think that's all it is? Stress? Dr Thomas did say there could be side-effects but I don't know if it's normal for them to go on this long."

"In my experience, patients can have side-effects for several days from certain drugs and procedures. I think it's most likely completely normal, but it wouldn't do any harm to check, would it? You seem to like this doctor and he seems approachable. I'm sure he wouldn't mind if you called to ask."

"Yeah, you're right," said Rose. "I'll call him tomorrow if I still have this headache."

"What has Nate said about the whole Alannah

business?" Helen's tone was caring, not probing.

"He swears she kissed him and he pushed her away. He's been so upset about the whole thing; keeps asking me if I believe him. Checking that I really mean it when I say I do. I don't know why, but my gut tells me he's telling the truth."

"I'm sure he is, sweetie. Nate's a good guy and he loves you."

"I thought Alannah loved me, but look how that turned out."

"She does love you, Rose. Come on, she's your sister — of course, she does. She's an idiot who makes stupid, hurtful decisions, but you can bet your life she'll be breaking her heart over this just as much as you are. What she did was terrible, though, and I can't imagine how you must be feeling right now."

"I can't believe she would do that to me, Hels. With Nate! She was the maid of honour at our wedding, I mean how sick is that? I just keep wondering, if Nate is telling the truth, how far she would have taken things if he hadn't pushed her away. Was it just a drunken kiss or a power thing to know she could have him if she wanted him? Or would she have slept with him, had an affair with him even? I can't believe my big sister would do that to me. We were so close… at least I thought we were."

"Don't torture yourself, lovely." Helen placed a hand on Rose's shoulder. "Have you spoken to her since?"

"I've had 57 missed calls in the last two days. It's almost as bad as getting the silent stalker phone calls. You'd think she'd get the message."

"Maybe you should speak to her and talk it through properly now you've had the weekend to process it all."

"I can barely talk to Nate," said Rose. "Even though I believe him, I can't help but be annoyed with him. I'm definitely not ready to talk to Alannah. I've never felt so angry with anyone in my life." Rose's words trailed off as tears interrupted her.

Helen tilted her head and smiled as she listened. "Oh, Rose," she said and shuffled closer to give her a hug. "At least you'll have the memories to watch back soon. That will give you and Nate something positive to cling to. And who knows, maybe if you can get the answers you need about the crash, you might have a bit more headspace to process and deal with all this Alannah stuff."

"I think I remember braking." Rose looked desperately into Helen's eyes.

"What do you mean?"

"While I was hooked up to the machine, I remembered. It was still really fuzzy, but I put my foot on the brake pedal and nothing happened. It was like pressing the brake with the engine off — it didn't feel right."

"Why don't you wait to watch it all back properly before you focus too much on the details." Helen looked concerned. "That way you'll be able to get a clearer picture."

A vibrating sensation took them both by surprise and Helen retreated to her seat on seeing that it was Rose's phone.

"It's Dr Thomas!" said Rose.

"Take it." Helen nodded and headed towards the patio doors that led to the garden with her coffee. Rose appreciated her lack of inclination to listen in. "Ask him about the headaches," Helen mouthed with over-exaggerated motions as she walked away. Rose gave her the thumbs up as she answered the phone.

"Hello, Rose, this is Dr Thomas." His voice sounded even more authoritative on the phone.

"Hi! I wasn't expecting to hear from you over the weekend."

"Research is a full-time commitment, I'm afraid. Am I disturbing you?"

"No, not at all, it's good to hear from you!"

"How are you, Rose?"

"Oh, you know," she said, unsure of how to respond truthfully without unloading on him again. He knew how she was. It was just a formality of polite conversation.

"Well, I have some good news for you. The memory extraction was a complete success."

"Really?" Rose felt her pulse quicken.

"The extraction went to plan and we have some clear data for you to view. I think you will be amazed at the results. I'm hoping it can still be a positive outcome from the experience."

"Have you watched it all? Were you able to get all the details of the crash?"

"I think it's best if you and Nate come for your viewing appointment as planned. It's not good practice for me to speculate over the phone. The data is very personal and is down to the patient to interpret accordingly. Are you both still willing to return?"

Rose felt the sagging disappointment of knowing she would have to wait even longer to get her answers. "Yes, we definitely are. Of course, I understand," she said. "When can we come?"

"I have appointments every day this coming week, depending on what time you—"

"Tomorrow," interjected Rose. "It should be tomorrow."

*

Rose was chilly as she sat on the bench. She could feel the cold wood of the seat through her jeans and the rigid metal frame digging into her back. It was a rickety old bench, conspicuous in its lack of maintenance compared to the modern memorial benches that were dotted around. Rose's mum had always joked about wanting her memorial to be something that involved less contact with strangers' bottoms.

Rose smiled at the elderly man who visited daily, tending to some flowers on his wife's grave. He changed them every three days and never let them look tired. Rose would often watch him as he polished the plaque on the headstone and muttered away as he picked out any weeds. She wondered if he was talking to himself or to his wife. She considered how comforting it must be to believe in an afterlife where your loved one could still see you, hear you, continue to be happy and at peace. She clung onto the thought of her mum being present somewhere even if it wasn't there. And better still, the notion they could one day be reunited.

"I love you," she said to the sky, but instead of making her feel better, it started the familiar tingle behind her eyes. The feeling made her head throb even harder than it already was — a symptom of no sleep and a morning full of tears.

Rose looked at the plaque on the wall of remembrance; etched in golden writing on shiny granite was her mum's name, date of birth and date of death. Three bits of information that left no doubt about her life and her fate. The plaque itself looked clean and new. Rose noted its position on the wall and how its appearance dated it. It was not dusty and fading like the older plaques — some were barely legible any more. However, it was not bright and spotless like the newest additions; it had become established on the wall yet everything still felt so recent to Rose. A year was no time at all.

It occurred to her that the concept of her mum being gone forever had not embedded itself until recently. It was like it had taken a year to process the finality of it all — a whole calendar of events; a year's worth of celebrations that were harder without her mum; 365 days of life's tiny details that she hadn't shared with her best friend. Her grief had changed over the last month or so — the raw tears had given way to a constant dull ache. The chaotic memories of life with her mum were gaining clarity and lingering for longer on specific images in her mind. Rose's pining to speak to her and hug her was becoming more painful the longer it had been since they were last together. The dust of the initial explosion had settled, leaving the ruins now lying exposed. And there, in the midst of it all, was the fundamental, heartbreaking reality of loss — a little girl who desperately missed a mother she would never ever see again.

As Rose gazed at the wall, her eyes were drawn to a fresh bunch of flowers directly below her mum's plaque. She got up and walked to the spot on the ground where she had sat for hours at a time in the weeks after the funeral. She picked up the bouquet and looked at the card.

'Taken too soon and missed every day. You'll always be in my heart, Elaine. Thoughts with you all. Love, James x'

One thing Rose could say about her ex was that he had always been thoughtful. He had a knack for remembering the important dates and marking them properly. This gesture really touched her, it may have topped them all.

Rose blew her nose and wiped her eyes, being mindful of her mascara. Her gaze was drawn to a shape moving across the field to the south of the church. She would recognise that shape anywhere — Alannah. She could see her sister's pace increase as she noticed Rose squatting by the wall. Rose stood up and walked away through the church gate in the opposite direction.

She had known that Alannah would visit at some point today. It was only natural. It was something they should have been facing together — united in grief and love. But Rose felt far from united with her sister; she felt betrayed, hurt and confused by the entire revelation. For a moment, Rose had considered not going to the memorial garden at all for fear of bumping into her sister, but the thought of not visiting on the year anniversary of her mum's death was unbearable for her. No matter what Alannah had done, Rose would never let her mum down... not again.

Rose's legs sped up as she turned left out of the church gate and down the pavement towards her car. She felt a surge of adrenaline as she worked harder to put distance between Alannah and herself. She had enough to deal with today without another argument.

"Rose!" Alannah's voice was far enough away not to

pose the threat of catching up, and Rose continued ahead, focusing on getting to the car. She unlocked it as soon as she was within range and hopped into the driver's seat, slamming the door behind her. She pulled off into the country lane that circled the churchyard and could see Alannah's jog slowing to a halt, a bunch of carnations drooping in her hand as she realised she had lost this race. Rose focused her stare on the road ahead and put her foot down a little until she was clear from view. She didn't know if the queasy feeling in her stomach was because of the near encounter with her sister or being behind the wheel.

"I never saw you," she said to herself as the figure of her sister diminished in her rearview mirror. "Besides, I have an appointment to get to."

*

Rose drove with a steady caution towards the garage. If anyone had asked her about her journey, she couldn't have told them a thing. Her mind was retracing the steps it had taken over the last year. She had experienced so many emotions since the morning she left the house to pick up her mum a year ago today. Such life-changing consequences from the need for a new sofa. Today felt poignant to Rose, and she had purposefully booked the appointment to coincide with the significance of the date. Today, a year on from her mother's tragic death, she would find out what had caused her to crash the car. She felt so sure that all of her questions would be answered within a matter of hours. All her demons would be laid bare, her torture eased, her closure finally achieved. She would know the truth and move on with her life, with her husband. Whatever she saw today when she watched back the memory video would mark an end to the darkness and if she was lucky, the light of her happiest memories would be what remained.

"Hello, you!" Gaz's voice crept out from behind the bonnet of a mucky Honda.

"Well, if it isn't our knight in shining armour." Rose leaned her head out of the window as she pulled up next to him. The handbrake creaked and Rose settled back into her seat with her elbow resting on the bottom of the window frame.

Gaz slammed the car bonnet shut and squatted down by the driver-side door to meet Rose's eyes.

"How are you doing today, darlin'? I know it's a tough one."

Rose sighed. "Mixed reviews," she said, trying to force a smile.

"Nate said you were struggling this morning. You know you can talk to your Uncle Gaz anytime don't you?"

"You're two months younger than me, Gaz,!" Rose

grinned gratefully.

"Yes, but so much wiser," joked Gaz as he placed his hand mock-patronisingly on Rose's arm.

"Love you, mate." Rose squeezed his hand.

"Get your hands off my missus!" said Nate with a smile as he walked from the office out towards the car.

"You're a lucky bastard, Nate. She's a keeper, this one." He winked at Rose and headed back towards the Honda. "Good luck, pal," he said to Nate as they patted each other on the shoulders.

"You OK?" asked Nate as he got in and did his seatbelt up. "I was worried you'd never get out of bed today the state you were in this morning. I'm so sorry I had to leave you to come to work. How did you get on driving?"

"It's fine. Better again, to be honest," said Rose. "I just needed to get the tears out of my system earlier. Going to the memorial garden helped. The fresh air was therapeutic."

"How was it?" asked Nate.

"Peaceful," said Rose. "Until Alannah showed up."

"Oh God, you guys didn't have a slanging match, did you?"

"Nope, you would have been proud of me." Rose pulled a faux angelic face. "I walked away before she could speak to me. I'm not having her ruining today. Today is Mum's day and all that is important is finding out the truth for her and then moving on with our lives."

"I'm proud of you," said Nate, squeezing her knee. "Best get on with it, then."

19

Nate

Sitting on the same sofa as their previous visits, Nate and Rose once again bridged the gap that formerly existed between them. Nate clutched Rose's hand within his own. They were physically connected even further, touching knees and forearms as their entwined hands rested jointly in the crevice between their respective legs.

Nate was working hard to control the thudding of his heartbeat. After concentrating on keeping Rose calm for the journey there, he found his own nervous anticipation rising as soon as they reached Dr Thomas's home-office. Now, he imagined his chest could be visibly observed, beating from within like a cartoon character.

Why the tension was tightening inside him, he couldn't explain. Something about being back in this room stirred anxiety in the pit of his stomach. The doctor had attempted to put them both at ease and introduced this stage of the therapy. He assured them the extraction phase had been successful; the clips they were about to view resulted from a digitisation of the neural images in their brains from when they had been responding to the photos in their previous session.

A black-framed screen was mounted on the wall behind where the doctor's chair had been positioned on previous visits. Nate looked at it and saw his own reflection staring back. That screen was about to spill out the inner secrets of his memories. The agitated feeling in his stomach increased as he contemplated the thought — a rolling tape of what had been in his head, with no control of his own to filter what was being reviewed. The reality of the situation gnawed at him. Even without feeling he had anything to hide, he felt vulnerable. Memories are meant to be served up with an element of bias. Fishing out the ugly parts when we don't want them discolouring the good stuff; holding back some detail when we don't want the good stuff to seem quite so good. Were these memories going to be filtered at all? Had he been able to exert any control over what pictures flashed through his mind when recalling the events they talked about? He'd soon find out.

Nate blinked and brought himself out of the trance of thoughts that came from looking at his reflection on the screen. Instead of seeing himself from this perspective, he tried to prepare for the unique experience of seeing events on that screen through his own eyes — and yet still being an external viewer.

Dr Thomas sat at his desk, introductions over with. He moved the wireless mouse around the desk, his eyes now fixed on the laptop screen. From his angle, Nate could only see the laptop lid. The doctor pointed a remote control at the big screen, bringing a menu into view. He moved the highlighted box down over a list of input choices, then made a selection. Nate presumed the screen was now showing the same picture as the laptop screen on the desk. Although it remained mostly black, a filename had appeared, emblazoned across the centre in white font; standard media player symbols were on a panel of buttons along the bottom. Nate braced himself for the unknown to become reality. The screen would become a window into Rose's mind and a portal into his own.

The cursor hovered over the triangular play icon in the centre of the panel. Nate felt the doctor's judgemental eyes connect with his own one more time. After a second's pause, a picture filled the screen. Mouth closed, Nate inhaled sharply through his nose as his eyes locked onto the image in front of him.

There was nothing startling about it, nothing unusual or incriminating. Had he privately thought there would be? Or was it just the place, the situation, the process up to this point which piqued a feeling of indiscretion, regardless of whether it was warranted. The scene unfolding was none of those things, but it was captivating, nonetheless. It was instantly recognisable, a strange mix of seeing CCTV footage and a promotional tourism video. The only difference was Nate was now watching himself as the star of this film, in a scene which he remembered experiencing all those years ago.

It was the picturesque market square, bustling with people. A cobbled stone floor was flanked by imposing grand buildings snuggled together, rising into a crisp blue-grey wintry sky. This was their first morning in Bruges. They had travelled on the overnight ferry, dropped their bags at the hotel and gone straight out to explore.

The view looked out from in front of one of the street cafes — Nate remembered them sitting there. On the screen, in the middle-distance, a woman was posing for a man to take her photograph, living out her imaginary modelling career. Her beige scarf was ruffled around her neck and chin, a long overcoat covered her body down to her calves where it met a pair of brown suede boots. She bent one knee forward and lifted her heel as she shifted position, striking a new pose. Her partner and personal photographer was moving around her attentively, his phone held out at arm's length, searching for the perfect angle. Nate wouldn't have brought a recollection of this couple to mind, but now that he saw it, a vague sense of recognition was stirred. This was Rose's memory, not his.

Then, as the viewpoint panned to the right, he saw himself close-up, sitting at a bistro table, a frothy cappuccino under his nose. The mixture of milky white froth and brown chocolate dusting was atop the drink and also across Nate's top lip. On screen, he laughed and heard the laughter of Rose accompanying him. On the sofa, he cringed a little.

A horse and carriage trotted past the table and came to a halt a few paces away. A young couple was seated below a light blue canopy, listening to the last of the city's historic tales from the leather-jacketed driver over his shoulder. Instantly, Nate recalled the chatty young chauffeur seated on this carriage. He'd tried to convince them to pay for a ride, too. He'd homed in on Rose, flirting and trying to shame Nate into forking out for a guided tour or otherwise feel like he was 'letting down the lovely lady' — that's what he said, those were the exact words that came right back to his mind as he watched the video. That canopy over the carriage, though, Nate had remembered it as green, not blue. Did they each remember it differently? Change a little detail like that or allow it to be reconstructed in the brain? Or maybe they had seen the colour of the canopy differently from the start when it was committed innocuously to each of their memories. And if colours could be seen or remembered differently, what else? Either way, they had shrugged off the local man's persuasions and taken a boat trip on the river instead. The interaction never appeared on screen.

Looking across the square to the coloured buildings with stepped roofs, the audio and picture faded simultaneously. The background hum of chatter and footfall drifted away as the picture transitioned into a black screen again. Nate was momentarily impressed by the technological skill in producing the fade-out. Dr Thomas clicked his wireless mouse again to pause the video, then interlocked his fingers upon his lap. The entire clip must have been only thirty seconds, but it was an immersive experience. The sights and sounds were captured, as if watching a fly-on-the-wall documentary. Nate could almost smell the chocolate fountain from the cafe outside which they were sitting. The tip of his nose had been cold, but he'd warmed it by blowing on the hot drink and feeling its steam rise.

The doctor smiled and glanced at them both, before aiming to coax their first response. "Just a quick flavour to begin with but how was that for each of you? Rose, this was from your memory. How did it feel to watch back?"

Rose inhaled gently and opened her mouth, but it took a few seconds for any words to come out. Nate looked at her, face awash with a mix of awe and content.

"It's wonderful, just… amazing. I'm not sure what I imagined, but it really is like being back there. The statue, the cobbles, the buildings are all exactly as I remember."

"Well, this is exactly as you remembered it, Rose. This is directly from your own memory," Dr Thomas reminded her. It was an obvious statement, but it danced around in Nate's head like it was a concept he couldn't pin down. "Tell me, was there anything unexpected in the video?"

Rose paused with a more intentional deliberation this

time. Her eyes rolled up and away from Nate.

"No, I don't think so, not really. Just… all those people around the market square. I know they were there; it was busy with people Christmas shopping and sight-seeing. But, I didn't think I would have remembered them all. They were just there in the background. I never mentioned them when I talked about the memory, did I?"

"What do I always say about you and people-watching?" Nate chipped in.

Rose gave him a look, which told him to shut up and be serious.

"It's a good observation, actually, Rose," Dr Thomas said, dismissing Nate's quip. "Even though you didn't verbalise every detail, you visualised it. Our brains store an incredible amount, more than we realise or need. We are very good at labelling these memories internally with what elements are important and what are simply peripheral. However, that doesn't mean those outlying details are discarded or lost forever. That's the beauty of this process. Our research in neuropsychology has found that by identifying what we call the engram, we can extract a fuller image of your memory than even you may have realised you had stored."

"That's crazy," said Rose.

Nate was equally astonished. His brain raced to keep up. He pictured a blackboard full of algebra from his GCSE maths lessons and had the same sense of inadequacy from not understanding a fraction of what was being described.

As if sensing his bewilderment, Dr Thomas offered Nate a smile that was probably meant to be reassuring but Nate interpreted as patronising.

The clips that followed were further snippets, similarly short but rich in detailed memories. Next was the view from the bell tower. Then, the comical sight of them running along the riverside to catch the last boat trip of the afternoon. After the relief of reaching the kiosk in time, they were soon sailing along with a group of other tourists. Swans paddled out of the way of the boat. Stone bridges passed them narrowly overhead and pastel-coloured buildings scrolled by in the background. Sunlight glistened off the surface of the water, but Nate felt the chill that came from sitting there in the sharp winter breeze.

Afterwards came an evening view of the same market square, looking even more romantic with the front of the buildings lit up. Nate's heart rate had settled, and he found himself enjoying the brief clips, opening up more freely in between them as he and Rose jogged each other's memories about what else they had seen and done.

There's no way Nate would have remembered what they had eaten for dinner, yet the contents of their table appeared on screen before them — a direct result of Rose's incredible memory for what each of them chose from any given menu. He might not have been able to recall the Flemish stew on his plate, but a reminder of the little restaurant had been joyous. The walls were crowded with colourful framed prints and there were a range of objects hanging haphazardly from the ceiling — musical instruments, watering cans, baskets of plants. They spent half of their meal looking up and around them, but it had been an idyllic night, followed by huge drinks of local beer before… oh, yeah, before the hotel.

As they joked on the sofa about their antics in the restaurant, then the bar, then the woozy walk through the narrow streets back to the hotel, Nate's memory flashed forward to the passionate scenes that followed.

Again, he felt like the doctor was listening directly to his thoughts. "Don't worry," he said in his smooth, knowledgeable voice. "We don't need to view everything here. You'll be able to take a copy of all these clips home with you on an encrypted flash drive."

If he wasn't feeling paranoid enough, Nate thought he caught a wink from the doctor as he spoke the words. Something about the entire process now made him decidedly uncomfortable. How could he claim to feel violated, though, when he'd agreed to it all? His pulse was quickening again as the doctor suggested they move to Nate's memory clips of the same occasion. Suddenly he felt like a rabbit in the headlights again, as if waiting to be caught out. He knew it was only his own happy memories of an altogether perfect trip yet vulnerability nagged at him.

The doctor's cursor moved down the black screen to the panel of buttons again and clicked play. An image sprang to life. Looming above everything else in shot was a huge shiny steel fermentation tank, rising between tightly packed buildings and protruding higher than the rooftops. In its wake was a pretty courtyard, packed with round silver tables and matching chairs. Ivy covered the cream-coloured walls of surrounding cafe fronts, contrasting with the red-brick walls of the brewery itself.

Nate pin-pointed the time and place immediately amongst their sight-seeing itinerary. This was the day after the river boat trip, their second day in Bruges. Touring the brewery had been his only real input into the plans. After they had been shown around the inside workings of the place, the courtyard is where they had sat and sampled the free beer.

The video playing in front of them was still catching up with Nate's real-time memory. Just as he recalled the fresh taste of the beer they'd been given, a half-pint glass of it came into focus on the screen. Behind it, Rose flashed him a smile and wrapped her hand around the glass to lift it to her mouth. He was now watching and remembering almost simultaneously. It felt like having two screens showing the same movie, but with a few seconds' delay.

"Ah, my bracelet. You remembered me wearing it!"

Rose exclaimed, not from the screen speakers but from the sofa next to him. Her commentary on the scene playing out reminded him she was scrutinising his memory with him; this is what he remembered, but she was now taking it in for herself. Had he remembered the bracelet? Yes, he'd bought it for her from a market stall the day before. But he hadn't even noticed it on screen until Rose pointed it out, let alone remembered it when he described this memory in the last session. He was amazed by these finer details his brain had held onto, without him even realising. The bracelet appeared to earn him some unexpected brownie points from Rose — so all the better.

Her voice coming from the video this time, Rose commented on not liking the taste of the beer because she was still feeling grossed out by the pungent smell of mashing grain inside the brewery. Nate laughed and suggested it was more to do with the skinful she'd had the previous night, before pouring the remains of her frothy beer into his almost empty glass.

The screen went black, but this time there was no stopping to discuss. The next clip was allowed to come straight on, which Nate also instantly recognised. Oddly, these were out of sync. He knew straight away the scene about to unfold in front of them was from the tour which preceded complimentary beers in the courtyard. He wasn't sure why these were chronologically mixed up, but he had described this moment during the memory extraction session, so it was no surprise to see it being played now. Even so, he shrank in his seat an inch with an uncharacteristic prudish flicker across his face.

The tour had taken them up and down various flights of metal staircases inside. At one point, it had led them right up onto the rooftops where they had an incredible panoramic view of Bruges from above. As the group of 20 or so people were shepherded by the guide from room to room, Nate remembered being either first or last into each area. First of the group to file into one area would be last to troop back out the same door. He and Rose had led the queue to see the stunning sight of the surrounding rooftops, which meant that when the tour guide was ready to move them on, they were last to file back down the staircase. That was the moment playing now on screen. Like a schoolboy, Nate felt his cheeks redden at what was coming.

On screen, Nate leaned against the rooftop rail, one arm hooked around Rose's back, knowing that it would take a while for the mix of strangers, viewed from behind, to descend.

As the last of their fellow group disappeared through the doorway, Rose stepped forward to follow. Nate watched himself grab hold of her waist and pull her back towards him. Rose gave a tiny yelp of surprise, followed by a smug grin as he held her close and wrapped both arms around the small of her back. With the beautiful Belgian city skyline as a backdrop, he kissed her. After a long, lingering smooch, they touched their foreheads together and Nate rubbed his nose against Rose's. If their own private cameraman had shot the video, then he'd just zoomed in so close that Nate could see the cute little creases either side of his wife's nose that only appeared with her broadest of smiles.

Before fading to black again, the image on screen ended with Rose turning to lead them into the doorway to the staircase. Nate reached forward and gave her backside a quick squeeze as he followed her. Watching it back with a third party for company felt like he'd been caught in the act of something naughty. He felt grateful they had not had to watch the hotel scene with the doctor as a shared spectator. That thought was immediately followed by the thought of the doctor watching it back on his own as a direct extraction from either of their memories. Nate squirmed and ran a finger inside his sweaty collar.

Dr Thomas stopped the video and looked at them both with a smile. "Nate, so how does it feel for you, watching your own memory back?"

Nate struggled to encapsulate the emotional fireworks going off inside him. The minute or two of footage was a technological marvel; an unparalleled rekindling of a distant time; a retching invasion of his private memories that he had so willingly offered up; a surreal experience; a reality check.

"It was… pretty strange," he offered.

"Strange in what way?" came the probing reply.

"Just… odd to see that, isn't it? I mean, great, yeah. Really cool. It just feels… odd!"

He had struggled to interpret most expressions on Dr Thomas's face since they walked through the door today. If paranoia hadn't taken complete hold, then right now he felt like he was being pitied by the doctor.

Rose looked at him like a soppy teenager. If he'd have been down on one knee, a box of chocolates in hand and the thorny stem of a single red rose in his mouth, he couldn't imagine a more gushing, dewy-eyed look from his wife. He edged closer still to her warm body and gave her thigh an affectionate squeeze. They snuggled on the sofa like they were watching a late-night rom-com, as the rest of Nate's Bruges memories faded in and out on the screen, punctuated with them waxing lyrical about any additional details that came to either of their minds as they indulged.

They were moments to savour — a textbook response to the memory therapy. It was evoking the behaviour and emotions from each of them, exactly as it was all intended.

20

Rose

Rose noticed an emotion swelling up inside her. It began in the pit of her tummy and spiralled up through her chest to the back of her throat. She stifled a sound that, left unchecked, may have resembled a tiny squeak. It wasn't a dramatic burst of feeling, but to Rose, it lit up like a neon sign, conspicuous because of its year-long absence; it was happiness. She allowed herself to bask in the contentment of having Nate's arm around her. It seemed like forever since she had felt comforted there.

She looked up at the face of her husband and realised that her motif of accusations had been unfair. He did care; he did notice the little things — he just struggled to express himself. His mind had clung onto the memories that mattered and Rose had watched them clearly on the screen — the bracelet he had bought her, his struggle to keep his hands off her on the rooftop and the way he had lingered on her face for so much longer than Rose had ever remembered him doing. The screen was displaying the aspects of life that caught Nate's attention. She could see the places his eyes flicked to — the parts of her body over which his focus hovered. The surrounding people ignored in favour of staring at her. Yet when the doctor asked for his reaction, he couldn't find the words. She could see now that she had been too hard on him, expecting him to react to things in the same way that she did. She had interpreted a lack of words as a lack of caring, when in truth they were just different people who expressed themselves in different ways. She vowed never again to force him to verbalise his thoughts in the way that she did.

The treatment was working. This is what they had come here for. She couldn't have imagined the strength of this power, seeing Nate's intimate memories through his own mind, unhindered by the need to articulate them himself. It gave her a pleasing new insight into her husband. Rose considered the irony of Alannah, despite her marriage-wrecking stunt, having recommended the doctor who may be the key to her and Nate cementing their relationship.

Dr Thomas clicked a few more buttons on the screen as he prepared to move onto the next memory. He paused and smiled at them.

"Right, that wasn't so bad, was it?"

Nate and Rose sat up and a laugh relieved any tension that had been building. They both wriggled in their seat and Nate stretched his back.

"Ready for the next episode?" asked Dr Thomas with a jovial tone that the couple were not used to hearing from him. He seemed pleased with his little quip, and Nate shot Rose a cheeky side glance.

"Go for it, Doc," said Nate as he settled himself back into the sofa. "What's next?"

"Rose's memory of the wedding is next in the schedule."

Rose put her head on Nate's shoulder and watched as Helen appeared on the screen in a baby blue bridesmaid dress with her hair curled and tucked into a beautiful up-do.

Rose's eyes widened as an image of herself came into view and behind it, the backwards furniture of her mother's bedroom. For a moment, Rose was stumped and held her breath as her brain worked hard to catch up. She could sense Nate's gaze turn towards her. No sooner had the realisation hit that this was her own reflection in the dressing-table mirror than a new one emerged.

"Mum!" Rose gasped as she watched the woman she loved more than anyone else in the world, appear behind her and place a precious string of pearls around her neck.

A punch to Rose's chest triggered a tremor that no amount of pressure from Nate's hand could restrain. The tears rolled quickly, burning her cheeks as they gathered in strength and magnitude. Her shaking hand covered her mouth in disbelief as she watched herself talking and laughing with her mum. Her mum who she missed and achingly longed to see just one more time. She heard her mother's voice speak again for the first time in a year. The words falling on ears that had taken every utterance for granted. She should have listened more carefully, absorbed each piece of advice and kind compliment to ingrain them at the forefront of her memory. But she didn't. Of course, she remembered the day, but this tiny interaction had been lost, swept away in the avalanche of micro events and conversations that had come since. If it wasn't for the memory therapy, this moment could have been lost forever.

"You look beautiful, darling." Her mum's voice like a soft comfortable pillow — the tone familiar and calming. "Your dad would be so proud of you today. He'd be proud of you every day, of course, but he would have given anything to be the one walking you down the aisle today. It would have been the biggest honour of his life."

Rose watched her mum come closer and hug her. Through the eye of her memory on screen she could see waves of her mum's blonde hair and for a moment, sitting there on the sofa watching it back, Rose could have sworn she smelled her perfume.

"I can't believe I have this forever," said Rose, sitting forward. "To watch whenever I need to see her or hear her. It's so much more than I could ever have wished for." She looked at Dr Thomas and with fierce unequalled sincerity said simply, "Thank you."

Dr Thomas's blue eyes connected with Rose's, and the sides of his mouth turned up. It felt poignant to Rose that he acknowledged the depth of her gratitude. She felt Nate's hand stroke the back of her hair as she continued to watch the screen, mouth open and eyes wide like a child fixated on Saturday morning cartoons.

The screen went black for a few seconds before flicking to the next image of Alannah, Helen and Rose's goddaughter, Mia, stepping out of a wedding car that pulled up in front of the church. The view was from the back window of the car behind that carried Rose and her mum. Rose heard herself say, "Here goes nothing," before handing her bouquet of sunflowers to Alannah who was waiting to assist.

"Ha! I almost tripped over my dress," giggled Rose from the sofa. "Do you know how hard it is to get out of a car in a lady-like fashion whilst sporting a lace cathedral train?"

"Um, can't say I do," said Nate.

Black again. Then the sound of an organ playing as rows of people in various hats and fascinators turned to look behind them. Rose could see every single guest in the church, and she felt her stomach churn as the nerves came flooding back to her. She remembered how nauseous she felt before spotting Nate's face in the front pew. Details long forgotten were there for her to take in the second time around. Gaz embracing his best man's duties with a little pat of reassurance on Nate's shoulder. The barrage of feathers protruding from Auntie Joy's hat, threatening to tickle anyone within a two-mile radius. The soft reassurance of her mum's voice as they prepared to walk down the aisle. Alannah and Helen fussing with the train of her dress to make sure it was laid out perfectly in her wake.

Rose urged her screen-self to look at her mum one more time, but she didn't. Her gaze was fixed on her husband-to-be in his grey, striped morning suit with a crisp white shirt, silk, ivory waistcoat and cravat that matched the blue of the bridesmaids' dresses. His dark hair was tousled upwards at the front in the way that Rose always found sexy. She turned to Nate who was grinning on the sofa beside her. "Look at you," she said, tilting her head. The screen faded to black.

*

"For better, for worse, for richer, for poorer, in sickness and in health, to love and to cherish, till death do us part." Rose could see her own face again, this time through Nate's eyes which never faltered from her as she repeated the vicar's words. The crystal detailing on the corset of her ivory dress sparkled in the sunlight that was seeping through the stained glass windows of the church. Rose remembered how much she loved that dress and how special she had felt when wearing it. This was the wedding video that no videographer could ever have captured; it was an intimate, personal and unique record of their combined memories of this day. If only people could experience their happiest moments in this way, knowing they could create their own individual perspective of the events. What a gift this technology could become. What a valuable, life-changing way of living. The endless possibilities fluttered through her mind before she refocused on her own special day playing back in front of her — not just her memory of it but Nate's. A double-dose of memory indulgence. Of course, she knew her husband had happy memories of them getting married. But to see it unfiltered through his eyes, that felt like being given a whole new blessing. She rubbed her hand along his forearm and beamed with contentment.

Fade to black again, followed by the sound of the organ fanfare becoming more distant as Rose and Nate walked out into the beaming sunshine through a tunnel of cheerful faces, flower petals being thrown into the air.

"Those petals got into *everything*," laughed Nate. "And I mean, everything. I was finding them for days." Rose playfully nudged his leg and smiled as she remembered pulling petals from inside her bra in the toilets at the reception.

The view panned around the churchyard and once again the couple expressed awe at the detail kept in Nate's memory.

"Who's that guy?" asked Nate.

"That's my Uncle Pete…" said Rose.

"I don't remember him," said Nate.

"You know," said Rose. "He talked to your dad about cricket all afternoon."

Nate's face looked blank.

"Wrote the lovely letter to us with tips for a long and happy marriage?"

"Nope," said Nate.

"He gave us the case of vintage port as a wedding gift."

"Ahh Uncle Pete! Yeah, nice chap."

Rose giggled and slapped Nate on his thigh.

"Wait, who's that?" asked Rose.

"Where?" said Nate.

"Can we rewind it?" Rose asked Dr Thomas.

"Of course," he said, moving the cursor on screen and clicking the button. The screen went black and then came back on to the image of Uncle Pete again. A few seconds later, Nate's on-screen gaze moved to another group of people near the gate that led to the road.

"There!" said Rose. "Pause it!"

Dr Thomas did as instructed and Rose stood up to get a closer look.

"That's Nina from the garage," Nate said. "Gaz

brought her as his plus one, remember? Before they split up and she left us in the shit with all the paperwork."

"No, not her… her!" said Rose, pointing to a figure who was not part of the wedding party. A woman with short dark hair was standing across the street from the church, partly obscured by a parked car. She was not in wedding attire but a pair of denim shorts, a white hoodie and pink trainers. She was clearly in a heated discussion with a man in a large grey overcoat, with the hood pulled up and his back to Nate's view.

"What the…?" Nate sat forward and seemed to search for words.

"Is that Nicola?" Rose's tone was sharp and accusatory. Nate's face coloured, and he stood up next to his wife to take a closer look.

"Did you see Nicola outside the church on our wedding day? After you'd already told her to get lost that morning?"

"I don't remember seeing her," said Nate. "I'm sure I don't, I mean… I don't think I did."

The doctor cleared his throat. Rose brought to mind the people she had seen in the background of their Bruges memories. Peripheral figures she never would have remembered in a million years. Yet there they were in her recorded memory as clear as day. Nate could be telling the truth and anyway, from the speed he averted his gaze, it was clear from his memory that he had no interaction with

226

her. But why was she there?

"Who's the guy?" asked Nate. "Was she shouting at someone?"

"Can you zoom in on the man she's talking to?" asked Rose.

"No, I'm sorry. The quality of resolution wouldn't be good enough. It would just pixelate," said Dr Thomas. He seemed flustered at this unexpected diversion from the happy memories they had been reminiscing over.

Nate sidled up next to the doctor, leaning over his shoulder. "Maybe if we scroll the mouse just here—" He reached over towards the laptop and Dr Thomas abruptly removed his hand.

"Please don't touch the laptop," he said. Nate raised his hands in the air as if surrendering. "Apologies." The doctor cleared his throat. "It's just on some very specific settings for memory playback and I don't want to risk something being altered by accident."

"Fair enough," said Nate, raising his eyebrows as he walked back towards the big screen.

"I'm sorry," said Rose. "But that is way too much of a coincidence. What was she up to?"

"Maybe it *was* just a coincidence," said Nate. "She does live in the same town, it wouldn't be the most ridiculous thing."

"Really? A town this big and she just happens to be having a heated exchange outside the church where her ex-fiancé is getting married at that precise moment. The ex-fiancé she went to visit that morning to persuade him not to go ahead with the wedding. You really think that is a coincidence?"

"Yeah, I guess it does seem odd," said Nate. "But I don't remember seeing her and I didn't see her again that day."

Rose sat back down, a little further away from Nate this time. "OK, let's carry on," she said louder than she had intended. "We can watch it back later. I'm not letting that psycho ruin this."

Nate pulled his foot up onto the opposite knee and waggled it. His brow furrowed and Rose wondered what he was thinking. She considered the vast breadth of information hidden deep within their psyches and wondered how many times Nicola had been lurking in the background. She had seen her in bars and clubs when they first started going out, never approaching them, just sitting on the sidelines pretending to be out with her friends. But Rose knew she was secretly watching Nate. She had always put it down to her feeling raw about their breakup, and Rose felt sorry for her. But showing up twice on their wedding day? That wasn't the emotional behaviour of someone who had just been dumped — too much time had passed by then for Rose to give her any sympathy. She did, however, feel very uneasy about Nicola's presence in the memories, especially if Nate was unaware of it. If they recorded all the memories from their time together, how often would Nicola's face appear unbeknownst to either of them? How many times might James — or worse still, Scott — appear in her own unfiltered memories?

21

A Confession

I saw you that day. Your wedding day. I watched you walk out of the church, beaming smiles, lapping up the attention and platitudes. I knew then that you would never be happy, I just needed to let you realise that for yourself.

Except you didn't, did you?

You carried on with the pretence that everything was a fairytale, but I could see through the cracks. I knew you needed my help to break free from those chains of obligation that were keeping you there.

That's why I did it.

Because you needed me.

If I hadn't stepped in to speed things up, you'd still be in a rut now, going about your day-to-day lives. Sure, you may have been content, but true happiness is more than that. You deserve so much more than that, and I deserve so much more than to be ignored. When no one ever notices you, you have to fight for attention, it's just something I've grown to realise over the years. When the sun doesn't naturally find you, you have to step into the light.

I know you saw me watching, even though you always pretended you didn't.

Well, I have my pride and I wasn't prepared to sit around on the sidelines for any longer. If you would not act, then I had to step in and release you.

I know you can't see it now. I know you think you're in love, but are you really happy with someone who doesn't make the effort for you anymore?

Are you OK with second best?

One day, you'll see why I did it.

One day, you'll look back and wonder why you didn't act sooner.

One day, you will thank me.

22

Nate

Everything that was previously calm and reassuring about the therapy room had been knocked off kilter. The plush sofa sagged too much beneath him. The perfectly conditioned air was now stuffy and oppressive. Anxiety and the uncertainty of what might come next infiltrated the comfort of rekindled memories.

Nate tugged the collar from his neck with one finger and briefly considered the irrational notion of being betrayed by his own memory. How could his own recollection leave him with such an overriding feeling of losing control? Yet, he had to acknowledge that he could not repress what details he remembered, what details were etched into the lesser accessible parts of his brain. He forced himself to stop re-examining all those doubts about even agreeing to be there in the situation he now found himself.

"Let's refocus," Dr Thomas said, exactly as Nate needed him to. He forced a smile, nodded, and searched for the enthusiasm that had built steadily until a few moments ago. The doctor's own composure had slipped a little too. "Can I get either of you more water?" He poured himself one from the jug.

Nate shook his head and glanced at Rose for her response.

"Shall we just get to the next videos?" she said curtly.

Dr Thomas inhaled but paused for a beat before his words flowed out. "Yes, that seems like a good idea. It's important at this point to reiterate that you should both concentrate on what the memories show of each other. Whilst the peripheral details can be important, we should keep in mind the purpose of why we're here. Try to remember the positive reasons you selected these memories to bring."

Nate braced himself. Moments earlier, Rose had articulated her joy at seeing the memories of her mum captured from her brain in a way she could watch and share repeatedly; a way that would never fade like memories do. Nate could only imagine the sense of delight it must have brought his wife to hear her late mother's voice again — audibly, being played to her, not just conjured inside her own head.

He had shared in the pleasure that their first videos had evoked. Being transported back to Bruges had been a cathartic experience. That's what this was supposed to be about — happy memories.

Instead of that positive expectation, the view of Rose's

27th birthday surprise filled him with tension rather than joy. As the screen came to life with colours and the sound of party chatter, his eyes scanned the edges of the display to see who or what had been captured without him realising. The picture was filled with the large open green space of his mother-in-law's garden. Tall, perfectly pruned conifer trees lined the right-hand side with the left dominated by blooms of pink hydrangea. A raised decking was in view at the foot of the garden. Framed by these three sides, in the middle and foreground of the shot were groups of laughing, chatting friends and family.

Lots of familiar faces caught Nate's eye. Rose's friends Helen and Tori were watching as a present was being unwrapped; behind them a bunch of other old school friends were in a group of their own — Cameron, George and someone else he couldn't recall the name of. Gaz was there towards the back of the crowd, getting his ear bent by one of Rose's uncles. Uncle Pete, maybe? No one jumped out who Nate hadn't remembered being there. This was Rose's memory. Nate wondered if she had better control than him over who or what she recollected? Had she been better at filtering out anything unnecessary or incriminating? He cursed himself for retreating to the cynical perspective.

On screen, he saw his younger self as Rose bounded over towards him. His face filled the screen before transitioning into a view over his left shoulder as she threw her arms around him and thanked him for organising the surprise. Rose squeezed her arms around his back. Nate spotted one of her work colleagues called Scott who he had never liked. The smarmy guy raised his wineglass and nodded with a half-grin towards them before Rose looked away. Then the memory faded to black.

"Let's keep going for now, shall we?" Dr Thomas interjected without stopping the video. His eyes flitted from Rose to Nate, and it felt as though he was scrutinising every reaction.

When a new picture faded back into view, it was of Rose's mum. This was her speaking directly to Rose, just to the side of any larger groups. Next to him on the sofa, Rose caught her breath in her throat and inched forward at the close-up sight of her mum again.

"Hasn't he done so well?" Elaine said to Rose. "Did you honestly not know anything of the surprise he was planning?"

"No, I really didn't, Mum. It's amazing! He's been so thoughtful. I just thought he was spending all his spare time in the pub with Gaz!"

Nate blushed a little at being privy to this exchange all these years later. The women continued their conversation, discussing the details that Nate had arranged — a huge Happy Birthday banner strung across the fence; the considerable guest list; the way he had decorated the garden with balloons and bunting. Eventually, the gardener, Nigel, interrupted. Nate had forgotten how much effort the old chap had put into this party, helping with various bits of the staging. He'd been a godsend. He was wearing an ill-fitting brown suit, continuing the extra effort with his attire. Nate had rarely seen him wearing anything other than work overalls and here he was as probably the only bloke present wearing a tie. He'd always seemed such a loner, but unquestionably loyal to the family over the years.

Nigel's eyes seemed to look straight into the camera — Nate had to remind himself that this was no camera, but his wife's eyes — and then fixed warmly on Elaine. "Can I just borrow your mum for a minute?" he asked Rose with a kind smile. Elaine happily complied with the request, and Nigel led her away by the arm. Rose's view scanned across to the left. She called out Helen's name and waved to her friend before this memory also faded to black.

"Do you reckon Nigel had a soft spot for your mum?" Nate asked.

"Don't be daft!" Rose responded without a thought. "We've known him years."

"Maybe it's you instead, then. Does he like a younger woman?" Nate laughed.

Rose dismissed the thought with her hand.

"Rose, is there anything that you felt was particularly poignant about seeing these memories?" Dr Thomas refocused the discussion.

"It was all lovely. I'd like to see what Nate remembered from the party, though," said Rose. The implication was clear that she had one thing she wanted resolved. She'd have to wait a little longer before the moment she was interested in.

"OK," Dr Thomas agreed. "Let's push on. There are four distinct segments that I've been able to retrieve from your memory here, Nate. Remember, Rose, what has happened is in the past. Deciding how we respond to events is what will shape our future."

The doctor clicked the play button, and an image faded into view of Rose and Alannah. Rose scoffed at the sight of it.

"Look at her — she's so brazen! I feel sick, knowing what she did later." Rose cast her eyes upward and shook her head.

"Rose, look at the two of you. This is your sister. Think how close you are," Nate said.

"How close we *were*. You'd better have pushed her away like you said you did, Nate."

Suddenly, all avenues were leading to one moment of recollection and nothing that preceded it in this process mattered. Nate contemplated whether his memory would betray him this time.

The video showed the close connection which flowed between the sisters. Nate wasn't within earshot to hear the conversation, but from his view, it was a picture of sibling love. Rose threw back her head in laughter. Alannah, telling some story, touched Rose's arm with one hand and waved around a glass of Prosecco with the other, entertaining the rest of the gathered crowd. Rose was obviously having a wonderful time, and Nate wondered whether the sight would soften her reception of the memory at all. A glance along the sofa to his left and the narrowed eyes of his wife suggested she was not softening very much.

Alannah was still holding court as some others in the group came into focus. Helen and Tori stood together, adding their occasional input to whatever tale was being raucously recounted. Rose's work friends appeared to be the audience, rather than adding to the details. That guy, Scott, was sidled up to Rose, on the opposite side to Alannah. He stood up close — a little too close actually, his arm brushing against Rose. Nate vaguely recalled thinking that very thing at the time. He was sure he didn't articulate it as part of his description when this memory was being harvested, but he found it interesting — the detail evidently stuck in his head and formed the image that was appearing now. Was it just him seeing it that way, though? Was it a jealous, over-protective thing of his own? Again, he glanced at Rose, but there was no sign she was seeing anything that changed her prior expression.

The second of Nate's memory videos followed. Gaz was helping him prepare the barbecue. The tray of hot coals, turning from black to ash-grey, dominated the foreground of the view. Occasional flames leapt up and licked the grill tray above. He had hired a DJ who had now begun his set of tunes right next to where the barbecue was smoking away. Nate smirked at the thought of his cooking apparatus doubling as a smoke machine. Standing under a gazebo, the guy had his headphones over just one ear and was fixated on a laptop screen whilst the sound of some 90s dance track blared. The usual DJ smoke machine wouldn't have had the unmistakable smell of a barbecue to accompany it. Maybe there was a business venture there, he speculated absently.

He remembered what a gorgeous late afternoon this had been with the sun beaming down on all the guests in the garden, giving their faces a glow and glinting light off half-emptied bottles and glasses in their hands. He felt himself being lost again in a pleasant memory that was seducing all of his senses.

"Hey, gorgeous, shall I bring the burgers out for you yet?" Alannah's voice cut through the dance music. She'd appeared into view from nowhere but had to lean in close to Nate's ear in order to be heard. It wouldn't have seemed noteworthy at any other time, but at this point, Nate was uneasy at the presence of her up so close, his line of sight aimed straight towards her neck and the mass of dark curls falling over her shoulder.

He didn't even hear his own reply as he watched

Alannah smile and walk away.

"Did she just wink?" Rose exclaimed. Nate hadn't noticed if she did. "She's got a damn nerve. I can't believe she just winked at you. Is this where she was plotting to come on to you when she got her chance?"

"Rose…" Nate began, softly.

"And this is from your memory, don't forget! This is how you remember my party. Being over there in the corner with a sly wink from my sister."

"You're making something out of nothing, Rose. Calm down," Nate said. His efforts at a mellow tone were either poorly delivered or poorly received, possibly both. Rose folded her arms and took in another deep breath.

Before the video faded out, Nate's view had turned to Gaz on his right, but Gaz wasn't looking. He was watching Alannah striding away, with a lop-sided grin on his face.

Nate's third memory faded in and out with little for anyone to pick up on. In different circumstances, they might have had more of a laugh about their group of friends sitting around playing party games.

George, who Rose knew from her secondary school days, was standing with a beer talking to Scott. Nate imagined them both introducing themselves to each other and saying they knew Rose 'from school'.

In front of them, Rose was pictured next to Helen, both of them with yellow Post-it notes stuck to their foreheads. Rose was labelled as 'Peter Kay' while Helen's scribbled note read 'Winston Churchill'. Nate wondered what kind of bizarre conversation those two famous figures would have with each other. It didn't feel like the time for a quip, though, as he knew what was coming next.

The last memory faded in. It was his view of the kitchen, as he flicked off the tops of two beers with a bottle opener. Alannah was standing alongside the worktop next to him, pouring Prosecco into a pair of champagne flutes. She was complimenting him on his organisation of the party, then asked if he would give her a hand to clear some of the empty bottles from the kitchen surfaces and take them down to the cellar.

Nate daren't look across the sofa towards Rose now, but he knew she still hadn't unfolded her arms. Even without looking, he could feel how tightly coiled she was.

"Here we go," said Rose. "Let's see the little harlot in action, shall we?"

The clanging of bottles echoed from the speakers, accompanied by a tipsy laugh from Alannah. She directly addressed the glass bottles and told them off for being too noisy as they reached the bottom of the cellar steps. Nate almost couldn't watch. Alannah turned towards him and put her hand towards his chest before a close-up of her face filled the display. Her bright, chestnut brown eyes looked straight out of the screen, her pupils dilating as her giggling face became more serious. No sooner had she leaned in with the obvious intention of a kiss, than Nate heard himself speak.

"Whoa there, I think someone's a little drunk." He had stepped back, putting more distance between them, and had his hands forward defensively, palms held out towards Alannah.

"Oh, come on, Nate. No-one's going to see us down here."

"Lana, no. Your sister is up there — my *wife* — who I love very much! Never mind that it's her birthday, for God's sake. What the hell are you playing at?"

"Yeah, but, Nate—"

Alannah's voice trailed off as the screen faded.

"But Nate, what?" asked Rose from the sofa. "What happened?"

"I'm sorry," Dr Thomas interjected, "that's the last of what was captured from that scene in Nate's memory. I think we may have been interrupted at the time."

"So, it was like I said. I told her no. I pushed her away." Nate pointed out. His heart was beating rampantly, but what they just witnessed surely vindicated him. He felt relief flooding in.

"And then what?" Rose persisted.

"Then I left her there to get herself together, and I went back up to the kitchen to get your birthday cake."

Rose eyed him for a second or two. His version of events hung there to be interpreted and analysed.

"The memory is as Nate described," Dr Thomas

added. "We can't see what happened next as it was not harvested. But remember, we're not here to test each other. This was an auspicious occasion that you selected, was it not?"

"It was until I knew what happened out of sight!" said Rose.

"I pushed her away. Nothing else happened." Nate protested, extending both arms out towards the screen. "You literally just saw that with your own eyes."

Again, Rose held his gaze for a second of contemplation before relenting.

"OK, you're right. This is what you said happened. I believed you anyway, but I guess your memory backs you up. I'm still mad at her, though." She flashed him the briefest hint of a smile. It was a look which conveyed much more, if he was reading her correctly. It was a 'we're on the same side' kind of smile; maybe bordering on an 'I'm sorry' kind of smile; he was pretty sure there were hints of a 'thank you' kind of smile in there too.

It thawed the frosty insecurity that had emerged between them. The tension lifted a little from Nate's shoulders. He felt like he'd been on trial and just received a 'not guilty' verdict from the jury.

"That's all from the birthday celebration. There is one further clip that I have to play you," Dr Thomas said.

Rose gave an audible intake of breath.

23

Rose

They both felt prepared for what was coming: the accident. Rose knew it was the crux of why they were there and the emotional state she had been in for the last year. She wondered if she would have been half as keen if it hadn't been for this memory. She was moments away from seeing what happened in the car that day; from finding out why she crashed; from discovering why her mum was dead. Her mum, whose face she had seen so clearly and in its prime in the previous memories. The images had given her the chance to refresh her lasting evocations of the woman who had raised her. They showed her mum at her best, the way any child would want to remember a parent: smiling, relaxed and in control. Rose knew the second she watched the next memory back, all that work over the last few hours could be erased and replaced once again with the image that haunted her. Her mother's memory would once again be reduced to a singular moment in time. With one rasping and terrifying breath, Elaine had become lost forever and Rose was about to relive it all over again. Was she strong enough to watch her beloved mum die twice?

"Are you sure you want to go ahead with this?" Nate's voice crept in and Rose realised she had been staring out of the window. "It's not too late to leave things there, we can stop now and go home on a positive note! It's been great watching the happy memories; let's not ruin it." He looked to Dr Thomas for support.

"Well, I mean, it's up to you, Rose. If you don't feel you need that closure any more, by all means, we can stop."

"Play it," said Rose.

"Honey…" Nate put his hand on her knee.

"Play it," she repeated. "We've come this far. I need to finish this."

Dr Thomas and Nate exchanged looks and hovered for a moment in each other's gaze. Rose felt irritated. Nate turned to look at her. She could feel his eyes, like those of a puppy, pleading with her not to do it, but she had made up her mind. She focused on the screen, avoiding Nate's stare, impatiently waiting for the picture to change. She noticed a slight nod from her husband towards the doctor and she felt her hackles rising. This was Rose's memory. Her property, her decision, and she didn't need permission to be granted from her husband to watch it back. She raised her eyebrows and looked at Dr Thomas who obediently pressed play.

The view was looking straight out of the windscreen from the driver's side of Nate's car. Rose could see the car parked ahead of her on the road outside their house. It was red. She thought she had remembered it as blue. The top of the steering wheel spun as the car pulled out onto the road. The outlook was unfamiliar — Rose rarely drove Nate's car, and neither of them had seen it since it was written off in the accident. She reached for Nate's hand on the sofa and squeezed it. He seemed keen to return the gesture.

She watched the road as she remembered it, a little busy with Saturday morning traffic. The Autumn sun was glaring, and the radio played in the background. For a few minutes, there was nothing of interest to anyone. Traffic lights, cars moving in the opposite direction. Her hands in Nate's gloves, which she had borrowed from the glove-box, holding onto the steering wheel. Only the quickest flash of sight towards the inside of the door, but it was over in a split second as the traffic moved on again and Rose's eyes stayed fixed on the road ahead. The familiar streets played out before them; it was a journey Rose had made thousands of times. Elizabeth Park was to the right and the semi-ruined stone walls of the ancient market town that led the way to the Abbey. It wasn't long before Rose could see the sign at the entrance to the village that had been put up just before she left for uni. It said 'Careful Drivers Welcome' and boasted its ageing accolade of *Derbyshire in Bloom Gold Award 2009'*. Rose's mum had always joked that it should have increased the value of her house. Nate liked the regular quip that Gaz clearly wasn't welcome in the village.

The Elephant and Spear pub stood at the heart of the village, bathed in sunlight that enhanced its white exterior. Rose and Alannah had spent many evenings in that pub with their school friends. Geoff, the owner, had always let them in under age but never served them alcohol until they were 18. There was no option of fake ID with him knowing the family so well. Rose remembered the night of her 18th birthday when she had gone for a meal in the beer garden with her mum and Alannah to celebrate. Geoff had brought out a bottle of champagne — on the house. Since then, the pub had always been a place of comfort and happiness. Reunions with friends during holidays from uni, New Year's Eve parties, Sunday lunches with Nate. It was the natural choice for her mum's wake and despite the unyielding sadness of the day, Rose had felt the atmosphere wrap her up in a familiar hug with Geoff like a father figure there to support her and Alannah, as they put brave faces on for their guests.

Rose held her breath as she saw her mum's house come into view. Any minute now she would see that smiling face again. The brick wall that surrounded her mum's property was decrepit. She saw it following the car — a parallel stream of reddish brown in the periphery. Then on the left, the gate posts which flanked the entrance to the house. The gate was always open; Mum had said it was a faff to get out every time to open and close it. The posts made an attractive feature, but it required a good swing to get the car around safely. Several visitors had suffered minor scrapes over the years, but it was second nature to Rose. On screen, she saw the car pull out before turning into the drive.

The sound of gravel under tyres took over the audio, drowning out the radio, and there ahead was the house that Rose had grown up in. The house that she now owned, jointly with her sister of course. She pulled to a stop outside the front door and Rose's view adjusted its focus to the passenger side window. A door slammed and footsteps on the gravel could be heard but Rose's eyes were focused on the line of trees behind the brick wall at the edge of the garden. Sitting on the sofa watching back, Rose wondered what she had been staring at. Maybe she was taking in the colours of the Autumn leaves that dominated the trees at that time of year. Bright oranges and yellows with the last of the summer blossoms that blew around the garden and piled up under the trees. When they were little, Alannah and Rose believed the blossoms were fairies and if they could catch one their wishes would come true. If only Rose had a fairy to grant her a wish right now, she thought.

The footsteps grew louder, and a figure approached at the edge of Rose's on-screen vision. 'Mum,' she thought. Within a split second, the figure was fully in view. Rose realised she had been holding her breath, but now she struggled to exhale. Her chest was full of pressure and her head was fuzzy. For a moment, she thought she felt the seat move beneath her and she put both hands down on either side to steady herself as the room spun. Every instinct within her body was telling her to run away, find a bathroom, lock the door, be alone to ride through the panic unobserved. But she couldn't. She was glued to the seat; her stomach was churning; her skin was clammy and covered in goosebumps.

"There must be a mistake! I don't understand."

"What the hell?" Nate's skin was pale and his mouth open.

"What's going on? Someone tell me now!"

Images on screen continued to roll, the sounds all correctly in line with what Rose was expecting. The cessation of footsteps on the gravel. The clunk of the car door being opened and the words, "Hello, my love," being spoken by the person getting into the passenger seat. Everything was right, but everything was wrong. It wasn't the memory she had recounted for the doctor under her drug-fuelled reminiscence. Rose's mum wasn't getting into the car. Nor was it her voice speaking.

It was Alannah's.

"Gosh, this is embarrassing," said Dr Thomas. "I'm sorry, I must have lined up the wrong video file." Becoming flustered, he knocked the mouse off the desk in an effort to switch it off.

Meanwhile, the scene on screen continued as Rose watched what she thought had been herself sitting in the driving seat of Nate's car waiting for her mother to get in. But this video was playing out very differently. Rose put both hands to her head and kept them there, holding back the hair from her face as the doctor scrambled to retrieve the mouse which had fallen under his chair.

"Did you miss me?" Alannah said on screen. Her face leaning in closer as she knelt across the seat. The same flirtatious smile was there that Rose had witnessed in the previous memory from her party when Alannah was speaking to Nate. The same tone of voice, trying to sound innocent but achieving only predatory and provocative.

The video paused as Dr Thomas finally found the mouse and his composure.

"Leave it on," said Rose.

"There's clearly been a mistake," said Dr Thomas. "I must apologise."

"I said, leave it on!"

"Honey… please," said Nate.

"If you don't press play, I swear to God, I will wrestle that laptop from you and do it myself."

Dr Thomas obliged, seemingly reluctant, and watched Nate's face as the scene continued.

On screen, Alannah moved closer and put her hand out at face level. The view moved up giving the impression she had tilted the chin of the person recalling this memory, moving their gaze from the tiny mole at the base of her neck, past the dark curls of hair to her golden brown eyes. Whoever this was, it sure as hell wasn't Rose!

The screen went black again, but the sounds continued, unlike before when the memory had ended. Whoever this memory belonged to had closed their eyes.

"Oh, God!" Rose spat out before covering her mouth with her hand. The sound of lips engaged in a passionate kiss was unmistakable, and the view over Alannah's shoulder came back into focus.

"Someone's pleased to see me," giggled Alannah. Rose's sister leaned in again for another lengthy kiss before releasing herself with a long sharp intake of breath, as if the act of resistance was too much for her to bear. "Put your foot down," she said, sitting down properly and reaching for her seatbelt. "I need to get you in that hotel room as soon as possible. You have no idea how hard it's been keeping my distance in case Rose sees us."

The wheels on the car rolled across the gravel driveway, creating a noisy exit from the house — and the memory.

Silence fell over the room, and Rose stared at the screen in total disbelief.

"I'm so sorry," said Dr Thomas. To Rose it seemed more aimed at Nate than at her.

"How? I just…" Rose was shaken and lost for words.

"What the fuck was that?" Nate's tone was both

accusatory and defensive.

"There must have been a mix-up with the memories," said Dr Thomas. "This must have been—"

"Nate's!" Rose interjected.

Nate swung his entire body around to face his wife, his mouth agape.

"When we go through the harvesting process, I collect many more memories than we watch in this session," explained Dr Thomas. Nate stood up and paced the room. "I only show you the ones I think will help you both as a couple. The rest are discarded. This must have slipped through the net. I'm so sorry."

Nate struggled for words. Sounds of confusion escaped, but no clarity could be found. On his forehead, Rose could see beads of sweat forming. "This is bullshit!" he said, redder in the face now and eyes darting all over the place. He headed for the door and Rose taunted him.

"And right on queue, you walk away and refuse to talk about it. See you, then, Nate. Just don't bother coming back this time, yeah?"

Nate turned on his heels with his finger raised. He opened his mouth as if to speak, but he paused and lowered his finger. "You know what? There's no point. I'm not listening to this." He threw the car keys towards the space on the sofa where he once had sat and turned again towards the door. Rose didn't protest this time. The door to the office slammed shut and within seconds the

252

external door had banged with such force that the entire house shook.

Rose sat silent and still with her elbows on her knees, hands over her mouth. "I'm right, aren't I?" Rose looked at Dr Thomas.

"You must understand, Rose, that I can't discuss other patients with you because of confidentiality," he said gently. "However, I can assure you beyond any doubt that this can't belong to anyone else other than Nate."

"But you only harvested three memories. When did this happen?"

"The mind is a complex place, Rose. In our studies we often find that during the recording process, linked memories can emerge. It's like a chain reaction. You think of one event or—" He cleared his throat. "—person and a related memory is sparked. They all get recorded, which is why I filter out the most useful."

A tear ran down Rose's cheek, followed by another and then another. She was exhausted. Too tired for any more grief. A familiar numbness set in and she could feel the walls growing up around her once more.

Rose picked up the car keys and calmly walked over to the desk where Dr Thomas had his laptop set out. Next to it were two USB sticks with each of their names on. It had been written in the information pack that part of the treatment package was to receive a hard copy of all the happy memories viewed during this session *'so that the healing reminiscing process can continue at home'*. Rose picked up both sticks and looked at Dr Thomas.

"Thank you," she said. "Not the revelation I was hoping for today but best I know the truth so I can move on. I think I'll watch the rest on my own if you don't mind?"

"Rose…" Dr Thomas paused as if he had changed his mind about what he was going to say. "Take care."

24

Nate

Nate stormed from Dr Thomas's building. After throwing the car keys down next to Rose on the sofa, he slammed the doors behind him and emerged out into the street. The brightness of the day made his eyes squint. He tried to blink away both sunlight and confusion.

By the time he reached the road, that bluster of energy was sucked out of him. He clutched one hand to a searing pain in his chest as he felt fresh air smacking at his face. He tried to force his surroundings into focus, steadying himself with his other hand against the upright pole of a pelican crossing. Traffic continued past in a blur with the sound of revving engines echoing in his head. His mind was reeling. The impact of what had been shown on screen felt like a sledgehammer blow.

The beeping of the crossing jerked him into stepping forward into the road. He staggered across towards the cafe on the park corner, struggling to order the emotions that surged through him. Rage was chased by bewilderment which was chased by regret.

Eventually, he reached the same spot where he had sat with Rose barely a week earlier. On the same bench where they had talked between memory harvesting sessions, he slumped. Alone, Nate leaned over with his elbows on his knees and shook his head. He cast his mind back through the journey of the weeks leading up to this moment, the doubts he had expressed over the whole process; his initial reluctance niggled at him all over again. A bitter resignation coursed through him — having reached a point that he feared, yet hoped would never occur.

In the park beyond where he sat, there were couples and families — a picture of normality. Did all of those people have secrets locked away in their minds? Did they all have normal lives? He scanned across the faces of the strangers, wondering what each of them might have buried in their memory banks were they to offer them up, without control or restraint.

Nate looked back down and picked at the skin beside his thumbnail. Half of him wanted Rose to stride over, looking for him. He pictured the scenario and what he would say. He felt his chest tighten again and the other half of him just wanted to sit there alone until the world around him had stopped spinning.

Shaking his head again, he muttered aloud under his breath, "How the hell did it get to this?"

Although the sight of that last video clip tortured him, his mind was drawn to earlier elements, too. Something niggled about Gaz. The way he'd watched Alannah walk away from the barbecue at the party. It had stuck in Nate's mind. It was like having the outer body ability to step back and see your own memory from a fresh perspective; to give a unique insight you might miss the first time around.

Nate pulled out his phone and scrolled to Gaz in his recent calls, then tapped on his best mate's name. As soon as the ringing was answered, he was keen to get straight to the point.

"Hey, mate. How did—"

"Don't ask. I've been stitched right up. But I need to ask you something. Have you ever had a thing with Rose's sister, Alannah?"

Gaz stuttered, "Er, why would you ask that now?"

"Just tell me," said Nate.

"Well, it was years ago, just—"

Nate hung up and slammed his clenched fist into the back of the bench beside him.

He was right.

It had occurred to him with the right nudge.

He pocketed the phone as he got to his feet, putting both hands to his head, turning back to face the doctor's place. There were all kinds of thoughts building inside now about his best mate. From the naïve to the vindictive, from the improbable to the unthinkable. He cursed himself for letting all of this mess with his judgement, making him paranoid. Then he cursed the memory therapy for being everything else it had become. Certainly not therapy.

He switched his mind away from Gaz. His brain was clogged with a hazy fog whilst also bouncing from thought to thought. There was so much more to unpick about those video memories.

Again, he sat back down and tried to order his thoughts. He quickly resolved that he needed to talk to Alannah. Just as quickly, he knew he wasn't ready for that yet; he should sort his own head out first.

He needed to speak to Rose. Of course. He kicked at the ground and wished that Rose's name had come to mind before Alannah's. It was like being at war with his own brain. Maybe that was another conversation that should wait until they could both be rational.

Against his better judgement, he also decided he needed to see Nicola. She was there outside the church on the wedding day. He'd seen her that day. He just hadn't wanted to admit the fact to Rose — either then or now. Nic was outside the churchyard, doing no harm so he'd blocked it out. Now he needed to know why.

He took out his phone again and stared at it for a moment, then his eyes flickered from side to side as he pondered the conversations ahead. He refocused and scrolled down to the third number on his recent calls list, tapped it and put the phone to his ear. It was answered on the second ring.

"Nate, I was just thinking about you…"

"Can I come over to yours?"

25

Rose

Rose sprawled across the width of the bed, her head wedged between the two pillows. The bed felt less empty that way. If she could somehow fill the space, then Nate's absence wouldn't feel so striking. She imagined she was back in her single bed at her mum's with no expectation of sharing it with anyone. She tried not to think about what was missing. The warmth of Nate's body, the natural way his arm pulled her close so she could lay her head on his broad, comforting chest. If this had been merely an argument, she could have drifted off to sleep, sad but accepting. But Nate wasn't sleeping in the spare room. There was no chance of him creeping back into her bed the next morning, full of apology. This felt more final than anything they had experienced before. The doors were locked, and she knew he didn't have a key. Rose's chest felt thick with grief, her head throbbed from hours of uncontrollable tears. She was cold and restless.

The sounds from outside caught her attention — a bin lid flapping up and down, the squeak of the gate in the wind. Goosebumps covered her, and she realised that for the first time in years, she was completely alone. She had never considered herself vulnerable, but now her breath caught in her throat and her heartbeat boomed in her ears. She had been raised by a strong and independent woman. The old Rose would never have craved a man's presence to feel safe. She cursed herself for allowing things to get this far and allowing Nate to make her feel like this.

She got up and pulled a hoodie over her pyjamas. Turning on every light along the way, she went down to the kitchen and boiled the kettle. As she stared out of the window, the darkness outside merged with her own reflection and formed shapes in the peripheries of the garden. Had she seen someone? She pulled the blind down and threw a tea bag into a mug before checking the door was locked.

Tea in hand, she plonked herself onto the sofa and switched on the TV. The warm glow of the screen didn't ease the all-too-familiar feeling of being watched. How could she have allowed herself to become this jumpy? She pulled the curtains tightly across the patio doors to eradicate any gaps and flicked through late-night channels, none of which offered anything worth watching. She considered putting on a film, but then a flash of realisation occurred: the USB stick from the memory therapy was still in her bag. She hadn't watched the actual footage of the accident.

She considered whether she wanted to do this alone. She should have been with Nate, in the safety of Dr Thomas's office. Two people there to support her: her husband and a professional therapist, but here, she had no one. She contemplated turning everything off and trying to go to sleep, but the pull was too strong. She needed to know.

Leaving the lights on, Rose headed back upstairs with her bag over her shoulder, tea in one hand and the laptop in the other. She climbed into bed and puffed up the pillows behind her back, fashioning a nest to cradle herself. How could this day get any worse? She may as well get comfortable and face all her demons head-on. Maybe this would bring closure. Perhaps she would sleep and wake up refreshed by truth, ready for the new start she needed to forge.

The laptop felt warm on her lap as it whirred. After several attempts at getting it in the correct way around, the USB slotted in and the whirring became louder. A window appeared on her screen containing thumbnails of several video clips. She squinted as she struggled to see the contents of each picture, but she could make out the beginning of that fateful morning. She clicked to open it, ready to watch the events unfold for the third time.

The memory began just like the mistaken one had with Rose looking at the interior of Nate's car. A blue car was parked ahead of her — she had remembered the colour correctly after all. The sound of the engine started as she saw herself removing the air freshener and placing it in the glove compartment. This is how she had remembered it during the memory extraction. The tiny details were clear now — how could she not have noticed their absence in the clip she had watched earlier in the day? Had the desperation to find out what happened swept her away? If so, it was a dangerous emotion that had made her careless. The unfamiliarity Rose had felt whilst watching the wrong memory had gone. Earlier, she had put it down to the lapsing of time and her emotional state, but seeing this now made her feel foolish for not realising before. This time, there was no doubt that this was her memory — authentic. She watched to where everything had blown up in Dr Thomas's office. Then came the most crucial difference — no Alannah here, just the smiling, comforting face of her mum.

Tears ran warm again, tears that should have dried up after all the day's events. Her head felt like it was going to explode, and she pressed hard on the point above her right eyebrow that always hurt more intensely than anywhere else. A sudden, shuddering inhalation made way for sobs and moans of pain. Desperation ran through every cell until her chest felt tight and heavy. She needed her mum so intensely, and the permanence of her loss was emotional and physical torture.

It surprised Rose to find her finger clicking the button

to fast-forward the video. She had expected the need to lap up every minuscule interaction, like a child hoarding treasures — looking, stroking, sorting, cherishing. But that was for another day. Right now, she just needed to know.

As she pressed play, *Dreams* by Fleetwood Mac began on the car radio — the song that had triggered her nausea at least once since the accident without her realising why. Now she knew. She watched as she chatted with her mum. Even from the safety of her bed, the speed at which the car was travelling made her tense up and hold her breath. She could see the traffic building up ahead of them. She felt her foot push involuntarily against the soft duvet, despite no brake pedal to engage with. And on screen, she heard the thud of her foot doing the same. Only that was a real pedal, and the image was not slowing down.

"What the fuck?" she heard herself say.

"Language, Rose," said her mum.

"The brake's not working at all now, Mum, it won't…"

From her bed, Rose watched the view on the video move erratically from the road to the floor of the car as her eyes instinctively darted to the point of the problem. She could see her leg moving violently, then the view changed again to the road and the traffic now stopped up ahead. Down to her leg again. Then, back to the road as the car edged across lanes. Hoots from horns and the distant screeching of brakes. A scream she didn't recognise although it could have been her own. Then darkness, the point at which Nate had taken her hands and brought her back to reality during the memory extraction.

Rose shook and struggled to shut the laptop. She felt herself sinking backwards, and she focused on the swirls in the Artex ceiling. The brakes failed. There was no doubt now. She had been driving carefully. The speed had been uncomfortable to watch, but only because she knew what was coming. She had witnessed herself check the speedometer as she cruised at 50mph on the A-road — not a dangerous or unreasonable speed. Her eyes were looking ahead, focused, checking her mirrors. She did everything right, but the brakes failed. It wasn't her fault.

What did this mean? Had the brakes just worn out naturally? No warning lights had lit up on the dashboard. Had something been long in need of attention or repair? Nate had serviced it just days before the accident, he wouldn't have missed something significant… unless he didn't. Or worse, he had seen to it. How badly had he wanted to be rid of Rose so that he could move ahead with his alternative life with her sister? It was his car, after all. He had every opportunity.

The questions left Rose aghast. Only hours ago, she would have fought with every fibre in her body to save her marriage to Nate. To defend him because, despite their troubles, he was a good man. She knew he loved her. Had she been wrong all this time?

She berated herself for even daring to think such

thoughts. Nate was a cheater, but he wouldn't want to see her hurt. He wasn't capable of… that. Rose picked up her phone and opened her chat with Helen.

'I need to talk to you. Need someone sane who I can trust. Can't even trust myself right now. Can you come over?'

After waiting a few moments for the buzz of a reply, she realised it was 3am. She had hours to spend alone in her own head with no chance of sleep now. She dreaded what state her thoughts would be in by morning.

26

A Confession

I sat outside your house in the dark. Like I have done so many times. Someone was in, but I wasn't sure whether it was you. Both cars were there, but it seemed to me like only one person at home. I sneaked quietly through the back gate, recalling through regular familiarity the precise angle it reached before it creaked. I cursed as a bin lid clattered noisily out of my control in the wind. Soon afterwards, I watched the trail of lights flick on from the bedroom to the landing to the kitchen. I was out of sight, though.

I couldn't see you and you couldn't see me.

But I felt a warmth at being close to you.

These are the moments where I can picture it being just you and I again. Moments that have kept me going during the darker times.

I tried to forget about you once. After those nights in the pub, watching you. I put distance between us. I moved away. But then you appeared back in my life like fate returned you to me.

I wondered what you would do if you came outside

and found me there. Would you freak out? Or would you finally see how much I care? The lengths I would be prepared to go to, just to be near you.

This lifetime in the shadows has been hard.

Eventually, you will see the light.

27

Nate

The red digital display of his old clock radio flicked over to 03:00 as Nate lay awake, eyes wide open. He could feel the rigid sofa bed frame through the flimsy mattress in his parents' spare room. It still seemed odd to refer to it as the 'spare room', given it was his own bedroom not much more than a decade ago. Bland magnolia walls now covered the marks where he once had posters stuck to the walls. New carpet had replaced the one in which he'd accidentally burnt a cigarette mark when he was 17.

It wasn't just the room that made him feel like a teenager again, though. He'd felt so helpless when his mum and dad arrived together to pick him up from near to Dr Thomas's place. Explaining to them how the session had evolved and how it concluded was just as painful as experiencing it first-hand. There was a feeling of guilt he couldn't shake, even as he described to them the events that were shown on the doctor's screen.

"So, what are you saying, Son? You don't remember picking up Rose's sister and her giving you this kiss in the car?" his father had asked as he drove.

"No! Dad, no! I'm saying I didn't do that. It wasn't me. That was not my memory, and it was not me in that car."

"Well, it's all very odd, Nathan," added his mother.

"Odd? Yeah, that's one way to describe it," he seethed. "Worst of all, though, I was just presumed guilty. She just believed it had to be me."

He had text Rose a while later, after pacing the garden of his parents' house. It was succinct and unapologetic.

'Staying at Mum's. Need to get my head straight.'

No kiss at the end. He'd originally finished the message with an *'x'* but deleted it and replaced it with a full stop. No reply came back.

Lying there now, in the early hours, there was still a niggling little part of him that was blaming Rose. She had pursued this whole memory therapy from the moment the idea was in her head. His instincts had been to steer clear, yet he convinced himself to go through with it for her.

He became aware that he was grinding his teeth. Stopping himself, he stretched his neck and rolled onto his back. It was a struggle to make the blanket cover both his shoulders and his feet together; he sighed and folded his arms across his chest.

He cursed himself for blaming her, then clambered aboard the same hamster wheel of emotions he'd been on for the last few hours: it wasn't Rose's fault, he should have stuck to his guns and not gone through with the therapy.

Then — how was he to know what would be in those videos that were played back? And then — what was that bloody doctor doing allowing that clip to come on, anyway. He stuck on that thought for a while. Soon enough, he couldn't help being drawn back to Gaz — that image of him and Alannah at Rose's party; worse — the thought of him and Alannah having some kind of thing together.

When he closed his eyes, he only saw images he didn't want to see.

After barely an hour of restless sleep that followed, Nate was up and dressed in the same clothes he had on the previous day. With no car, he'd considered asking for a lift again from either his mum or dad. They were still in bed and he didn't want to wake them. Instead, he decided the walk of a couple of miles would do him good, anyway.

The harsh morning air hit him as he quietly let himself out of the front door and closed it behind him. His eyes were puffy and red. He ran his fingers through his hair, a feeble replacement for brushing it properly. Around his neck, he turned up his collar, hung his head towards the ground and walked.

It was still early when he arrived at his own house. His front door key was in the same bunch as the car keys, which he'd thrown next to Rose before walking out of the doctor's office the previous day. He'd been unsure whether he wanted any conversation with her now, but he had to press the doorbell to be let in.

It took a second ring before Rose answered the door, initially just a crack to peer through. When she saw him, she pulled it open wider and walked away back into the house. She looked as groggy as Nate felt — still in her pyjamas, dark rings under her eyes and hair unbrushed.

Nate stepped inside and followed her, the silence weighing heavily. Rose threw herself onto the sofa, pulled one knee up towards her chest and tucked the other leg underneath her. She picked up the remote control and brought the black screen of the TV to life. Nate had hovered for a moment and got the signal that she was not about to instigate a chat, so he moved straight through the house and headed upstairs.

Ten minutes later, he was back down with a few clothes and other essentials stuffed into his gym bag. He walked back in to see Rose in virtually the same position. It took a moment's deliberation of whether to walk straight back out or whether to get off his chest the one protestation he had been holding in. He didn't so much choose the latter option as simply find it blurting out from his mouth.

"That wasn't me, you know, in that video. It wasn't my memory, I wasn't in that car."

Rose swung her head around and looked straight at him. The outer corners of her eyes creased.

"How the hell could it not be you?" she responded.

"It just wasn't. I wouldn't do that. You were so quick to

believe it was me. Didn't even want to ask or hear my side."

"What d'you mean you wouldn't do that? Kiss my sister? You did do that — or was that not you in the cellar either? Or you sat in the doctor's chair, describing the whole episode at my birthday party, of all times?"

"Yes, you know it was. You know that was different, and you saw what really happened. It was all her. I pushed her away. This thing in the car is nothing to do with me. It's not me."

"Why did you throw your keys at me and walk out, then?"

"I just panicked. I didn't know how to handle it. I just felt... I don't know, overwhelmed."

Rose's stare lingered on him. He held her gaze like they were in competition to see who would blink first.

Nate held strong.

"What do you expect me to say?" asked Rose. "I don't understand what's happened. I can't get my head around all this."

"Fine. Maybe 'sorry' would have been a start," Nate fired back.

"Don't take the moral high ground. You're certainly not in that kind of position."

"It's not a competition, Rose. I'm just telling you the truth. I'm going to stay at Mum's for now. We need to talk, but maybe we both still need some more time to cool off and think."

"If that's what you want," Rose turned back to face the TV, and flicking absently through the channels as she spoke. "Your USB stick from Dr Thomas is there on the side, if you want it. I brought them both away. We have a copy each. Maybe there's a video you want to watch and enjoy again on your own."

Nate shook his head and scooped up the device without offering the satisfaction of a response. His hand was on the door, but before he was through it, Rose called out.

"Actually, Nate, before you go, there's something else," she said. He hesitated and then looked over his shoulder, giving her the opportunity to continue without responding. "Just so you know, I watched the memory of the accident."

"And?"

"And it wasn't my fault. I braked. I tried and tried, but the brakes didn't work. There was nothing I could do. I watched it all play out again, and it was like seeing it clearly for the first time since it happened."

"Rose, I…" Nate's voice trailed off. He was still in confrontation mode. Something much softer tugged at his emotions that caught him off-guard and no words came out at all.

"Why would that happen, Nate? The pedal felt different at first, soft, but everything had been fine from here to Mum's and then…" Now it was Rose's turn to hesitate. "… well, you said you'd done the car's service that week. Surely you'd have checked the brakes? I remember because you said it would be fine for picking up that sofa Mum had ordered."

"Yeah, I know I did. We've been through this. What are you trying to say?"

"I don't know. I'm just telling you what I remember. And what I've seen from the memory."

"You weren't supposed to be driving that car, though! I was. It was my car. I was meant to take your mum that day."

"Yes… but you didn't."

They looked at one another, both bereft of the right words. Yet Nate sensed that just as many cogs of interpretation were grinding in Rose's head as they were in his.

*

He sat in the car and pulled the door shut. He put his hands on the steering wheel and locked his arms out straight. Then his head slumped back into the driver's seat and he felt tears prick the corners of his eyes. The events of the last 24 hours crashed over him in an overwhelming new wave.

He put the key into the ignition, started the engine and spun the volume of the stereo up high. The short drive and blast from Metallica's drums and guitars drowned his thoughts as he let *Nothing Else Matters* reverberate through him. He pulled up outside his mum's house with a new resolve taking over him. He was determined to figure out what had occurred. But first, he had to check out something else.

Still sitting in the stationary car, he scrolled to Gaz's name in his phone contacts and tapped the entry.

"Hello." Gaz's answer was monotone. Nate could hear the clunk and clatter of the garage in the background, where he should also be.

"Gaz, something's not sitting right with me here and I need answers."

"Look, I tried to tell you yesterday, mate. I don't know why this is being dragged up. There was something and nothing between me and Rose's sister. It was a one-off, ages ago. I don't know why it matters."

"It's not that. It's something else. Well, at least I hope it is."

Gaz must have walked outside as the background noise faded before he replied. "What's up, pal? Talk to me, will you?"

"This is going to sound random but hear me out. The week of Rose's accident…"

"Yeah?"

"We serviced my Volvo, right? I did the service, and you checked everything for the M.O.T. — remember?"

"Well, yeah, I think so. I dunno for certain when… but if you say it was that week, then yeah. Would have been me, I suppose. I can get Linda to check the records, if you need. Why?"

"No need. I've got the records with me. I took them the other day. Rose is sure the brakes failed on her. Like completely failed. And it's something that's always bugged me since the accident because I know the car had just been in. But I don't see how they could have failed if we'd checked everything a couple of days before. It's got your signature on the M.O.T. certificate, but it's got Andy's initials next to the work done."

"Why have you got the records? What are you saying, Nate?"

"Nothing. Just putting the pieces together. Did you do the work or just sign it off?"

"It was over a year ago, mate. I can't remember. If it's my signature, then I checked it, I guess. I don't get where you're going with it, though?"

"Never mind."

"I dunno what's going on in your head, mate but just talk it through, will you? Gimme a clue."

"Forget it. Doesn't matter."

Nate hung up.

He hadn't learnt a lot, but he was gradually clearing the

fog.

There was one more call to make. For now. It was a tricky one.

In his contacts, he scrolled further down to the entry that read '*Nic*'. Did she still have the same number? There was one sure way to find out.

With a tap of the screen, her name filled the display and his chest felt a little tighter.

One ring.

A second ring.

He was ready to change his mind and abandon the thought.

"Hello? Nathan?"

The only other person apart from his mum to call him by his full Christian name.

"Hi. Nic. Yeah, it's me. How are you?"

"Erm… I'm feeling a little surprised. Can't say I was expecting your name to be popping up on my screen."

"Yeah, I know. Look, I really need to talk to you."

"Go on." She elongated both words, so they sounded like they were loaded with a mixture of both intrigue and apprehension.

"Not over the phone. Can we meet? Tomorrow, maybe?"

"Is everything OK? Is Rose OK?"

"It's a long story, but I want to ask you some stuff and I'd just rather it be in person. Are you free?"

"Fine. I mean, more than fine, obviously. You know I'd be happy to. OK, at mine?"

"What about the cafe opposite the church? Tomorrow morning, 10ish?" Nate suggested, wanting somewhere a bit more neutral.

"Alright. That would be lovely. It's been a while since you bought me a coffee, Nathan. I'll see you there. Just one thing, though. Does Rose know you're meeting me?"

"Not yet."

*

Inside the house, Nate turned on his dad's computer and inserted the USB stick. His eyes skimmed over the thumbnail images until resting on the apparently incriminating one that he sought. When this played in the doctor's office, it didn't quite sink in. It was just a confused blur. Now he watched it again. Over and over. He scrutinised it. He knew it wasn't him in that car, but he needed proof to show Rose to clear his name. More than that, he needed to understand it himself.

When he became frustrated and his vision was blurry from staring at the screen, he paced the garden, made a drink and then watched some more. In between, he watched the other video memories again. Painfully, he watched Rose's real memory of the accident. Watched her thrusting her foot into the brake pedal and screaming at her mum that it wasn't working. He spent the day and the evening barely leaving the computer screen, watching the same clips over and over, hoping that something would seem out of place, something to latch on to.

Most of all, he watched the clip that was not his memory but someone else's. Someone else going to pick up Alannah. It looked like his car — the same Volvo that was destroyed in the accident. It was easy to see why the beginning of the clip could have been mistaken for Rose's recollection of her own journey at the start of that fateful day. Same dashboard, same steering wheel. It even appeared to be his leather gloves on the hands holding the wheel — gloves that he had not seen for the last week, now he came to think of it. Most of the image looked ahead out of the windscreen. It was the brief journey from their house to Rose's mum's — all familiar.

The day gave way to darkness outside the window as he continually fended off questions from his mum, asking him if he was OK or suggesting he take a break. He sipped on a coffee, having lost count of the caffeine hits he'd taken in the preceding 16 hours.

When the clip finished, he went back to the start again and again. He studied each turn of the journey, scanned the edges of the screen to look for flickers of clues that came into view. Nothing grabbed his attention, though. Each time it ended up with Alannah walking out of the house, entering the car and leaning in to plant a kiss on the driver's mouth.

And then there it was.

Something finally triggered in his coffee-addled brain.

It was almost subconscious. A complete aside from everything he'd been studying.

He didn't go back to the start of the clip, but clicked and held the button to go back through the frames. He stopped as the car was turning into the driveway. It was only just in sight, but it was clear — the wall!

The new brickwork that Nigel had built just the other week. This so-called memory or video was recent — as recent as this last fortnight. That meant there was no way this was his car. His car had long since been consigned to the scrap yard following the accident. This was the same — or very similar — make and model. It was almost like it had been chosen to mimic their old Volvo.

He let the clip play for the next few seconds again. Now, it was like choking back the bile in the back of his throat as conspiracy theories ripped through him. He watched Alannah come smiling out of the house. On a roll and with his senses back on full alert, he clocked something he should have spotted all along. Something Rose should have spotted if she was looking for it. Something that showed this wasn't him in his car 12 months ago. The bag on Alannah's shoulder was new. Rose had bought it for her last birthday a few weeks ago.

This clip was recent, and Rose would know that Nate didn't have this car to drive anymore.

He sat back in the chair, and his breath caught in his throat. Slowly, he exhaled as he digested the significance of what he'd discovered. He felt the tiny hairs on his arms and neck prickle and shuddered at the realisation of what he was processing. He already knew this wasn't his memory. Now, the thought cascaded over him that it was more than just someone else's mixed up recollection. This was a deliberate act to mislead — a video that had been made to look like it was him; a video that had occurred in the last few weeks — maybe even since he had given up his own memories.

This was malicious.

He swallowed hard. There was so much he needed to say. He looked at the time on his watch. Nearly 11:30pm. It was late, and he suspected Rose would be in bed as she would normally be by now.

There was no way he could wait until morning, though, and he would not rely on trying to convince her of this over the phone. He needed to show her. Explain it.

He snatched his car keys and headed home.

28

Rose

Rose lifted her upper body and awkwardly rested on her elbow as she flipped her pillow over. She flopped down again and stared at the ceiling for a while. When this didn't help her sleep, she moved onto Nate's side of the bed. She scooped up half of the duvet, held it close to her body and wrapped her leg around it as if she were cuddling a person. The rain had been battering the windows for hours and heightened anxiety replaced her usual love for the sound of a thunderstorm. As the wind blew, the noise of clattering debris outside made her veins flush with adrenaline. Twice in the last week, Rose had lost her breath for a moment at the sight of a movement in the garden. She knew it must be her mind playing tricks on her — a fox moving in the bushes or the shadow of a tree branch, but since Nate left, she had been plagued with a jumpiness and the feeling of being watched. Now everything sounded like footsteps, like objects being smashed, like doors being slammed. Lying on Nate's pillow, she pulled hers over her head to block out the noise.

Rose wasn't sure how long she'd been asleep, but she must have drifted off. The force with which she sat up in bed and the nauseous feeling in her stomach were telltale signs of having woken suddenly. The room spun and her heart rate was racing but she didn't know why. Had she been dreaming? She sat still for several moments, listening to the silence. The room seemed darker despite her eyes being open now. She could feel the pounding of her heart in her chest and the pulse in her wrists.

A movement downstairs made her terrified to breathe.

Footsteps.

In the hallway perhaps, or were they coming up the stairs?

Her ears throbbed. For a few moments, she considered pulling her dressing table up against the bedroom door and hiding under the covers. She slowly reached for her phone, being careful not to make a sound. She slipped it underneath the duvet to hide the light and turned on the screen. Midnight. Who could she call at this hour? Helen, maybe? Dial 999? The footsteps grew louder. Definitely not a figment of her imagination. Rose felt tears rushing as she picked up the lamp from Nate's bedside table. She pulled out the lead and clenched it, her hand shaking. Could she make it to the door to close it? Or should she stay frozen where she was? She tried to rationalise her thinking; it was probably a drunk student heading home from the Willow Tree, confused or messing around. An innocent mistake by someone. She must have forgotten to lock the door.

"Rose?" A voice came from the bottom of the stairs, whispering loudly.

Shit. It was someone who knew her.

"I've called the police!" she shouted. "My husband will be home any minute."

"Rose, it's me!"

Trembling, she flung herself out of bed, scrambling into a hoodie. The lights were all on already as she opened the door of the bedroom a fraction and looked down the stairs. There, on the doormat, was Nate — keys in hand, shivering and dripping wet. She opened the door now, aware she was crying but not caring enough to pretend otherwise.

"What the fuck, Nate?"

"Sorry, did I wake you?" Nate seemed preoccupied.

"Wake me?" Her voice was raised. "You scared the fucking shit out of me! It's the middle of the bloody night! Couldn't you have knocked?"

"It's my house," said Nate. "Sorry, I just meant, I didn't think. God… sorry!"

Rose stomped into the bathroom to grab a towel. She marched down the stairs and threw it at him without stopping before heading towards the kitchen.

"This couldn't wait," said Nate. He was shaking and didn't seem to be aware of his surroundings.

Rose rolled her eyes as she put the kettle on. She sniffed and wiped her nose, allowing a little whimper of relief as the adrenaline eased off. She pressed her hands against the worktop, closed her eyes and shakily took some deep breaths. When she had composed herself, she turned, with arms folded, defensive and preparing for a conversation she was too tired to have. She was angry that Nate was pushing this and had caught her off-guard.

"Tea?" she said. But Nate hadn't followed her in as she had expected. He had gone straight to the lounge. He didn't reply but came marching in with the laptop and placed it on the kitchen table.

"Sit down," he said.

"*Please!*" said Rose, as if talking to a child. "Let me just make a cup of tea."

"No, you need to see this, please, sit down." Nate sounded odd. His voice was quick and louder than usual. He was still shivering, but it wasn't just the cold — he was wired. His hand shook as he pulled a USB stick from his wet jeans pocket and shoved it into the port. The whirring began, and the window appeared with thumbnails of their memories.

"Nate, just give it a rest," said Rose. The chair screeched on the kitchen floor as she pulled it out and slumped down, resting her chin on her hands. The house felt cold. Steam billowed from the boiling kettle, condensing on the glass of the kitchen windows. "I'm not in the mood to go over all of this again now — I'm so flippin' tired."

Nate ignored her and continued to click the touchpad until the video of the Alannah kiss was full screen. He pressed the button, and the scene skipped along until the car was approaching the gate to Rose's mum's drive.

"Look! There!" Nate paused the video. "What do you see?"

"I see a road and my mum's drive and you steering your way into it to pick up my sister."

Nate rotated his head. "Do you see me in this video, Rose?"

"Who else could it be?"

Louder now. "Can you actually see *me*? My face?"

"No," said Rose, barely parting her lips.

"Right, let's focus shall we?" Nate's tone irritated Rose. "What do you see at the entrance to the drive?"

Rose paused before speaking. "Some hedges and a brick wall."

"Right!" said Nate as if that cleared everything up.

"You're not making any sense, Nate. Have you been drinking?"

"Coffee," said Nate. "I've watched this hundreds of times today, I needed to prove it to you."

Rose felt herself soften.

"Nate, I can see you're tired and full of caffeine, but I am just tired. You're going to have to spell it out for me."

"Sorry." Nate shook his head quickly and pulled the screen and his chair closer to Rose. The lid of the kettle juddered as the water inside boiled. "The brick wall. It collapsed in the storm just before the accident, remember? Nigel was fixing it that day. I remember because he was there when I was trying to find Alannah after the police couldn't get hold of her."

Rose looked closer at the screen, realisation was hitting. A click from the kettle signalled the water had boiled, and the lid rested again. She glanced at the image and opened her mouth to speak, but the thoughts were still settling in her brain.

Nate continued, "Nigel never finished fixing the wall that day because he offered to help me look for Alannah. You were with the police and I wanted to get back to you as soon as possible. After that, Nigel stopped coming for a while until Alannah asked him to start back again a month ago. Do you remember he was there on the day we went to sort your mum's stuff?"

"That's when he started fixing the wall." Rose spoke slowly.

"The wall in this video is fixed," said Nate. "I drive past your mum's everyday on the way to the garage and that wall was only finished last week."

"Right, so it was before the wall collapsed or you've been having a recent affair with my sister, brilliant!" said Rose.

"Look at the car, Rose! The steering wheel, the interior. I know you're not a car person, but that is not our Toyota. Even *you* can see that. That's the old car, the Volvo — that's why you thought it was you picking up your mum to start with. And look at the bricks, they're not the original. Three of them are a different colour, much newer."

"That car was written off when I…" Rose's voice trailed off as everything slotted into place. Her mind spun. The Volvo put the memory at over a year ago, yet the fixed wall meant it must have happened in the last couple of weeks. She rubbed the palms of her hands over her face. "I'm so confused."

"It's not just that." Nate let the video play for a while longer until Alannah appeared in it. "It's the bag we bought her for her birthday. The one I picked up for you in Matlock. This proves that this memory was a couple of weeks ago at the most, yet that's not my car anymore, Rose. Do you see?"

"I see that," said Rose. Doubt was creeping in. Her resolve that this had to be Nate was being chipped away, but it wasn't enough.

"This doesn't prove it wasn't you," she said. "You could have borrowed a car from the garage."

"That's not all," said Nate. He skipped backwards through the video until the drivers' hands could be seen. "Those are my gloves, right?"

Rose once again felt slow for not being able to catch up

with the coffee-fuelled thoughts of Nate. He had been examining this video for much longer than she had, and she felt like she was fifty steps behind.

"How does that prove it's not you?" said Rose.

"I lost those gloves last week, after the memory harvesting appointment. Remember, I've been looking for them everywhere. You helped me look for them, you know they went missing. They're my warmest ones and I needed them for going out on recoveries, but I left them in Alannah's car that day. I lost them *before* Nigel had completely fixed that wall."

"So this couldn't have been you?"

"No, Rose. I swear on my mother's life, it is not me in that car. I have never kissed Alannah willingly. I have never cheated on you with anyone. I wouldn't, I couldn't, I…" Nate's voice broke, and he put his knuckles to his mouth. Rose had rarely seen him cry, and she felt shocked by the man who sat next to her. This was stress like she'd never seen it before on Nate's face, and she couldn't keep her hands from pulling his head into her chest.

"I'm sorry." Rose could feel the barriers dissolving and the anger of the last few days escaping through her eyes. She felt like a plug had been pulled and the release was enormous. "I'm so sorry."

Nate looked at her intensely. His dark eyes never breaking contact, both faces wet and tinged with red. He leaned in and rested his forehead on hers, noses touching.

"Please, Rose. You have to believe me."

"I do," said Rose gently. "I do." She kissed him and could taste salty tears. She didn't know which one of them they belonged to. Probably both. She kissed him again, harder this time, and he placed his hands on her cheeks, pulling her face closer to his.

"I love you," said Nate, not showing any sign of letting go.

"I love you too." Rose was almost laughing through the tears. "I've missed you so much, I hate being here without you. Everything is so fucked up."

"It's OK." Nate was quick to interject. "I'm here now and I swear to you I am on your side, Rose. Everything's going to be OK. But you have to trust me. If we're going to find out what all this is about, then we need to be a team. We need to go back to being the Nate and Rose we used to be — unbreakable."

"That's all I want," said Rose, kissing him again. "Will you stay?"

Nate nodded. "This is my home, it's where I belong. With you."

Rose kissed him one more time before pulling away and staring at the screen again with her head on his shoulder. "If it's not you, then who is it?"

"Look closely at the bag," said Nate. "Where have you seen that before?"

Nate pointed to a small metal keyring on the strap of

Alannah's bag — one half of a pair and in the shape of a teddy bear. Rose's brain was blank as she stared at the keyring. A familiar feeling of having seen it before swept across her. After a few moments, she gasped.

"Oh my God! That's the same keyring that Dr Thomas has for the medicine cabinet. I thought I recognised it. Alannah's had it for ages."

"It's the other half, I'm sure of it," said Nate.

"What are you saying?"

"I'm saying that our marriage therapist has been sleeping with your sister. I'm saying that this is his memory. This is him kissing Alannah. After all, they knew each other from school and she was the one who recommended him."

"Oh, God!" The reality of what they had discovered hit Rose. "So that's why she wouldn't tell us who her boyfriend was, she knew it would freak me out and I wouldn't have gone. This is too creepy."

"At best it's a conflict of interest," said Nate. "A violation of our privacy."

"Privacy? You don't think he's told her anything about what we've said?"

"You've got to ask yourself why Alannah was so determined to get us to see him. Why did it matter to her so much that we went to couple's therapy? And why him specifically? There are hundreds of therapists."

"I don't understand? How much do you think she

knows?"

"I don't know! I mean, she could have seen the memory videos for all we know."

Rose stopped for a moment, aghast. "She had access to the videos. He's one of the few people in the country capable of carrying out this kind of therapy. Do you think she was trying to find out the truth about Mum?" Rose's voice trailed off.

"Maybe," said Nate.

"Typical," said Rose. "I get that she'd want to know, she was her mum too but why does she have to be so conniving? She could've just talked to me about it."

Nate smiled and stroked Rose's cheek. "Maybe because it wasn't just about your mum."

"What do you mean?"

"I'm really sorry, Rose. I know she's your sister, but all of this is too weird. Maybe she started off wanting to find out about your mum, but you're forgetting about this memory!"

"So you don't think the doctor got his own memory muddled up by accident?"

"If that was the case, then why would he not just have admitted it and changed the video?" asked Nate.

"I don't know, maybe he was embarrassed. Worried he'd look unprofessional?"

"You're really telling me that a man who is so uptight that his clothes barely crease would make a stupid mistake like that. He is so pernickety about every little detail; his entire office is perfect, every bit of paperwork meticulously completed. You think he accidentally leaves the wrong memory in a file for a client?"

"So you think Alannah planted it? What would she have to gain?"

"Think about it, Rose. She's always been jealous of what we have — flirting with me, she tried to kiss me at your birthday party for God's sake. She did it to break us up. Dr Thomas has probably got loads of files in his computer, there's no way he hasn't extracted his own memories for his research. She saw an opportunity, and she took it."

Rose thought for a moment. "But everything you've said about Dr Thomas is true; he's careful to a fault. There's no way he just leaves his stuff lying around, insecurely stored. Like you said, he's anal about everything."

"So he planted it for her," said Nate. "She's manipulated him into helping her. You know what Alannah's like. She can get anything she wants out of a guy."

Rose raised an eyebrow.

"Most guys!" Nate corrected himself, and they smiled at each other.

"But she's been so against this memory therapy from the very beginning. If this is what she wanted, then why didn't she encourage me to do it?"

"Maybe it wasn't initially part of her plan. She knew if you went along with the memory therapy, then there was a risk you'd find out about her trying to kiss me. But we went ahead, she couldn't stop us, and so she saw a chance to take control. Revenge maybe for me telling you about the kiss."

Rose slammed the laptop shut. "There's nothing more we can do tonight. We should go and see her in the morning and confront her. She'll probably just lie through her teeth, but if I can look her in the eye, I'll know."

Rose's thoughts wandered a little further than she was prepared to admit just yet. She thought of the memory she had watched back the previous night. The accident, the brakes failing. Just how far would her sister go to get Nate for herself?

"Agreed," said Nate. "We can go first thing. Oh, actually there is someone else we need to see first. You won't like it."

*

Rose woke up the next day feeling a little stronger now that Nate had slept beside her. Confusion and anxiety still plagued her, throbbing away within her chest. The anger and mistrust of the last few days had left their mark, and the remnants of unease still circulated. But Nate being there was a comfort and her gut was telling her she could trust him. The overwhelming sense of loss and fear was dissipating, and she felt energised with determination to find out the truth. She needed to know what her sister had done. She wouldn't rest until she knew the extent of the betrayal and regardless of how devastating the outcome, today she would find out.

"I still don't understand why we need to meet Nicola," she shouted over her hair dryer. "She's got nothing to do with my sister and the therapist. We need to get to Alannah as soon as possible."

"I can't explain it," said Nate. "But something has been bugging me about the memory of the wedding. Why was she there? It's just another thing that doesn't add up in all of this. At the very least, let's see what she has to say about it."

Rose sighed. Nate had been right until now. She had been so quick to accuse him of cheating, the least she could do was let him follow his gut on this. The thought of seeing Nicola again made Rose's stomach turn. That woman had done everything in her power to break them up; she had followed them on nights out, showed up at their house drunk and abusive, tried to stop their wedding, and now they were off to meet her for coffee. Where did she fit into this mess? Rose resigned herself to sitting quietly and letting Nate do all the talking. She didn't trust herself not to lay into Nicola, but part of her was curious to see what she had to say.

"Are you ready? We're going to be late." Nate called up the stairs, the Autumn wind filling the house as he stood with the door open.

Rose looked at her phone and saw that they needed to leave now if they didn't want to keep Nicola waiting. She took out her straighteners and decided she needed to spend a little longer on her hair.

29

Nate

Nicola was seated at a table in the far corner of the cafe. She looked up and the brief smile faded from her mouth. Nate weaved over towards her through a maze of tables with Rose a step behind, clutching his hand.

"I didn't realise she—" Nicola began, rising to her feet.

"I know. Neither did I when I spoke to you yesterday, honestly. But let's all be grown up about it shall we? It's been long enough." Nate held his palms towards her in a conciliatory fashion.

"Easy for you to say. I've tried—" Nicola was cut off again, this time by Rose, as all three of them stood at the small bistro table.

"Listen, I'm not here to start an argument. What's been said and done is in the past. There are just some things we both want to ask," Rose said calmly, although Nate sensed it was through gritted teeth. "Can we all sit down?"

Nicola resumed her place at the table in submissive response. Rose took the single seat opposite. Nate turned and grabbed a spare chair from the adjacent table, sliding it in between the two women to whom he had proposed.

"Right, I'm gonna get straight to the point, Nic," he said. As he spoke, Nicola's eyes locked onto him. Rose kept her gaze on Nicola, then baulked at Nate's over-familiar shortening of his ex-fiancée's name. The cafe was moderately busy with only a few customers, mostly middle-aged women, dotted around. Nate made a point of trying to keep his volume low.

"That'd be good. I can't stay long," Nicola said curtly. Rose leaned back in her seat and folded her arms.

"OK, I know this might feel like raking up the past," Nate began, "but on the day of our wedding—"

"You turned up at Gaz's house and tried to stop Nate going through with it, didn't you?" Rose butted in.

"What's that got to do with anything now? Nathan, what's this all about? I'm not staying here to just get accused of things from years ago." Nicola pushed back her seat and put her hands on the table. A grey-haired woman on the periphery of Nate's eye-line sipped her coffee and looked across at them not too subtly.

"Stop! Wait a minute." Nate's voice rose as he looked from one woman to the other, needing to address them both. "Rose, let me do this, will you? Nic, please, hear me out. It's not about the morning."

Rose tightened her crossed arms. Nicola mirrored the expression. Nate took a breath before continuing. He thought he heard a tut from the grey-haired woman.

"It's about the church later. Outside the church after the ceremony. You were there, weren't you?" He pointed towards the window, indicating the significance of the street outside. The stone wall and grassed bank of the churchyard was a stone's throw from where they now sat.

Nicola blinked, glanced at Rose, then back at Nate.

"You saw me? But why bring it up now?" she asked with genuine intrigue prickling her tone.

"It's a long story. But you were with someone else too — why?" Nate quizzed. He'd softened his tone again and clung to the hope of prising something useful out of Nicola, suspecting her presence was too much of a coincidence — both then and now in his video-captured recollection.

"I... I..." Nicola floundered, shaking her head and closing her eyes. "I shouldn't have turned up. I'm sorry. It was a stupid thing to do. I just got talked into it. I suppose I was still infatuated, I hadn't got over you properly then, Nathan. I was just young and naïve."

Rose quietly but conspicuously snorted her contempt and looked away.

"I'm not doing this to blame you, Nic. I simply need to understand. You said you were talked into it? How do you mean?"

"You know, having the idea planted in my head that you two weren't really happy, that you probably wanted a way out, an excuse to call it off."

"That's rubbish!" Rose chipped in again. Nate delivered her a cutting sideways look. He felt he was getting somewhere, but Rose clearly couldn't see it, and he needed her to bite her tongue so as not to ruin any momentum he had. He put his hand on her thigh, hoping to placate and not patronise her.

"Nic, I get that part and I know that's why you came round in the morning but I thought we resolved it then. Why still come to the church but not actually do anything?"

"It wasn't my idea. I just went along with it. The idea was to interrupt the wedding, make an objection in front of everyone, force you to face the truth about you not being right for each other. But by the time we were at the church, I couldn't bring myself to do it, so we ended up arguing on the street and that was it."

"You say 'we', Nic, and that you were talked into it? By who?"

"Just some guy. I didn't even know him. He just approached me. Said he knew Rose and knew that you and I used to be together." Rose shifted forward again, leaning her elbows on the table.

"Someone who knew me? Who?" she asked.

"I'm not sure I can even remember his name," said Nicola.

"Scott?" Nate ventured.

"Scott?" Rose echoed but turned towards him. "What

the hell? Why would you say Scott?"

Nate had not addressed the doubt in his head — and his memory — about her colleague and everything he thought about him.

"No, that wasn't it." Nicola shook her head. "Andy, maybe?"

"Andy? Jeez, from the garage, but…" Nate's head spun towards Rose.

"I didn't even know Andy from the bloody garage then! I barely know him now! She's making stuff up, Nate. Nothing's changed a bit. She's still trying to cause a rift — she's said herself that's what she was trying to do back then — break us up!"

"Of course I'm not," Nicola shot back. "What would I have to gain now? I'm perfectly happy, thanks, and in a relationship with a lovely bloke. You called me about today, Nate, remember?"

"She's right, Rose. This is us asking Nic for help to understand. She hasn't instigated this. It's just, Andy, I mean… Garage Andy is odd sometimes, but he's just quiet. I know we take the piss out of him a bit but… surely not. Do you know another Andy?"

Rose threw her head to one side and arms in the air. It appeared much more likely she was dismissing the very idea rather than even contemplating whether she knew anyone else by the name.

"Hang on, maybe not Andy, maybe Adrian?" Nicola

suggested.

At this, Nate and Rose looked at each other. Based on the moment he saw Rose's eyes widen, he suspected that she'd made the link only a second after him.

"Shit! Adrian!"

30

A Confession

Getting that girl involved was embarrassingly easy. I'd almost forgotten about it until talk of the wedding day reared its head. I still curse that day.

I'd seen her so many times at the bar, lusting after a fading memory.

She was persuaded easily enough at first to prevent proceedings. She willingly turned up that morning to confess her undying love. Not that she has any idea what love is. What we have goes so much further, so much deeper. I still picture you from all those years ago at school. We have so much history.

Anyway, when the first plans failed with the girl, I convinced her she had one last chance at the church. She wouldn't go through with it, though. I even drove her there myself, but she didn't have the conviction to go inside.

She could have brought a halt to the whole sorry affair then and made things much easier. After that, I knew it was going to be down to me. If I wanted you single and available to notice me again, Rose, it was me who would have to make it happen.

31

Rose

Nate was walking so quickly that Rose could barely keep up. He was holding her hand, but it felt more like he was dragging her along behind him. As Rose turned her head, she could see Nicola still sitting at the table, stunned by the speed at which they had stormed out of the cafe.

"I'll kill him," Nate fumbled for his keys from the pocket of his jeans.

Rose knew better than to talk to him when he was angry. She clung to the dashboard as the car sped out of the car park and towards the road before she had engaged her seatbelt. She let out a whimper of fear. "Nate!"

Nate stopped at the entrance of the car park and looked at her as she tried to plug in her belt as quickly as she could. Her hand was shaking and her face must have given away the panic that was exploding inside her.

"Sorry," said Nate. He paused and waited for her to be ready. He had been very mindful of her trauma since the accident and had made a point of always driving more carefully when she was in the car. Today, however, emotion had taken over and Rose couldn't blame him.

The couple sat in silence as Nate drove.

Finally, Rose spoke. "I take it we're not heading to Alannah's anymore?"

"We can deal with her later," said Nate.

"But how do you know he'll be there? Should we ring first?"

"And give him time to get his story straight or more likely go somewhere we can't find him?"

"Promise me you won't do anything stupid." Rose wasn't sure what she thought Nate might do. She had seen him angry before — lash out even — but never like this. She had never witnessed him lose control, and she was frightened of where it could lead.

"He deserves what's coming," said Nate through gritted teeth.

"Nate… he's not worth getting yourself in trouble for. Let's try to get our heads around this first."

"Look, if I beat him senseless, which is what I would love to do right now, then he won't be able to tell us what the fuck is going on. Don't worry, I'll wait until we have the whole story before I pummel him."

"I'm serious, Nate. You ending up in prison is not a good way to get closure."

"I promise I won't do anything that will land me in prison," said Nate. "Maybe just some community service."

Rose stared at him with irritation. This was not the time

for his dry sense of humour.

"Maybe we should still speak to Alannah first," said Rose. "Get her version. After all, she's still involved somewhere in all of this."

"That's the trouble," said Nate. "Alannah's involved, Nicola's involved, and now this two-faced bastard's name comes up again, but I can't work out why. Why is he involved as far back as Nicola?"

Rose felt uneasy. Her mind spun webs that trailed back through her life. Names, faces, places. School, work, home. Family, friends, professionals. Some could be linked, but others shouldn't link at all. Not in the timeline of her life as she knew it. All together the names made no sense. The reasons for those people wanting to hurt both her and Nate so much made even less.

And of all the names whirling around her mind, Alannah's stood out the most clearly. Her only sister, in fact, all the family she had left in the world. Had she been too quick to think the worst of her? There was no doubt she was caught up in this, but as a puppet master, determined to ruin Rose's life? Rose didn't know if the conclusions she had jumped to about her sister were justified or the product of anger and betrayal.

"I really need to speak to Alannah," said Rose.

"I promise that we'll go round there next. Don't worry, honey, we're gonna sort this out now if it kills me."

"That's what I'm worried about," said Rose.

32

Nate

There was a surge of adrenaline pumping through Nate as he drove. His temples throbbed. His shoulders tensed. He leaned over the steering wheel like he was urging the car on.

"Slow down, Nate. Take it easy, will you?" Rose pleaded.

They had got what they needed from Nicola — but not what they had expected. Now, there was a whole other line of questioning added on top. It zapped around his head as he tried to plan what to say and where to begin.

The car screeched to a halt. They had visited this place several times but never arrived unannounced. Enormous trees draped their branches over the driveway with the house set back from the road. The immaculate lawn lay between them and a front entrance they had never used. A wall-mounted metal sign pointed down the side and to the rear of the building. Nate and Rose followed this path as they always had before. It had previously felt so professional, everything about the place so tidy. Now it felt creepy, too sterile, too private.

Instead of pressing the buzzer and waiting, as on previous occasions, Nate grabbed the door handle and marched straight in. The hallway which led from this door was empty, apart from the tall glass side table with a vase of flowers and unfathomable prints on the walls. They headed for the only door on the right side of the hallway, ignoring the two doors to the left. Nate continued his charge, barging straight through the office door which was slightly ajar and had a wooden plaque on the front which read '*Dr A. Thomas, MClinPsychol*'.

The doctor was sitting behind his desk, focused on the laptop in front of him, one hand on a wireless mouse to the side. He shot to his feet as the door swung open.

"Nate. Rose. What are you doing here? You can't…" His flustered voice petered out as he looked from one of them to the other, then sheepishly to the door through which they had just entered. Nate strode straight over to the desk which separated him from the doctor, slamming his palms down onto the surface and leaning over it.

"You've got some serious explaining to do, *Adrian*," he demanded. Rose hung back, a step behind. Dr Thomas cleared his throat and picked up a pen, rolling it between the thumb and fingers of both hands.

"I'm not sure what this is about, but it is not a good time — nor is it appropriate to arrive without appointment. Please, you're going to have to leave," he said. His voice maintained much of its usual calm, reassuring tone, but there was just a hint of something more strained and agitated lurking beneath.

"No chance. We're not leaving here till we have some answers, so take a seat." Nate demonstrated by sitting himself down in the place where he and Rose had been paired many times in their previous sessions. He sat back, folding his arms and crossing his legs. Rose had not spoken yet, but followed his lead and sat beside him on the edge of the seat cushion.

The doctor was the only person still standing. "Look, whatever the problem is, I'm sure we can address it in the proper manner, if you just—"

"I'll tell you what the first problem is…" Nate began. He clamped his hands together and interlocked his fingers, leaning forward instead. The nervous energy oozed from him. He knew his face was burning red, and he was working hard to keep his emotions from bubbling over. His heart pounded as he tackled the subject. "I've watched that video over and over that you decided to show us — the one which you said was a mistake; the one which you wanted us to believe had come from my memory. Well, I know for a fact that it wasn't me in that car, so I want to know what you're playing at."

The doctor's eyebrows raised a barely discernible amount and for a moment, he seemed to regain a touch of composure before responding. With a hint of reluctance, he lowered himself back into his plush leather office chair.

He put down his pen, closed the laptop lid and folded his arms.

"I suppose I was expecting this reaction at some point. I am sorry you both had to see what you did. Sometimes, we cannot control what is captured from the therapy sessions. They can be memories we have buried deep inside our minds, ones which we don't want to recall or don't even believe ourselves. Maybe you didn't want this memory to be revealed and therefore it is natural for you to claim it was in fact not you. Maybe you genuinely don't believe this event happened because you have blocked it out from your conscious mind."

Nate shook his head at the accusation and forced his tongue against his teeth. He could feel the heat in his face and the rapid beating of his heart. He remained calm enough to let the doctor dig himself a deeper hole if he was willing.

"I believe him, Dr Thomas," said Rose, adding her voice. "That wasn't Nate in the car and you know it, too. Why are you lying to us?"

The doctor glanced from Nate to Rose and flicked his eyes once more to the open door before addressing her with a reply.

"Rose, it is admirable of you to support your husband. As I explained to you previously, I'm afraid this memory can't belong to anyone else, despite what Nate might have you believing."

"You're a fucking liar!" Nate shouted and sprung to his feet again, pointing aggressively at Dr Thomas. In response, the doctor leaned back in his chair. One upturned corner of his mouth gave him a look which was morphing from calm to something more akin to smug. Nate was determined to wipe it off his face. "I'll tell you why. Not only is that video definitely not me, it is not my car. That video — whoever's memory or wherever else it came from — was made only a few weeks ago. We know for sure because of the bricks used to rebuild the wall of the driveway."

"Then one must presume you have visited your wife's sister recently," the doctor said, too quickly to have any air of calm now. For the first time, a trickle of aggression infiltrated his voice.

"You better be careful what you're accusing me of," Nate said. "Nothing about the interior in that car matches the car I have now. It's the same as the Volvo I used to drive, as you well know — the one which Rose was driving on the day of the accident that never came out of the scrapyard after they towed away it."

"If memory serves me correctly, I think you do work in a garage with access to any number of cars, do you not?" the doctor fired back, raising both his voice and the argumentative tone.

Nate slammed his fist down onto the desk and could feel himself losing control. From behind him, Rose's voice cut through the mist he felt descending around him.

"There's something else, Dr Thomas. At first, I thought it had to be my sister pulling the strings — that she had manipulated you somehow into inserting that video. But it's not, is it?"

There was a lull as the doctor took in a long breath before getting to his feet but ignoring Rose's question.

"I apologise but I really am going to have to ask you both to leave and we can address this properly with an appointment. In fact, perhaps it's better if we were to make individual appointments for each of you," he said. Whilst speaking, he moved from behind his desk around the room towards the open door and placed a hand on the edge. Glancing out, then ushering them towards the exit with his other hand.

"Not a chance," said Rose, shaking her head and also standing up. "Like Nate said, we're not going anywhere without answers. We've just come from a meeting with his ex, Nicola, as well. You remember her from the video, don't you? In fact, you probably remember her in person too!"

The doctor's pupils widened as his eyes flicked between Nate and Rose. His mouth opened, and he blinked rapidly. Almost absent-mindedly he moved back towards his desk and began tidying the items that lay there.

"Weren't expecting us to know about that were you?" Nate could sense an advantage building as the revelation seemed to have caught the doctor by surprise.

"I have no idea what you're talking about." The doctor shuffled some papers.

"Maybe you've forgotten, Doc. Maybe we need to hook your brain up to the computer because Nicola certainly had a clear memory of you persuading her to try to break us up. On our wedding day… three years ago! We didn't even know who you were back then, and now we end up in your therapy session. You're not telling me that is a coincidence!"

"Alright, I don't know what you think you know, Rose — but I promise you, it's not what it seems." The doctor's paper shuffling became rapid, and Nate could see wet patches forming on his shirt beneath both armpits.

"Maybe you'd care to explain, then." Nate slammed his hand on top of the doctor's papers, forcing him to stop still. The doctor's gaze remained focused on the desk and the hand of the man who was breathing down his neck.

"It was all for you, Rose," he whispered.

"You what?" Nate hissed.

"So, it was you?" asked Rose. "You admit it?"

"It's not how you think. I can explain."

"The video — you did that deliberately? But Nicola, years ago? You were trying to split up me and Nate, then? Why on earth? I don't understand!"

"It's always been about you, Rose. All these years, I've loved you. Since school!" he pleaded.

The revelation slapped Rose around the face.

Nate put his hands to his head.

Rose's mouth hung open, and she muttered, "But I… you…"

"You haven't noticed me for years, but you were everything to me," the doctor said as he stood and moved around the desk towards her. "I thought if only you weren't married or if you two weren't together, it would mean there was a chance that you and I—"

Rose staggered backwards, sending one of the neatly placed metal tissue boxes clattering to the floor.

"You lying little…" Nate spat out the words but didn't even finish as he launched himself at the doctor. He slammed his right forearm across the top of Dr Thomas's chest and used his other hand to pin back the doctor's own rising right arm. The two men clattered into the wall beside the open door, the doctor's back hitting the plasterboard with Nate's full force.

Rose was screaming Nate's name behind him and tugging at his shoulder to peel him away. Dr Thomas squirmed and wrestled his weight back against Nate as each of their arms flailed with similar force.

In less than a handful of seconds, a door opened from the opposite side of the hall, halting the untidy melee. A familiar voice trailed across the narrow space.

"What's going on with all the noise?" came the panicked shout. It preceded the entrance through the office door — surrounded by the swish of a pink, silk dressing gown — of Alannah.

Nate pushed the doctor back into the wall again and stepped back, locking eyes with his sister-in-law. Alannah stood aghast in the open doorway. Her hand shot to cover her open mouth.

"What the hell are you doing here — dressed like that?" demanded Rose.

33

Rose

"What on earth is going on?" Alannah marched across the hallway, pulling her dressing gown tightly around her waist and chest.

She placed herself between Nate and the doctor, almost squaring up to her brother-in-law. Adrian used the opportunity to manoeuvre out from behind her and replace himself in the leather chair. Nate's gaze followed him, and Alannah was quick on her feet to jump around in front of him again.

"How did you find out?" Alannah asked.

"He just admitted it," snarled Nate.

"I'm so sorry," said Alannah. "I know I shouldn't have kept it from you, but this is such an overreaction, Nate. It was all my idea, not Adi's. How is beating him up going to help?"

"Oh, it will help to make me feel much better." Nate fixed his eyes on Dr Thomas.

"I only had your best interests at heart. I knew you wouldn't come to see him if you knew he was my boyfriend. I just didn't want to complicate things for you."

Rose briefly shut her eyes and shook her head. "This has gone way beyond you sleeping with our therapist, Alannah. Or moving in with him, it would seem." She looked her sister up and down, standing there in her nightwear from another life that Rose had known nothing about. "As messed up as that is, we know the memory wasn't Nate's."

Alannah broke eye-contact with Nate and stood down from her defensive stance to look at Rose. "What are you talking about? What memory? This isn't about me and Adi?"

"We can get onto your sordid little affair later," said Rose. "But right now, your boyfriend has got some explaining to do."

"What are they talking about, Adi?" Alannah looked to the doctor who was sitting back in his chair with his legs crossed. He was pale and had a weak smile on his face.

"I have no idea," he said. "They barged in here, shouting and being aggressive. It would seem that a memory involving infidelity on Nate's part has caused a rift, and now they are trying to blame me. All I've done is try to help them."

"There was no infidelity on my part," Nate hissed. "You just admitted it!"

"What a very dysfunctional family you have, Alannah." said the doctor, calmly. "I think it's best if we don't see each other anymore. None of you. I'm invoking my prerogative to step down as your doctor." He flashed his eyes from Nate to Rose and then to Alannah. "Please gather your belongings and kindly get out of my house. All of you."

Alannah looked shocked. "Adi, I haven't done anything wrong. Please don't do this, I've been honest with you from the start. You knew she was my sister, you said you wanted to help her because you remembered her from school and because you cared about me."

Rose looked at Adrian. Everything she felt about him had changed. He had gone from someone she trusted, someone she believed wanted to help her to someone she was frightened of. She felt cold and noticed the hairs on her arms were raised. His calm, assuring voice now gave her chills. Her head spun and the beginnings of panic fluttered around the peripheries. She breathed deeply and sat on the sofa.

"I don't even remember you from school!" She was staring at the framed certificates, dumbstruck. "I think I can remember Alannah talking about an Adi in her class, but…" Her voice trailed off and her eyes refocused on the people in the room. "Did we ever meet? I mean, have we ever actually spoken before we came here for therapy?"

The doctor opened his leather notebook and grabbed a pen. "I've said all I intend to say on the matter. Please, leave."

Rose could feel anger rising through her in the form of tears. She began to speak, but Nate got in first.

"Oh, no you don't, mate. Tell your missus what you just told us. About you being in love with Rose. Tell the truth you dirty little liar."

"What?" Alannah's mouth opened, and a pallor swept her face. She glanced at Rose before moving towards the doctor. "What the fuck is he talking about, Adi?"

Adrian shifted in his chair and cleared his throat.

Nate looked into Alannah's eyes for several moments without speaking. Rose had seen him like this before, overwhelmed and unable to verbalise his emotions. His fists were still clenched. Alannah looked from him to Rose, then back to Adrian. Something switched inside her, as if she had suddenly made a firm decision. She walked over and slammed the door shut. She grabbed the spare seat and pulled it over so that it was in front of the door before sitting down in it with her arms and legs crossed.

"Right, nobody is going anywhere until you explain what the bloody hell is going on," she said. Rose couldn't help but admire her sister's assertiveness. It was rare that anyone messed with Alannah and got away lightly.

"Agreed," said Nate, perching himself at the end of Adrian's desk. "I think you're forgetting that the other key witness is now in the room."

Rose turned to her sister. "The doctor here showed us a memory of you getting into what looks like Nate's old car and kissing the driver. He made it to look like Nate was driving but—"

"Whoa! That wasn't me!" Alannah protested. "The barbecue was a one-off, Rose, I swear to you. I was pissed and lonely and stupid, but I've told you how sorry I am. It never happened again. Nate pushed me away, and it was humiliating."

"You must remember this occasion, though — it has to be recent. You got into a car that looked like our old Volvo?" Rose persisted.

"That was at the weekend!" Alannah turned to Adrian. "The hire car. You said yours had gone for a service?"

Adrian slowly screwed the lid back on his fountain pen and set it down on top of his notebook before straightening it.

"Your little lie seems to have unravelled here, Doc," said Nate.

The doctor ran his palm along the edge of his desk before tapping the top of his notebook. He raised his finger as if to speak, but paused when the words seemed to get lost. Instead, he inhaled deeply and tilted his head as if considering what to say next. He laughed, tossed his pen across the desk and combed his fingers through his hair with total abandon for the perfect line by which his hair was usually parted.

"How can you say you don't remember me, Rose?" He was almost whispering and staring down at the desk. "We met at the party that Ben Lloyd's mother put on for the French exchange students."

Rose blinked and desperately thought back. "I remember having a student stay with us and I remember going to the party but I was only about 15, I don't really remember who else was there."

"You spoke to me as we sat on the sofa and you told me you had a secret. You smiled at me like no girl had ever done before. You told me you were rubbish at French, that your student had been speaking English the whole time but not to tell Mrs Reeves… said it was just between you and me. Then you demonstrated the extent of your linguistic ability by bidding me 'Bonjour' as you got up to walk away. The way your face lit up as you left on that witty remark stuck with me, Rose. It was so attractive to an 18-year-old boy — beauty, wit, charm and confidence. Everything I didn't possess."

"I don't remember that at all," sighed Rose, rubbing her forehead with the palms of her hands. "It was years ago! I was a child!"

"Well, after that, I smiled at you when I saw you in the corridor at school and you smiled back. You have such a kind smile, Rose, you can make anyone feel noticed, feel special." Nate moved from the desk to the sofa next to Rose and took her hand.

"I smile at everyone," said Rose. "It doesn't mean anything, it's just polite!"

"I found myself bumping into you a lot after that, not that you noticed me. You became caught up with your friends and you rarely raised your head for long enough to see me but I could tell that if you had, we would have been friends. Sometimes I was lucky enough to stand behind you in the queue for the canteen. Even your hair shone in its cute little pony tail. I was sad when I left Sixth Form to go to university and I couldn't see you every day."

"You're a psycho," said Rose. "I don't even remember talking to you!"

A sharp intake of breath from Alannah caught Rose's attention. Rose looked at her sister who was crying. She moved to kneel beside her and give her a hug. "Come on, babe. Get dressed. You can come back to ours. This guy is a complete nutter, we need to get you out of here."

As if she hadn't heard her sister, Alannah said, "You told me it was me you noticed at school, that it was me you were thrilled to bump into again last year." Alannah's eyebrows were raised and her mouth ajar.

"You don't remember me at all?" Adrian ignored Alannah and stared longingly at Rose. He looked both hopeful and hurt. "I got a summer job behind the bar at the Elephant and Spear when I was back from university. I served you drinks. You smiled, always smiling! Surely that was your way of telling me you felt the same? But you never said any more afterwards, so I assumed you were shy. I've always been shy too — I couldn't ask you out, I couldn't bear the idea of you rejecting me. I would rather have lived in agony but with hope than be told no, even if it meant having to bide my time and watch you from afar. But you never said more than a few words to me."

"I'm not surprised! Weird stalkers aren't exactly a woman's type," Nate said bitterly.

"Ah yes, I know what her type is," the doctor aimed at Nate, oblivious to the women in the room. He stood up and walked towards him. "Idiot mechanics who show up with their grubby, oil-covered mates, drinking pints and doing shots of Jaegermeister. As if becoming a blithering moron is some kind of attractive quality."

Nate stood up and the two men were face to face.

"Say that again," said Nate.

"You're not exactly an intellectual match for Rose are you, Nathan? You can hardly articulate your own feelings, let alone be enough to support someone as deep and as complex as she is."

"Nate!" Rose said from the corner of the room as his body became tense. "Don't rise to it, he's just shit-stirring. He's not worth it."

"You're right, he's not," said Nate, raising his chin and pointing his finger close to Adrian's face. "You want locking up, mate. Stalking women, watching them, going out with their sisters to get close to them. It's sick!"

"Not as sick as you two all over each other in the pub. I mean, it's nothing personal, but you know Rose is in an entirely different league from you, don't you, Nate? It's no surprise that you two ended up here. It was hardly difficult to persuade Alannah to recommend me to you when it's so obvious to everyone around you that you're not right for each other. You never were, I could tell that as soon as I saw you trying to chat her up. Her giggling and touching your shoulder. Such a shame she didn't feel confident enough to just ignore your advances. She's too good for you, she always has been. You should have stuck with the other one."

"Nicola?" Nate was surprised that Adrian had brought her into it, incriminating himself further.

"The sad looking one who would prop up the bar at the weekends. You call me a stalker, but she never took her eyes off you, Nate. Watching from the far end of the bar. I saw her face, the pathetic longing like a puppy who'd just been kicked. The tears that betrayed her feelings for you when she saw you two dancing together, kissing and petting without an inhibition in the world."

"You took advantage of Nicola too," said Nate, angrily. Rose suffered a pang of jealousy once more, like she had in the cafe when he'd used her shortened name.

"She practically threw herself at me. One free gin and tonic and she spilt her guts like a wind-up toy. Telling me how hurt she was and how much she wanted you back. I couldn't see why. I never understood the attraction, but if it got you away from Rose, then it was an opportunity I couldn't ignore."

"You tried to convince her to stop the wedding?" Rose's voice was feeling weaker. The more she heard, the more violated she felt. Like someone had been staring through her bedroom window with binoculars — in fact, maybe he had! This guy had been watching her for years without her even realising.

"You said you noticed me." Alannah seemed to have zoned out from other parts of the conversation.

"I watched you both," Adrian continued. "You get a unique perspective from behind the bar. No one notices your face. You're just part of the furniture, a means by which to get inebriated. You were certainly good at that, Alannah. Flirting with any guy who would buy you a drink. I'm sorry, but you have just never had the same class as your sister."

"Don't speak to her like that!" For all the feelings Rose had experienced towards her sibling recently, she was now coming out the other side of the smog. Alannah was as much a victim in this as she was.

"I'm sorry, Alannah," Adrian continued coldly. "I think you're a great girl, lots of... fun. But it was no accident that I bumped into you last year."

"You used me. I asked you not to put my sister through that ridiculous therapy. That night in the Willow Tree when we argued, you convinced me you were just passionate about helping her, that you were sure it was the best way to make her better. I believed you. I believed you loved me. How could I be so stupid?" Alannah raised her legs onto the chair and hugged them with her face down.

"I'm afraid you were a last resort… collateral damage, shall we say? All of my attempts to get close to Rose had failed. Conversation at the bar never got beyond polite chitchat, which I can't bear. Taking a job round the corner from where she worked. Recruiting Nate's ex to stop the wedding. None of it was getting me anywhere, but then I saw you at a bus stop, Alannah, and I remembered you. Becoming romantically involved with Rose's sister? Well, that was guaranteed to get me into her life. And I knew you'd fall for any old line — girls like you never change. If I was the model boyfriend for long enough, you'd have to introduce me to your sister eventually, and then the opportunities would be plentiful. Family get-togethers, cosy meals and cups of tea. I thought Rose would have no choice but to get to know me for me. Realise how much we had in common, see what a perfect match we were. Little did I know you'd be so dead against me meeting your family. I had to take matters into my own hands."

"By manipulating me into recommending they come and see you for therapy," said Alannah. "So that you could try to split them up."

"This memory therapy has been in progress for years. Its benefits are enormous and it will change the world. It just so happens that everything fell into place at the right time and I could use it to my advantage. It should have worked. It would have done if it wasn't for that piteous cow Nicola."

"I would have found out the truth without her," said Nate. "It was only a matter of time."

"You must understand, Rose, no matter what these two say, it was all for you. I know we are meant for each other. I love you. You are perfect and I can look after you so much better than anyone else. I know your soul."

"You're deluded!" Rose was incredulous. "Did you really think you'd get away with all this and you and I would go running into the sunset?"

"It should have been easy with this technology," said Adrian. "I mean, how perfect! To have access to your innermost secrets." He looked into Rose's eyes, appealing to her. "Your precious memories. My God, I've enjoyed watching them back, Rose. Being inside your head, seeing the world as you see it. It's made me feel closer to you than ever. Shame this neanderthal had to feature so heavily, but I very much enjoyed seeing you in the mirror. Your brain is as beautiful as your body."

Rose let out a gasp of alarm. "I feel sick!" Alannah put her arm around Rose's shoulder.

Nate was back in the doctor's face, pushing him back into the wheelie chair next to the memory extraction equipment. "You sick, sick bastard! How dare you! That is my wife!" He lifted the doctor by the collar of his shirt and threw him to the ground. "I'm calling the police. Pervs like you shouldn't be allowed anywhere near other people."

Adrian laughed. "And what are you going to tell them? It's not exactly the crime of the century — a bit of video editing, a mistaken clip. It was lucky, really. With Rose's memory to refer to, I near-perfectly recreated that day. And I came so close to success. I have to say Nate, something as subtle as a few bricks is a good spot for you, you're not the sharpest of tools."

"Fuck you!"

Rose knew from her husband's tone that he was heading over a precipice. The point at which the humiliation was too much to bear, the perceived threat to his marriage too strong.

She placed her palm on his arm, about to convince him to back down in the calmest voice she could muster. Instead, her attention was caught by a flash of lilac on the floor behind the desk where Adrian had been sitting.

"Fucking hell! Is that my scarf?" she asked.

Adrian stepped into her line of sight, shielding her view of the garment, but she'd recognised it instantly. She'd searched for it several times in the last few weeks.

"What?" Nate responded with some confusion.

"I never wore that here to an appointment. Oh my God! Nate, we need to leave," she protested. "We'll let the police deal with it. At the very least, he will get struck off.

His career will be ruined, his precious memory therapy. It will all have been for nothing when they realise how it can be abused; how vulnerable the memories are to being twisted, by a sicko like him."

Nate appeared not to have heard. He was bearing down on the doctor, staring intensely as if the smallest blink could weaken his position. The doctor, despite his smug demeanour and determination to push Nate to the breaking point, looked small and vulnerable. Rose placed her hand on Nate's shoulder. "He hasn't won, Nate. He's lost everything. We have each other, nothing can ruin that, you've proved it. I know that you'll do anything to fight for us, and I'm the same. We're a team. Please, we need to get Alannah home."

Nate shrugged his shoulders to remove Rose's hand and pointed at the doctor. "You'd better watch your back, mate."

Nate turned to walk away and guided his wife and sister-in-law out of the office towards the front door. The doctor, finding bravado in his aggressor now being a good few feet away from him, stood and brushed himself down. Rose could sense him following them as they headed out onto the driveway.

"Wait," she said, once her, Alannah and Nate were all outside. "You tampered with my memory video. You made me believe Nate was cheating on me. Who knows what else you've done. But the video of the accident — please, tell me the truth — was that real?"

34

Nate

Everyone stood on the driveway waiting for an answer to Rose's question. Adrian smirked. Nate felt his blood boiling. He raised his eyebrows to encourage a response from the doctor. But it was Alannah who broke the silence.

"The accident? What have you found out about the accident? Was there something in your memory video?" She was still in her dressing gown and stood on the doorstep to the office entrance. She pulled the two sides of the garment and overlapped them across her chest, tucking one hand under the other as she clutched the thin fabric. Adrian stood a few paces from the door with Rose and Nate further down the block-paved driveway towards the front of the building.

"Yes, I've watched it back," Rose confirmed. "It was horrible. I saw it all again — everything I knew, or thought I knew. Right up to slamming my foot on the brake and feeling the pedal go loose under my sole. I couldn't have done anything, Lana. I'm so sorry, but it wasn't my fault, I'm sure of it now."

Nate swallowed back a lump which was forming in his throat and felt Rose's pangs of grief tug at him. The thought of her mum and the fate that Elaine had suffered; the thought of Rose and what she had been through for the last year. It all washed over him with renewed force. He wanted to grab his wife and squeeze her tight. He also wanted to grab the doctor and shake the hell out of him.

Alannah put a hand to her mouth. Her eyes welled. "So?" she said to Adrian. "Was that real? Or is that something you've meddled with somehow too?"

Rose tilted her head upwards to the grey sky, her chin quivering. Nate rested a reassuring hand on the back of her arm and she slowly inhaled. Both of them looked expectantly at the doctor.

"Of course it was real," Adrian replied, folding his arms and dropping his gaze towards the ground at his feet. His usually pristine demeanour was ruffled. It was the first time Nate had seen him that way. Previously, he thought of the doctor as unflappable, oozing authority and knowledge. Their scuffle earlier had instead left him with one side of his shirt untucked; his hair was disturbed, not slicked neatly into place. Rather than commanding respect, he now appeared broken and weak, his shoulders sagging with resignation.

"Oh my God! That's awful, Rose. I can't believe you've been able to watch that moment back. It could have been any of the three of us driving that day. You're right about what you said when we argued, it should have been me. It would have been if it wasn't for Adrian booking a hotel and us having to change my plans."

"Wait. What?" Rose was yanked from her own sorrow with the sudden realisation. "You two were together way back then? All that time ago?" She took a hostile step towards her sister.

"I thought it was the real thing," said Alannah, cutting a look across at Adrian as she spoke. The three of them were entranced in a triangle with a current of emotion humming between them. Nate was on the edge of it but flanked Rose. Alannah looked back at her sister. "I wanted to keep things quiet — just at first — and then Mum died, and it didn't seem like the right time to be introducing a new boyfriend. I wanted to just focus on being there for you, being there for each other. After that, I realised maybe he could help you and it was weird with him doing your therapy and stuff. I thought you'd freak out, and Adi always persuaded me not to say anything. You have to believe me, I thought I was doing what was right for you."

"Hang on," Nate added, waving his finger back and forth at both Alannah and Adrian. "You're saying that you two have been seeing each other in secret this whole time? Right back to the time of the accident — or even earlier — and it was because of him you didn't drive your mum that day?"

He screwed his face up as he cast a glance at Adrian,

who remained with his arms crossed. Still looking down, the doctor's head shook subtly from side to side before he looked up and straight at Alannah with a withering stare.

"Just be quiet, will you?" Adrian said to Alannah.

Her face crumpled. For a second, Nate thought of how much she'd had to take in during the last few moments — not just the memory revelations, but everything she thought about her own relationship being turned upside down.

"Alannah was supposed to be driving her mum to pick up that sofa, but she bailed because you booked a hotel — for what?" He aimed his question at Adrian. The doctor stood, arms folded across his chest, bottom lip sticking out. He shook his head almost imperceptibly as he stared at his feet. It looked like something was building inside him and about to explode.

"It's not a crime to book a hotel is it? Have you never performed a romantic gesture for Rose? Maybe it's you who should do some soul-searching, Nate. You're the one who sent Rose instead at the last minute. Unreliable as ever. If you hadn't gone to work that day, it might be you who had died, and we'd all be better off."

Nate darted forward, but Alannah got there first. "How can you say such an awful thing?"

"Get out of my face, Alannah."

"No! You're a sick bastard." She shoved him in the chest as all the anger and grief spilled out.

The doctor's body became tight and agitated. His fists clenched, and he fought to keep his eyes looking away from hers.

Alannah shoved him again. "We lost our mum and you're making comments like that." Another shove. "Our mum is dead!"

"It wasn't meant to be her!" the doctor screamed.

The words slipped uncontrollably from his mouth as his tear-filled eyes finally met hers. He paused, shocked at his own outburst, and for a moment, there was silence.

"What?" Nate's eyes sprang wide open.

Alannah stared, mouth open, wrinkles creasing across her forehead.

The significance of the doctor's words dawned on everyone.

"Excuse me?" Rose's eyebrows had shot up towards her hairline. Now the penny dropped. "Why the hell would you say that?"

"Rose, just listen to me—" Adrian began, now with a much softer tone.

"Oh, fucking hell, were you involved in this?" Rose interrupted in horror. "You wanted Nate to drive? Why? You couldn't have known something was going to happen. I can't be reading this right. Please tell me you didn't have something to do with those brakes and my accident."

"Rose, we can talk about this, but not here. Not like this." Adrian unfolded his arms and held his palms out to her as he stepped forward.

Nate instinctively stepped in front of his wife. "Answer her!"

Adrian ignored him and tried to look past Nate's shoulders at Rose with pleading eyes.

"Rose, please—"

"You're not actually denying it, are you?" Rose screamed. "I knew that something didn't feel right. Did you do something? Something deliberate? For what?"

"Please, let me explain, Rose. It wasn't meant to be like that. You weren't supposed to be driving, remember? Your mum shouldn't even have been in the car."

"So, that's why you wanted me to be driving?" Nate jumped in. "I know those brakes were fine. Gaz checked them — just that week. I've gone over it again and again, paranoid that we'd missed something. I thought I was going crazy, but I've checked the paperwork. What the fuck did you do? What did you want to happen?"

"Work it out for yourself." Adrian spat his words at Nate.

Alannah dropped to her knees at the doorstep, wailing as the revelation hit her too. The enormity swept over Nate and he lunged forwards towards Adrian. As he grabbed two fistfuls of the doctor's shirt beneath the front of the collar, Rose tugged hard on his arm. Adrian snatched back at Nate as their arms tangled.

"None of this would be happening if I'd got rid of you

then!" Adrian shouted as he grappled at Nate's arms and face, trying to push him away. "Sure, she'd have been sad at your loss, but I would have counselled her through it. Helped her to get over it and fall in love again. Only this time with someone who could meet her emotional needs."

Rose dragged at Nate too, attempting to pull him clear of the doctor.

"Leave him, Nate. This is sick. I can't be near him any more. We need to go straight to the police." Her words were drowned as the two men scuffled and shoved each other. Nate swung a fist but caught only Adrian's shoulder, then another which connected with the side of his head. His knuckles burned. They twisted and flailed at each other, Nate's sleeve tearing in the process before the volume of Rose's shouts and yanks took over.

"Stop, Nate. Leave it." She dragged at him with all her force. Eventually, he let go of Adrian's shirt and pushed him away as he stepped back, panting. Rose held onto his arm and moved around to the front of his body, placing herself between the two men with her palms on Nate's chest, trying to force him backwards.

"You'll pay for this, you sick bastard," Nate yelled over her shoulder.

"Huh. You're embarrassing, Nathan," came Adrian's reply. "You've never been good enough for her. You don't appreciate her like I do. I'd have looked after her if it was you that died in that crash. She'd have been better off with me."

All of Adrian's words were being shouted over the top of Rose's soft but direct commands right in front of Nate as she continued to push and coax him backwards. "Ignore him. Don't listen to him. Look at me. Come on, come on…"

Nate continued to jab an angry finger over Rose's shoulder in Adrian's direction, warning him it was not over. He allowed himself to be eased backwards by Rose, though. Gradually, he was catching his breath, his lungs and chest pounding hard. Little by little he was calmed by Rose's pleas. He obeyed her and looked into his wife's eyes as she kept nudging him back further towards the roadside. Adrian was rooted in the same spot, rubbing at his jaw and smoothing down his shirt and his hair.

"Listen to me," Rose continued, directing him. "We're going to take Alannah away from here with us. We're going straight to the police and we're telling them everything we know. This needs to be dealt with properly. You can't do anything stupid. Do you hear me? Just breathe, will you?"

Nate did as he was told. With Rose still pressing one palm against his chest and holding his cheek with the other hand, he took a deep breath and swallowed. His pulse pounded in his ears but he felt the composure he had lost now swelling back inside him.

"OK, you're right," he said, rolling his shoulders and cracking his neck. "He's tried to kill me. He's… he's… he's responsible for what happened to your mum."

"I heard him." Rose looked like she was doing all she could to hold herself together. Nate now saw she had tears streaming down her cheeks, despite appearing to be in control of manoeuvring him. Her entire body was trembling.

"Get in the car. I'll get your sister."

He glanced at Alannah, crumpled on the floor in a sobbing mess with her dressing gown draped partly around her and partly across the cold, hard paving stones of the driveway. Nate took his keys from his back pocket. The image flashed through his mind of throwing them across the sofa to Rose inside that office a few days ago, leaving her alone with this man, this killer! Now, outside the same building, he felt like an avalanche of events had descended on them. He placed the keys into her hand. Rose kissed him, then turned and walked to the pavement to head to the car.

Nate shot a glance at Adrian, then focused on Alannah, not straying from the instructions he'd just had instilled in him. As he reached her, he crouched down and tried to gather Alannah in his arms while instructing her to stand and follow him. He turned his back to Adrian who sensed one last opportunity. The doctor wasn't interested in Nate, though. He marched down the driveway after Rose.

Nate put one of his arms around Alannah and draped one of hers around his shoulder. She held onto him limply as he raised her onto her feet and faced her towards the road.

Rose pointed the key fob at the car and zapped the lock to open the door. She glanced left and right as she readied to cross to where they had parked. Behind her, Adrian dashed down towards the pavement as he called after her.

With Alannah sprawled over him, Nate watched Rose step out into the road. Halfway between them, Adrian had made it to the bottom of the driveway, shouting to Rose as his pace picked up. Nate knew he would have to drop Alannah to the floor again to race after him. He tried to hurry her along while keeping hold of her.

"Rose, wait!" Adrian shouted as he reached for her in the middle of the road. He grabbed her shoulder and stopped her in her stride. Rose spun her head around in response to the doctor's touch.

"Get off her!" Nate dropped his hold on Alannah and ran towards the pavement.

"Don't come near me!" Rose bellowed, trying to yank her arm from his grasp.

"Please! There's so much I have to say." Adrian tightened the grip he had gained on her upper arm.

"No! Get away from me!" she screamed. She pulled again, desperately trying to free herself from Adrian's clutches.

"Listen to me. It was all for you," he pleaded. Rose screamed and wriggled. From Nate's poor vantage point several metres away, it looked like she dug her nails into his arm with her free hand as he yelped in pain.

"Please—"

"No!"

A blurry flash of white came out of nowhere.

Then the sickening screech of tyres, skidding on tarmac, as a transit van hurled into vision.

Rose and Adrian disappeared from Nate's view.

Nate heard Rose's ear-piercing scream, followed by a gut-wrenching thud.

Then silence.

"ROSE!" shouted Nate, sprinting into the road. The van had stopped, and the driver sat gasping in shock from the front seat. There was a nauseating smell of burning rubber. The windscreen of the van was shattered, the bonnet dented.

Nate bounced off the vehicle as he hurtled to the other side of it. He stopped dead as he looked towards his car and his wife's body lying face down on the tarmac next to it. Beside her, the doctor was also lying still. A pool of dark blood was gathering between the two of them.

Nate lost his breath. The world was spinning and he couldn't move for panic. Behind him Alannah had appeared, crying and gasping.

The sickening whirlwind of motion and sounds ended as abruptly as they began. Through the stillness, a scream began to broadcast across the busy street. It carried through the cold, silent air as Nate saw Rose raise herself up onto her knees. She stared helplessly as yet again she found herself face to face with a dead body on the side of a road.

35

A Confession

I hope you never get to read this, Rose.

I hope somewhere in the future we will have reached the point where it's Adrian and Rose. Everyone will talk about us being perfect for each other. We'll tell stories about the funny journey we both took from our school days before finally becoming the couple we are meant to be.

Perhaps if you are reading, though, things have not worked out how I've always hoped they will.

Much of what I've written in this journal was just for me.

A record.

A purge.

A catharsis.

But there are things I will want you to know, and maybe this will be my way to tell you. I hope not.

You were not to blame for your mother's death. I hope you come to realise that. You shouldn't have been driving Nate's car that day. Your mother shouldn't have been in the car either. Nate was meant to be driving it. Alone.

That's how I'd arranged it. If anything was going to happen, it was Nate that it should have happened to. Maybe if it had gone to plan, you would have then found your way back to me.

I didn't even know if it was possible to cause the brakes to fail and lead to an accident. It happens in the movies, so I thought, why not? It was worth a try.

It's amazing what you can find out on the internet. I learned it would be better not to sever the brake hose completely. Nate would have realised something was wrong straight away. The brakes wouldn't have worked at all. But a slight cut to the line, a slow leak of brake fluid. That was different. Maybe the brakes would feel strange. Maybe they still wouldn't work at all and he wouldn't go past the end of the road. Or maybe, just maybe, he'd start driving the car and think nothing of it until he was out on the A6, travelling at speed. I even learned which of the electrics to disconnect so that the warning lights wouldn't illuminate on the dashboard.

Only it wasn't him, it was you.

You took the car that day and I wish now I could have warned you not to.

I don't think I ever dared to imagine I'd achieve the fatal accident. At the time it was the ideal scenario... so long as it was Nate to have succumbed. But when Alannah received the call to say it was you and your mother, I felt sick. It was not what I ever wanted.

I called you on the phone so many times afterwards to explain and apologise, but I could never find the words. I couldn't speak and had to hang up.

I watched you. Any chance I could. I found ways to be near you, without you ever knowing, hoping my invisible presence somehow brought you comfort. Like loved ones who can't be together. Just knowing I was there for you, made me sleep easier. The smell of you I've held near to me was a comfort too.

All the time, I've kept the pretence of being with your sister. I didn't know what to do next. Only that I had to give you more time again, that I had to be patient again. I had waited for so long and proven the extent of my patience. A little longer wouldn't make much difference. After all, the setback was my doing.

When Alannah talked about you and Nate struggling, I saw there was another opportunity. The university does not know that I've conducted the trials. The research is ongoing, and I always hoped it would have some use for you and I. Not from the start; it was my area of study, my PHd. But it also became my project for you and I.

I had access to everything I needed, and when I persuaded Alannah that you two should consider me for therapy sessions, the opening became clear. Fate was back on my side. Suddenly I had a way of not just being in your physical presence, but in your mind and your soul.

Of course, I had to put up with Nate being there, but I

was getting closer to you. The patience was paying off. I couldn't believe it when you walked into my office for that first session. I was so close and couldn't wait to talk to you — really talk. I thought you'd find comfort in the familiarity between us, but you didn't recognise me. I've watched my own memories of you so many times. I know your face so intensely, and yet you didn't know mine at all. It felt like a punch in the gut.

It was such an unexpected gift when Nate babbled the confession about his indiscretion with your sister. But it turned out to be still not enough. Why do you always see the best in people? It's one quality that makes you so special, but in this case, it has turned out to be a curse.

When I watched back the memories that were harvested, it presented me with an idea. All I needed was the footage of me driving to pick up Alannah in a Volvo that was a close enough interior match to your old 4x4. It was easy to pass off playing it as a mistake after it reached the crucial moment. Everything up to that point was my recreation of your journey. It was the little details that I was proud of, though. Sourcing the hire car, which was an identical make and model; being able to take Nate's gloves without him realising.

The footage looks like a perfect replica to me. I have just shown it to you. I couldn't have hoped for a better reaction. Nate has stormed out without even denying it. You believe that it must be his memory.

You have just left, and I am alone again, watching you smiling in the sunlight in Bruges. Watching your face as you kissed him and pretending it was me. Imagining that sexy look you gave him as you entered the hotel room was intended for me. It's all I have for now. But hopefully not for long.

I'll give it a couple of days before getting in touch. If things go well, I might soon burn this entire journal.

If, for any reason, they do not and if you are reading this, I'm sorry.

It was all for you.

Please believe me.

It was always for you.

Epilogue

"OK, love you too." Rose hung up the phone, replaced it in her pocket and perched on the bench next to her sister.

"Nate?" Alannah asked.

"Yeah. Gaz's been called out on an emergency pickup, so he's going to be late tonight. He's just going to come straight to yours and meet us there."

The two sisters sat in silence for a few minutes, staring at the memorial wall.

"How can two years have gone by without her?" Alannah asked.

"I still don't feel like it's sunk in properly," said Rose. She could feel a tightening in her chest and at the back of her throat.

Alannah put her hand on Rose's knee. "I'm sorry we had to do this alone last year."

Rose squeezed Alannah's hand. "We're together now, and that's all that matters. She'd be proud of us, you know?"

Alannah began to cry. "Tomorrow is going to be hard." She fixed her stare on their mother's memorial plaque.

"I can't even think about it." Rose's face felt flushed as the tears ran warm and fast.

"Let it all out!" sniffed Alannah. "It's healthy to release the emotions rather than trying to hide them."

"I'm really glad I bought you that mindfulness book for your birthday," Rose giggled through a large sob.

"I'm dragging you to yoga next week!" Alannah playfully nudged Rose's arm.

*

"Knock, knock!" Nate's voice reached the kitchen as Rose was stirring the casserole.

"It's open!" she called back to him.

He walked up behind her and ran his hands up her back, under her top.

"Fuck! You're freezing!" squealed Rose.

"Good job you're here to warm me up, then," grinned Nate, moving his hands further around to her tummy.

Rose squirmed free. "Nope!" She giggled, and he spotted the dimples on either side of her nose.

"Wow, it looks so different in here," said Nate. "You OK?"

"It doesn't feel like Mum's house anymore." Rose was quiet.

Nate put his hands back around her waist, over her top

this time, and made a point of pulling his sleeves over his chilly hands. He pressed himself into her and kissed her on the cheek, then rested his chin on her shoulder. "I know how hard this is for you, honey. It's OK to feel shit. I'm sad, too. But I'm here for you and I'll get you through it."

"I can't imagine not being able to just pop in for a cup of tea. Even without Mum here, being in the rooms makes me feel closer to her."

"I know." Nate spun Rose around and she stared up at him with tears in her eyes. He pulled her in close for a hug.

"Ugh, get a room." Alannah came up from the cellar with a bottle of wine.

"Ahh you can have a hug too," teased Nate. He grabbed Alannah and pulled her into the embrace.

"You two are so weird," she joked, making no attempt to release herself.

"Right," said Nate. "Is this dinner ready or what? I'm bloody starving."

The three of them sat down at the big table and reminisced about the memories that were absorbed within the surrounding walls. Rose and Alannah told stories of their childhood that Nate had heard hundreds of times. They teased him as they remembered the first time he came round for dinner, trying to impress their mum. Rose fondly shared the moment she had confessed in a mother-daughter heart-to-heart that she believed Nate to be the one. She grinned to herself as she pictured her mother's warm smile and the advice she had given her about checking if he knew how to use the washing machine.

"Think of all the washing these mechanics must produce," her mother had laughed. "You don't want to get lumbered with all that if his mum is still doing it for him now! It's these little details you need to establish before committing too much."

Rose stood up suddenly. "Right, I know this is a strange thing to bring up right now, but I have a proposition."

Alannah looked at her sister suspiciously before turning to Nate to see if he was any the wiser. He wasn't.

Rose had taken a phone call a few days earlier that she had decided to deal with herself. It had been suggested that she bring Nate along with her for moral support, but she needed to prove to herself that she was on the mend, that she was strong enough to face her past alone. Besides, she had wanted some time to contemplate her next steps.

Detective Constable Hayes had been friendly on the phone, warm and gentle in his approach to their conversation. He had reminded Rose of his involvement in the case investigating Dr Thomas and the events of that day. But Rose needed no reminder. She instantly recognised the voice who had been so caring at the side of the road. The voice who had talked her through the next steps, who had sat with her until she was ready to tell him everything that had happened. The first person to listen, really listen, to every detail of her mother's accident, the phone calls, the missing items, the therapy that had held so much promise to fix all that was broken.

"Rose, we've got some items here that we can return to you now that the inquest and investigation into Adrian Thomas's death have been closed. If you want them back, that is…" he had said on the phone.

Rose had met with DC Hayes. Not because she wanted her stuff back, but because she wanted to dispose of it herself. She wanted to be in control of what happened next.

Rose walked over to a box. A huge label on the side displayed the word '*EVIDENCE*' with a black marker line through it.

Nate looked at his wife with concern.

"What's that, honey?"

"Well," said Rose. "I had a coffee with DC Hayes the other day. He didn't need to meet me. I'm sure returning random stuff is way below his pay grade but he was keen to see how I was — which I thought was really lovely."

"You never said! Has something happened?"

"Nope," said Rose. "The investigation's closed, so he wanted to give me this."

"What is it?" asked Alannah, inching her chair closer to peer inside the box.

Rose pulled out each item one at a time. A hairbrush that had gone missing from her bedroom. A bottle of

Chanel perfume. A pair of men's black leather gloves. A lilac and grey scarf. All things that had gone missing well over a year ago. Insignificant items presumed lost in the chaos of everyday life but, placed here on the table as a collection, they sent a shiver down Rose's spine.

"Fuck!" said Nate. "You should have said, I would have come with you."

"I know," said Rose, "but I needed a bit of time to decide what to do with them."

Nate put his hand on Rose's shoulder.

"That's so horrid," said Alannah. "Sis, I'm so, so sorry."

"And then there's this," said Rose. She pulled out a brown leather book. It was thick and well-worn with faded patches and frayed edges. Papers and photos were stuffed inside and every page was covered in immaculate fountain pen.

"I don't recognise that," Nate said.

Rose shifted in her chair and could sense Nate looking directly at her face.

"It's not mine," said Rose. "It's his."

"What?" Alannah sounded confused.

"It's full of letters and confessions. He must have written them with no intention of sending them, but it's creepy as fuck." Rose paused and could feel her hands shaking. "Shit! There's a Polaroid here of me in our kitchen. It's taken through the window from the back garden!" Her head spun.

"Jesus Christ," said Nate, taking the photo from Rose. "Why have you got it?"

"I shouldn't have it. Not technically," said Rose. "But DC Hayes said it would only get archived. They can't use it as evidence against Adrian, he's dead. Plus, he has no family left, no will. So, no one owns it any more. DC Hayes thought perhaps it would help me to read what's inside. He thought it might help me understand."

Rose stared at the book. Everything about it screamed Dr Thomas: the style, the writing, the intensity of its contents.

"Do you want to read it?" asked Nate.

"No," said Rose. She was pensive, but something inside her clicked into place when Alannah retrieved another item from the dresser drawer behind her and waved it in the air provocatively.

"Whoa," said Nate on spotting the cigarette lighter. He sounded surprised and impressed in equal measure.

Rose got up from her chair. She downed her remaining half glass of wine and grabbed another bottle from the side.

"You're on my wavelength. Lana: follow me. Nate: blankets," she said assertively.

*

The warm glow of the fire reminded Rose of bonfire night when their mother would take her and Alannah to the village display. The crackle and sparks that she associated with comfort. This metal pit was on a much smaller scale but aroused in her a sense of safety.

"Shall we read them out before we throw them in?" asked Alannah, ripping out a page.

"Nope," said Rose. She looked from side to side, towards her sister and husband who flanked her on the outside seats — all three of them huddled under blankets. The wine was warming her insides as well as her confidence. "Wherever he is, I want him to be looking down at this, knowing that his words never reached me." She stood up from her chair, tilted her head back and shouted to the sky. "Do you hear me, you crazy psycho?" She lit the corner of the first page. "This is for you, Mum. I love you so much."

Rose tossed the page into the fire before ripping out another. Alannah followed suit, and soon all that was left was a melting clump of leather surrounded by ash.

*

Rose and Nate headed for Rose's old bedroom. The bed was all that remained amongst a mountain of boxes.

"What time are the movers coming?" asked Nate.

"Nine-ish I think," said Rose. "They're going to take all of Alannah's stuff to the new place first and then the charity van is coming for the rest of it. Are you sure Gaz's van is big enough for the stuff we're taking back to ours?"

"Yeah, it'll be fine. He's going to come over to give us a hand once the movers are all out of the way."

"So weird to think that some new children are going to live here. One day, they'll be lying in this room with a lifetime of memories spent in this house."

"Memories are a precious commodity," said Nate, drifting off.

"That's pretty deep for you," laughed Rose as she stared up at the ceiling. There was no response but the steady breathing that confirmed he was asleep.

Acknowledgements

Special thanks to our early readers: Katy Johnson, Toni Skitt, Christine Gunton-Bunn, Jessica Cooper, Andy Guy, Deb Mahon, Philly Cranwell-Hayes, Katy Jones. As the first people that we shared our story with, your support was invaluable. We really appreciate your encouragement and feedback, which helped us to develop our characters and plot. Thank you for taking the time to read our early draft and for being honest and constructive. You gave us the confidence to believe in what we have created.

We would like to say a huge thank you to Przemek Sikora for creating our fabulous cover design. We're so very grateful for you being so generous with your time and patience.

Thanks from Kirsty:

To Nick, for always having more faith in me than I have in myself. Oink. And to Barney and Beth for being so patient while I was busy writing. You all make me so proud.

To Mum. Sharing this adventure with you over virtual cups of tea has meant the world to me. I love you so much.

To Deb, for unyielding love and encouragement. You're my person and words aren't really enough so [PLEASE DRAW A PIG HERE].

To Philly, for sharing my excitement about this project. Your input has been invaluable and your friendship means more than you will ever know.

To my Whales and Fen Family for always being enthusiastic whilst listening to me constantly talk about writing. I honestly don't know what I would do without you all.

Thanks from Steve:

To Katy and Liv, for putting up with the constant book questions and progress updates of the project. I appreciate you humouring me with all the decision-making or just letting me talk it out. To Katy especially as our very first reader and to Liv for being TikTok content manager.

To both of you and also to Mum and Dad, for all the love and support; for always just being there.

To any other people - especially Angela Rogers and Karen Vine - who have offered opinions and answered queries about titles, covers and any other musings along the way. To those of you who have expressed an interest at any point in what we're doing, which has spurred us.

And to everyone (in advance) who helps to spread the word and let more people know about the book.

About the Authors

Kirsty

Kirsty grew up on the island of Guernsey before moving to England to study Primary Education at university. After 6 years as a teacher, she stepped out of the classroom to focus on mumming and writing stories for children. She has spent the last 4 years writing picture books for an educational publisher. She now lives in Cambridgeshire with her husband, two young children and oft-woofing mini schnauzer, Otto.

Steve

Steve grew up in the Black Country but has spent most of his adult life living in South Yorkshire. He spent nearly 20 years as a teacher in primary education whilst always pursuing a passion for writing. His first published book was a biography of former world speedway champion, Bruce Penhall, in 2005. More recently, he has spent several years writing fiction and creating teaching resources for children aged 7–11. He lives with wife Katy and daughter Liv along with their three cats (and furry writing companions) Eva, Judy and Tommy.

This is Kirsty and Steve's first adult fiction and first co-authored novel. The project began in the Spring lockdown of 2020. Ironically, the writing partnership came to fruition as a result of being confined to their houses, 115 miles apart. The entire process was completed remotely without ever being together in person thanks to video calls and collaborative writing software.

Kirsty and Steve are looking forward to continuing their writing collaboration and have ideas for more stories in the pipeline. If you would like to get in touch or follow the progress of future projects, then you can find them on the following social media channels:

facebook.com/twosyourwords
twitter.com/twosyourwords
instagram.com/twosyourwords
tiktok.com/@twosyourwords

We look forward to hearing from you. Share your thoughts about the book with the hashtag #WhatYouDontRemember and if you've enjoyed reading it, please consider leaving us a review on Amazon.

Printed in Great Britain
by Amazon